A mirror of questionable origins appears out of nowhere in a shipment of furniture. It calls to those it finds compatible. The owners soon find out why, and wish they hadn't. Can a mirror actually be possessed? What happens to the people it encounters?

This chilling story takes place over several decades as the mirror becomes the possession of many different people. Who is immune from the call of the mirror, and what is it in the mirror that beckons? Pray you don't find out…

KUDOS for *Mirror, Mirror*

In *Mirror, Mirror* by Leonardus G. Rougoor, everyone who comes into close contact with an ebony-framed mirror is in danger of disappearing forever. Over the decades, the mirror calls to certain people, who have no idea of the danger they are in. Buying the mirror comes with a price far more than any money paid for it—a price no one would willingly pay if they knew the true cost. Well written, fast paced, and chilling, this is, in my opinion, one of the best books the author has released so far. A really great read. *~ Taylor Jones, The Review Team of Taylor Jones & Regan Murphy*

Mirror, Mirror by Leonardus G. Rougoor is an excellent example of how very talented and versatile this author really is. The story follows the ownership of an unusual mirror, which is made of smoked glass framed in ebony. What the buyers of the mirror don't realize, until it's too late, is that the mirror is evil and means them harm. Can they resist it? And what happens to them if they can't? Is the mirror possessed, or is there something evil inside it? Beautiful and unique, the mirror ensnares many innocent victims, who thought only of how beautiful and exotic it was, and what a great deal they got on it, not knowing the real price was yet to be paid. I was very impressed with *Mirror, Mirror*. Chilling, intense, and compelling, the story grabs you by the throat and holds on from beginning to end. You won't be able to put it down. *~ Regan Murphy, The Review Team of Taylor Jones & Regan Murphy*

OTHER BOOKS
BY
LEONARDUS G. ROUGOOR
AND
BLACK OPAL BOOKS

Waiting in the Shadows

The Clock

The Chase

The Murderer and the Lost Treasurer

The Revelation

MIRROR MIRROR

Leonardus G. Rougoor

A Black Opal Books Publication

Dedicated to my dear friends,
Marita, Maureen, Bill, Karlina, Elli, and Richard.

Mirror, Mirror, on the wall,
Old and young, it does call.
Pray the Lord your soul to keep,
For it beckons while you sleep.

PREFACE

James parked the car on the side of the road. Getting out, he walked unsteadily toward the garden outside what he knew to be Margaret's bedroom. Slowly, being careful not to make any noise, he snuck toward the French doors. When he felt safe he leaned close to the glass. Looking through the window pane with anticipation, he saw the sleeping form of the girl he wanted.

Off to the side, he noticed a slight glow in the mirror on the wall above the dresser. There seemed to be some movement reflected in it. Suddenly, he saw something unholy in the glass of the mirror, and immediately there was a sensation of extreme pain in his head.

As fear took over, he screamed in agony, running away from the house. The swing in the garden wasn't even seen, and he hit the protruding upper support beam with his head. Falling to the ground, he cursed and tried to regain his footing. The fear in him was so great that he didn't even feel the gash on his forehead.

Stumbling off the farmer's property, James ran to the car. The lights had come on in the house, and the front door was opened. James didn't even see the man holding a shotgun in his hands as he sped away.

The only thing in James's mind was that he had to get away from there. He knew, without a doubt, that he would never return to that place. His hands were trembling uncontrollably, and he almost drove off the road into the ditch several times.

CHAPTER 1

New York, New York, 1912:

Come on, Bobby, we have to go. Mom and Dad are leaving," Jenny yelled. "Hurry, they're getting me a new dresser."

"Awright, awright, I'm coming. Gee whiz, what's the big rush? It's just a place to put your stuff," Bobby returned with a sigh.

Out the front door they went, with Jenny, thirteen years old, bouncing up and down with excitement. Bobby brought up the rear at a much slower pace. They got into a shiny two-year-old Packard. This vehicle was their father's pride and joy. He owned several stores that sold ladies clothes and was fairly successful so he could afford this kind of luxury.

All the neighbors were so envious when Father drove it home for the first time, Jenny thought as she got into the back seat with her younger brother. Because of the success of the ladies stores, Mother always dressed quite stylishly. Others had to pay full price for clothes, but Father acquired them wholesale and sometimes for even less if he could find a defect. Father, of course, didn't let Mother know there was a defect.

Father drove slowly making sure everyone around could see him in the black 1910 Packard. It was 1912, and very few people could afford an automobile such as this. It was wonderful living in New York City. Now and then when he had time, he would drive the family to Central Park to spend the day and sometimes they even ended up at Coney Island, if the day started early enough.

That day they were going to visit a friend of their father's who sold furniture. The two men bartered back and forth, giving each other far better deals than regular customers got. The streets were a little rough, but it was far nicer in the automobile than it was riding in a horse-drawn carriage like they used to do. It was also far quicker getting to their destinations.

After half an hour of navigating the streets to the store, they finally arrived, parking in front of the sign, *Benson's Furniture*. The usual people stopped to admire the car, but Father walked right past them without a word.

"Come, come, children, we don't have all day you know. I have a business to run," he said as he opened the door leading into the large store.

"Good morning, Marcus. How do you do, Abigail?" the store owner said as the Weatherbys entered.

"Good morning, Franklin. We're here to look at a dresser for Jenny. Can you show us what you have?" Marcus asked.

Leading the family to the section reserved for bedroom furniture, Franklin chatted with Marcus about business. Bobby, ten years old, got distracted, as usual. He stopped in front of a bunk bed set. He wondered if he had a brother, who would get the top bunk.

Jenny was shown the inventory of dressers available.

She inspected each with a critical eye. She knew what she liked and what she wanted. As Jenny checked one after the other, she dismissed most and reserved judgment on only two.

Coming back and opening drawers in each she finally decided on one, except there was a slight problem, as far as this young lady was concerned.

"Mother, may I speak with you please?"

"Yes, dear, what is it?" Abigail asked her daughter.

"I like these two," she said, pointing her finger at the ones that were her favorites. "The problem is that the one I really want doesn't have a mirror. A mirror is such an important thing as you well know, Mother."

"I'll speak with Mr. Benson. He may be able to help you." Turning to face the proprietor, she asked, "Oh, Mr. Benson, may I have a moment of your time?"

"Why, certainly," he replied as he walked over. "Have you made a choice already, Jenny?"

"I have, sort of. I like these two here," she said, pointing again to her favorites. "But I really, really like this one. The only thing wrong with it is that there's no mirror."

"Oh, I see. That does present a problem, doesn't it? I have a few in the back that might do. Why don't you come with me and you can decide if any will suit your needs," he said as he led the way to the storeroom.

Abigail and Marcus followed the pair as they went to inspect the much-needed mirror. Marcus thought, *Gosh, twelve years old and she is already so much like her mother.*

Franklin made his way past the crated items that would soon be put into the showroom. At the side, off to the right, were several mirrors that he proceeded to show Jenny.

"The dresser you have chosen is made of a rather dark

wood, so in my opinion, a dark mirror would be the best choice. Do you agree, Jenny?"

"I do, Mr. Benson, sir."

"I have two here that may be suitable. Do you like either of them?" he asked the well-mannered young lady.

"Oh, they are beautiful, but do you have any others?"

"I'm sorry to say that—" He stopped in mid-sentence and thought, as an idea came to mind. "There is one that was sent here by mistake. It is a rather odd mirror, and I wasn't sure you would like it. Here let me show it to you."

With this, he moved a crate out of the way and pulled a mirror from behind a piece of packing. Holding it in two hands, he grunted with effort as he lifted a truly unique mirror.

"This one is made from a wood imported from Africa. It's called Ebony and is a very strong exotic wood. As you can see it has a very different style to it and almost looks a trifle lopsided. I checked it over, and it really is uniform. It's the texture and coloring of the wood that makes it look odd. The glass is also unique as it has a smoked effect in it. Kind of spooky, don't you think, Jenny?"

A warm feeling came over Jenny. "I absolutely love it. Can we get this one, Father, please?" she asked as she gave him that special pleading look, the same one that worked so well when Abigail used it.

"Gosh, Jenny, it is a trifle different. Do you really think it will look good with the dresser for your room?"

"Oh, yes, indeed it will, dear Father," she said with a smile.

Turning to Franklin, Marcus asked, "Do you know anything about it?"

"I've checked it over and there are no markings indicating who made it or where it was produced. It is of very good quality. The piece came here by mistake, and even the shipper doesn't recall anything about it. It's almost as if it appeared in the shipment out of thin air. I can let you have for a very reasonable price," he said.

The two men bartered back and forth and came to an agreement. The mirror was brought out and placed on the dresser, just to make sure it looked all right. Jenny squealed with delight as she visualized it in her room. Delivery preparations were made, and Jenny was one happy young lady.

It took several long days for the dresser and mirror to arrive and be carried by two workmen up into Jenny's bedroom. The men had been instructed to mount the mirror on the wall above where the dresser was to be placed. Jenny had decided ahead of time the best spot for the dresser and so it took very little time for the mirror to be hung in its proper place.

When it was all finished and the packing materials were removed, Jenny sat on her bed. Looking at her new treasures. Out of the corner of her eye, she saw a slight movement in the mirror. She was actually looking at the dresser when it happened. Stunned for a moment, she approached it and gazed at her reflection in the smoky glass. Taking a hard look at this beautiful mirror, she realized that the open window off to the side must have had a light breeze come through it and rustled something in the room. This must have been what she saw in the glass. Funny thing was, she never felt the breeze.

Her friends would be so envious of her. None of them had anything quite this exotic. "I love my mother and father," she said softly to herself.

The door opened and Bobby entered the room.

Jenny scowled. "You're supposed to knock before you come into my room. You know that, Bobby."

"Ah, geez, I forgot. What's the big deal anyway?"

"You're just supposed to, so please do it from now on," she retorted.

He looked at the new dresser and then the mirror. "Why did you pick this one, it's so dark? How can you see anything in it?" His head reached just high enough to see his face and that was about all.

He saw nothing special there so he left. Jenny walked over to her doll house and played make-believe with her favorites. In the mirror, a shadow moved, but Jenny was unaware of it.

"Jenny dear," her mother called. "It's time to come down for supper."

Off she went, closing the door behind her. Bobby was already at the table, but his mother had a word to say.

"Bobby, your hands are filthy, please wash them, and use soap this time."

"Awh, Mom, I washed them a little while ago." Receiving a look, he said, "Okay, okay. I'll do it again, geez."

Supper consisted of roast beef with potatoes and carrots. Marcus and Abigail chatted as the children were silent and ate. Desert was a slice of apple pie and a glass of milk, accompanying the evening meal. Marcus had a business acquaintance coming over shortly, so the children were asked to go upstairs.

"For heaven's sake, please be quiet."

School was out for the summer, which made Bobby happy, although Jenny missed her friends. As the two ran up the stairs, Jenny announced that she was going to have a bath, and Bobby occupied himself in the temporary tent made from a bed sheet in his room.

Once the water was drawn, she got in and relaxed in the fragrant bubbles. Now and then she scooped up a handful and blew them into the air to land at the other end of the tub. After half an hour, she was eager to cast her eyes on her new dresser and possibly rearrange her clothes in the drawers.

Drying off and putting her nightgown on, she entered her bedroom. There it was, the beautiful new piece of furniture and the wonderful mirror hanging on the wall directly above it. She studied the looking glass, inspecting every detail. She could see that it was a very-well-made item and wondered how it came to be included in the shipment to Benson's Furniture. There must have been a mix up when the workers loaded the other things to be shipped.

As she walked toward the closet, there was the movement of a shadow in the mirror. Looking back quickly, she studied it intensely. She was sure she had seen something move. Looking around the room to make certain Bobby wasn't in there trying to frighten her, she saw that she was alone. Again as she turned to look at the glass, she saw movement out of the corner of her eye. By the time she was actually looking at it, there was nothing out of the ordinary to be seen.

"I think my imagination is getting the better of me. I'm sure that the light hitting the glass is making me see things that aren't there," she said to herself.

The door opened and Bobby stuck his head in asking, "Who are you talking to?"

"Oh, nobody, I'm just playing."

The door closed again, and she was alone once more. "It had to be Bobby that made the movement in the mirror," she mumbled.

Picking up a book, she lay on the bed and read *Rebecca of Sunnybrook Farm*. This book was almost as entertaining as *Anne of Green Gables*, which she read a short time ago.

Getting lost in the book, she read till her eyes started to close. She put the book down and cleaned her teeth before retiring for the night.

Hearing her daughter upstairs, Abigail came into her room and tucked her in, saying, "Goodnight, dear."

"Goodnight, Mother, thank you so much for the dresser and mirror."

"You're welcome, dear."

With the lights out, Jenny closed her eyes. Just as she drifted off to sleep, she thought she heard a soft whispering, but couldn't be certain. Falling into a deep sleep, she woke in the middle of the night having to make a trip to the bathroom. As she was about to get out of bed, half awake, there was a faint whisper again.

She couldn't make out what it was and wasn't even sure that she actually heard anything at all. It might just have been the sheets rustling as she was about to get out of bed. This, however, was doubtful as the soft voice seemed to speak just before she moved.

Wow, this has been a strange day. First shadows moving in the mirror and then sounds in my room coming from nowhere. What is going on?

CHAPTER 2

In the morning, Jenny woke to the birds chirping outside her slightly open window. There was a large maple tree outside her room, whose branches were only ten feet away. Sometimes a sparrow would land on the sill with a tiny click of its claws and look in, but this only happened occasionally. Maybe a bug or some other morsel enticed it to come this close to the glass.

It was seven-thirty, and her father was already up and sitting at the kitchen table. Mother had prepared the coffee and a light breakfast for him. He'd always been an early riser and claimed this was one of the reasons he had succeeded in business.

"Good morning, dear," her mother said.

Her father just smiled in her direction as he continued to read the newspaper. Watching the stock markets had paid off for him. There was always money to be made if you were aware of the opportunities. Marcus Weatherby had done well in life and was a pillar of the community. He served on numerous committees and was respected by all.

Abigail was an avid churchgoer and did what she could to help those who were in need. There was a women's movement starting to gather momentum. There was, of course, much resistance to this, and tempers of the male population flared out of control at times. Abigail didn't see what the fuss was all about, but then again, she had a husband who looked after her needs quite well.

Bobby made his appearance at this time, and his mother asked what he would prefer for breakfast. The choices were few, but he liked the idea of having porridge that morning. He had awakened with a slight chill and felt that warm porridge would hit the spot.

At eight-ten, Marcus got up, hugged his wife, and patted his children on top of their heads as he headed for the front door.

Their mother had a church meeting later in the morning and asked, "Do you want to come with me? You can keep yourself occupied in the Sunday school for an hour if you like. Or you can stay at home, and I'll ask our neighbor, Mrs. Richards to check in with you periodically."

Jenny had plans other than sitting in a room with Bobby for an hour or more, so she said, "I think that I would prefer to arrange things in my new dresser, if you don't mind, Mother. Bobby and I will keep ourselves busy, and with Mrs. Richards next door, I'm sure we will be just fine, right, Bobby?"

"Yeah, we'll be okay, Mom."

Plans made, Abigail set out to wash the dishes and clean all the items that had gotten dirty. Half an hour later, she was getting ready to go to the church meeting. Colleen Williams was picking her up, and she found that she was actually looking forward to the short ride in the horse-drawn buggy. She and Colleen had had a close bond for years. The two had gotten together on many occasions when each needed someone to talk to. In this modern new world, the second decade of the nineteen hundreds, things had changed far more quickly than some had been able to adapt to.

Looking out the parlor window, she saw the buggy approaching and called out to her children. "I'm going now. If you need anything, just ask Mrs. Richards."

Both kids said goodbye with Bobby running down the stairs to give his mother a hug. Jenny, however, was far too mature to do this and just answered from the top landing. After she left, Bobby locked the door as instructed. Having heard the sound, Abigail felt safer, as far as her children were concerned, knowing that the lock was of a superior type.

Waving to her friend as she walked down the front path beside the gravel driveway, she felt happy. She had had to persuade Marcus to install the pathway because he saw no need for two ways to get to the front door. Abigail told him that the gravel would damage her good shoes and they would then have to be replaced. Unless he wanted his wife to go out in public with shoes that looked old and worn.

Since appearances meant a lot to Marcus and the fact that he hated to spend more than necessary, he had the path put in rather quickly. Over the years, she had learned how to approach these kinds of situations. It had paid off more than once.

CHAPTER 3

The two children played together for a short time till Jenny asked, "Bobby, do you want to help me straighten out the clothes in my new dresser?" She already knew the answer, but this would make it seem like the choice to play by himself was his idea.

"Yuck, I don't want to touch your stuff. I'll play in my tent. You take care of it yourself," he said, pulling a face as he ran off preparing to fight the Injuns that had surrounded his wagon train camp.

Jenny entered her room in order to find some answers. She wanted to see the back side of the mirror, but that was impossible since it had been mounted to the wall with hooks and wire. The only thing she could do was open the curtains on both windows and turn on the lights.

Picking up her magnifying glass, she studied the wood holding the glass in place. The joints in the frame were flawless. The craftsmanship was truly remarkable, and she was pleased that she picked this one over the others. Climbing on the dresser she looked at the top and then down the side.

When she had her head close to the dresser in order to inspect the bottom of the frame, something in the mirror drew her attention. A slight movement in the darkened glass startled her. Looking around the room, she tried to see if Bobby had come in unannounced. No one was there with her, and so she quickly looked back at the mirror. Again, there was something that just managed to evade her attempts to catch a good look at it.

She no longer had any doubts that there was an odd quality about this new addition to her room. If she couldn't find out what it was, she might have to enlist Bobby's help, a thought that was unappealing to her.

In an attempt to get to the bottom of this mystery herself, she stepped out of the room, leaving the door partially open. Walking down the hall loudly, she stopped, turned around, and snuck back on tiptoe. When she got to the door, she looked through the gap between the door and the frame where the hinges were.

Once again, she was just quick enough to see something move, but not fast enough to actually see what it was. It was almost as if whatever was making the reflection knew what she was trying to do. Jenny loved a good mystery, and this was proving to be a very formidable one.

She wondered if it was possible that there could be someone hiding in her room. If so, how could she find out without endangering herself or Bobby? She hadn't seen anything or anyone, and there really were no good places to hide. With this in mind, she re-entered her room, staying in the doorway.

Looking slowly around the room, she felt a slight tingling in her fingers. There was an eerie feeling going through her as she carefully scanned all around her, trying to discover a prankster. Nothing was found, and so she walked over to the closest window and looked to see if anyone was outside. Seeing nothing but the tree, and no one in it, she went to the second window. Again, there was nothing to be found.

With the search done, there was only the mirror itself that could be the source of this mystery. She looked at her reflection and asked, "What is going on here? What do you want from me?"

Of course, there was no answer. She really hadn't expected one, and when there was only silence, she hadn't been surprised.

Thinking it might be a good idea to check on her younger brother, she exited the room. At the last instant, she turned her head quickly. There was no faint flash of movement in the glass this time. Either that or she had been just a bit too late to see it. Maybe she had been imagining it. She couldn't be sure. Either way, this was becoming frustrating.

CHAPTER 4

T he front door closed with a slight thump, and Mother called out, "I'm home, where are you?"

"We're up here, Mother," Jenny said as she arrived at the top of the landing. "How was your meeting?"

"It was just fine, dear. Do you and your brother want to come down for lunch?"

"I'll go get him, Mother, and be right down," she said, walking to his room. "Bobby, Mom's home, and it's time for lunch."

"I'll be right there. I'm being attacked and have to shoot them Injuns before I go."

"I'm sure they'll still be here when you get back," she said.

At this, they both went downstairs for a fried bologna sandwich and a glass of milk. A cookie topped things off and, as Abigail watched her children eat, she asked, "Do you want to go to the park? We can drop by the butcher on our way back."

Both wanted to go, and once they were cleaned up, they headed to the green space. The park had the usual swings and sandboxes, but what made things interesting for them were the large ponds with their assortment of wildlife. A few pieces of stale bread had been brought along. The ducks just loved this treat.

All three had a wonderful time at the park, and by the time they had had their fill, it was time to go to the butcher and then home. Abigail took the items from the butcher to the kitchen and, once they were put away, she began preparations for the evening meal. Marcus would be home in one and a half hours, and he liked to eat right after he had his evening cocktail. Sometimes, they each had one, but quite often Abigail would not.

Today, the two sat down together in the study and chatted while they had their drink. The children were in their rooms with Bobby playing and Jenny reading more of *Rebecca of Sunny Brook Farm*. At least she was trying to read. Her eyes kept shifting to look at the mirror, hoping to see something.

So far, the mirror was just that, a mirror. Nothing unusual was going on, so she decided that she might as well enjoy the book. Another half hour and she heard the voice of her mother asking her and Bobby to get washed up for supper. After this was done, the two ran down the stairs to give their father a hug.

"So do you still like the mirror?" Marcus asked.

"Oh, yes Father, I really do."

"That's good. I would hate to have paid a tidy sum for it and you not have been happy with it," he stated with a smile.

CHAPTER 5

Life had been good to this family, and both Marcus and Abigail knew it. At church on Sunday, they gave their tithes quite willingly. They knew that New Life Baptist Church needed their help. Not everyone in the congregation could afford to contribute enough to keep the church functioning as it should.

At one point in his life, Marcus had considered going to seminary to become a pastor. He soon realized that he was more cut out to be a businessman and could help the church in what he considered a more practical way. He had strayed for a time after that decision had been made, but when he met Abigail, she soon showed him the error of his ways.

When the children came, he knew he had made the right choice. Life got better and better with the woman he loved. It took years to develop the ladies fashion stores. There were a few moments when things got a little precarious, and he was on the verge of losing it all. What saved him was having made a few contacts in the supply end of things who gave him some real breaks in cost for favors to be repaid in the future.

This he did, and the playing field had been leveled

with all debts paid and favors repaid. Ladies fashions changed quickly, and he had to stay on top of procurements constantly. Luckily, he had an arrangement with his suppliers that allowed him to sell things off at a reduced rate when the items were just not moving. The supplier then took a cut, but this was better than having items returned and not sold at all.

Yes, life was good. Jenny was growing up quickly and seemed to have inherited many of the good qualities her mother possessed. Bobby was still very young and not as mature as his sister but did show promise. In the next few years, as the boy became a teenager, he would be gently brought into the business.

Boys were the lifeline of a family. Girls grew up to marry and the family name ended there, but boys retained the name their entire lives, and through them, the name lived on. There was a change, called the Suffragette Movement, building momentum. What on earth did the troublemakers think they would accomplish? Good grief, where would it end? The next thing you knew, they'd be asking for equal rights, maybe even asking to vote. Strange times were ahead for this world.

Marcus had seen things come that he would never have dreamed possible. The automobile was a perfect example. It had been almost ten years since those crazy Wright brothers actually flew that contraption through the air. Imagine being so reckless as to risk your life sailing through the air, twenty feet above the ground. If a man was meant to fly, the good lord would have given him wings. What on earth did these people think would come of this foolhardiness?

Marcus let his mind wander for a time and then came back to reality. It was time for bed, and he had to get to work early to supervise a shipment that was due to arrive.

CHAPTER 6

Abigail lounged for a time in the evening after the children were in bed and her husband was in his study. Her friend Colleen had been going to meetings where the wives of prominent men were having a speaker come shortly. Through the grapevine, it was said that the lady was part of the Suffragette Movement and looking for recruits.

Colleen had always been somewhat radical in her views. She had even gone so far as to say women banding together could accomplish much in the way of change. What kind of change these women thought would come about was beyond her.

Abigail had serious reservations about the motives of the women leading this charge. If Marcus found out she was contemplating attending a meeting, he would be so upset with her. He would say, "A woman's place is in the home. Are you lacking in anything? I provide for you and the children very adequately, and you should be more than satisfied. What do you actually think will be accomplished by this act of rebellion? I'm certain this whole fiasco will end in disaster. Can you imagine what the people at church will think of this?"

These thoughts and others went through her mind and bothered her greatly.

CHAPTER 7

Jenny lay in bed in a shallow slumber. There were whispers in the air that were preventing her from falling into a deep sleep. The soft, barely audible voice came from the mirror on the wall and was ever so faint, it almost seemed to be only in her head. Jenny was unaware that it was even happening or of what was being said, as it only entered her mind subconsciously. If she knew this was happening, she would have been frightened, very frightened indeed.

Because of the whispers, she had dreams of being pulled into a pool of quicksand. It was almost as if the soft voice was telling her what to dream of. It started with Jenny being pursued by an unknown person. She ran through the woods in an attempt to get away. No matter what she did or where she ran, she wasn't fast enough to get away. In the end, she broke into a clearing and ran right into the sticky muck.

There seemed to be no end to the depth of the quicksand, and she had no way to get out of it. As she sank, deeper and deeper, she screamed more and more. When she was up to her neck in the sticky mess, the person chasing her came into the clearing. Her back was to her

would be captor, and she couldn't see the face. Jenny
heard the heavy breathing behind her as she slipped under the mud. A scream escaped her lips, and she found
herself awake in her own bed.

CHAPTER 8

There was the sound of a door opening and the voice of her mother softly spoke to her. "Are you all right, dear? Were you having a bad dream?"

Jenny shook all over. "Gosh, Mother, I was running through the woods being chased by someone and fell into a pool of quicksand. It was so frightening. I couldn't do anything."

"It was just a dream, sweetheart. There's nothing to be afraid of, dear," she said as she hugged her little girl and tucked her in for the night. "Just put it out of your mind. Everything is all right, these things are normal and, in the morning, you will laugh about it. Goodnight, dear."

In the dark, with only a little light shining through the window, Jenny lay in her bed. She wondered why she had this nightmare. This was highly unusual for her. She had always had such pleasant dreams in the past.

Hanging on the wall was the mirror. Looking at it, she saw a slight illumination in the glass. *It must be as a result of the light coming in through the window.* She looked at it and didn't remember any light on the wall where the mirror was before it hung there. The light must have been hitting the glass because of a reflection from something that had been moved lately. This was all very strange. She fell asleep and the soft whispers were no longer there, allowing her to rest.

The morning sun shone through the window, illuminating the room. Jenny woke to the sound of birds chirping in the tree outside. The dream she had during the night was but a distant memory and hardly seemed real anymore.

Downstairs at the breakfast table, Mother asked, "How did you sleep, dear? Were there any more dreams to wake you?"

"I slept very well, Mother. I don't know why I had the dream, because I normally don't have scary ones like that."

"That's good. What would you like for breakfast, dear?" Mother asked.

Marcus sat at the table, reading the morning paper, oblivious to the conversation going on around him. If there was anything important to talk about, he would be told. With his breakfast done, he said goodbye to his family and went to work.

CHAPTER 9

In her room, Jenny thought back on the previous night. Sitting on the bed, she tried to discover where the light coming through the window would be reflected back into the mirror. Walking to the open window, she looked at where the street light came from. Moving to the wall behind her, she tried to locate something that would reflect it back to the mirror.

The dresser and mirror were placed on the same wall as the window, so whatever reflected the light should be very near where she was standing. Knitting her brow in concentration, she delved into the problem. There was nothing in the immediate area that had a reflective surface. So where the light came from that illuminated the glass was a mystery.

Unable to resolve the problem, she walked to the dresser and attacked the problem in reverse. Looking around the room, she tried to ascertain how the light could have hit the spot where she was standing. There was nothing she could see that indicated a solution to her dilemma.

As far as she could determine, there was only one solution to this mystery. That evening when it got dark, she would have to sit on the bed with the lights out. When she saw the light in the mirror, she would walk to it and see where the reflection came from. A smile crossed her face at the thought of being able to come up with a method to resolve the problem.

As she left the room and glanced back, she saw yet again a slight movement. This was now being looked at as a challenge. Jenny thought that some kind of game was being played and that she was smart enough to figure out who was behind it. With that in mind, she waited eagerly for the day to pass.

"Do you two want to go to the park this afternoon? I have some stale bread that we can feed the ducks with," Mother called up.

At the top of the stairs, the two answered together, "That would be great." Bobby continued, saying, "Can we bring a snack with us?"

"I don't see why not. Let's go at one-thirty. That will give me time to tidy the house and prepare lunch."

"I thought that was the housekeeper's job," Bobby said, slightly perplexed.

"It is, but I like to do the little things myself. What would I do with my day if I let someone do everything for me?"

In the afternoon, the three walked to the park nearby and, as they approached the pond, Bobby made a run for it. Because there was a downhill slope leading to the water, he misjudged the stopping distance and with the grass being slightly wet, he slid feet first into the pond. The water had the murky look it always got during the hot weather.

A few duck feathers floated on the surface. The warm water had soaked the boy's clothes. As he got to his feet, he stood knee deep in the water with a stunned look on his face.

"Bobby, what on earth are you doing? You could have been drowned," his mother shouted.

"Aw shucks, Mom, it was an accident. How was I to know that the grass was wet? I'm only a little wet, and it will dry up in no time," he said.

"I can't have you running around soaked to the bone. What would people think?"

As he walked on the grass, the squishing sound coming from the wet socks and shoes filled the air. Off they went back home to change the boy's clothes and wash him up.

"God only knows what you could have picked up in that dirty water. I don't know what to make of you sometimes, Bobby." Abigail said to her boy.

Aw, gee whiz, Mom, it really wasn't nothing, you know."

"Wasn't anything, not, nothing. Learn to speak properly, please."

Sorry, Mom. Can we go back to the park now? We still have the bread and snacks. It would be a shame to let it all go to waste."

"What do you think Jenny, should we go back?"

Looking at her younger brother, she saw a pleading look on his face. She was tempted to say no but realized that she may need him to help solve the mirror mystery. Smiling at her brother, she said, "It seems to mean a lot to Bobby, so yes, I'd like to go back too."

Bobby gave a sigh of relief and was already putting his shoes on by the time his sister and mother got to the front door. He gave his sister a smile as he opened the door, and they all left together. Back at the park, Bobby made sure he didn't make the same mistake again.

Supper was finished and Marcus asked the children to play in their rooms while he and their mother talked about adult things. When they were gone he said, "I hear that your friend Colleen is involved in that movement that is causing such a ruckus. I certainly hope you steer clear of it. There are going to be very big ramifications for those who try to push this issue."

"Why do you say that? Don't you believe that women should have a few more rights? We aren't all simple you know."

"I know you aren't, but not everyone is as forward thinking as I am. One day women may even be allowed to vote, but I can't see that happening in the near future. What I'm saying is, be careful, I hear things," Marcus said seriously.

"I'm not involved with anything at this point, and I'll discuss it with you before I do. Does that make you feel better?"

"Yes, it does, thank you. I have a reputation to maintain and something of this nature could adversely affect my interests," he said with a concerned look on his face.

The discussion drifted to other topics and the mood became lighter. The children occupied themselves for a while. Soon it was bedtime, and each brushed their teeth. This was something many of their friends didn't do, but their mother insisted on this ritual.

Abigail tucked them in, saying their prayers with them. Marcus was busy in the office and shouted his goodnights from there.

CHAPTER 10

The door to Jenny's room was closed, and she waited for her eyes to adjust to the darkness. As they did, there appeared a soft glow in the mirror again. It was so faint that she had to stare at it in order to know it was really there.

"Maybe it's not dark enough in here to see the reflection," she mumbled.

Waiting for fifteen minutes, she got out of bed and carefully walked close to the mirror. The very faint light was still there and so she placed herself in a position where she could see where the light was being reflected from.

No matter where she stood, there wasn't a light that she could see. She turned to look at the mirror. There it was again, that ever so slight movement. By the time she was looking directly at it, there had been nothing to see. *Maybe it's just an imperfection in the glass,* she thought, trying to look at every possibility.

The soft glow was there and, when she moved sideways, from one side to the other, the glow could always be seen.

"How can this be? If I'm right, there is no reflection,

which can only mean that the light is coming from the mirror itself. No, this cannot be. There is no light in or behind the glass. I was here when they put it on the wall. I looked at the back of it when they unpacked it too. What's going on?" she asked herself in a mild state of disbelief.

Studying the glass, she attempted to come up with a viable reason for the glow. Try as she might, she could not fathom any reasonable answers, no matter how she studied the problem. There was only one thing to do, un- pleasant as it may be, she'd have to ask Bobby to help her.

Going to his room as quietly as she could, she snuck in to see if he was still awake. "Bobby, Bobby, are you asleep?" she whispered.

There was a soft groan before he answered saying, "What do you want?"

"I need your help. Can you come to my room and look at the mirror for me. I think there's something funny happening."

"Can't it wait until morning?"

"No, it has to be dark to see what I want to show you. Don't say anything. I don't want Mother or Father to hear us," she said, almost pleading.

Reluctantly, he got out of bed and followed his sister into her room. They closed the door and slowly, not wanting to bump anything, they moved to the dresser. As their eyes adjusted to the darkness, Bobby asked what he was supposed to be looking for.

"Wait a minute. I don't think our eyes have adjusted enough yet." They waited a while longer, but nothing happened. It was dark and there was nothing to see. "I don't know what's going on. There was a light coming from the mirror earlier. I don't see it now," Jenny said, perplexed.

"Aw, how can that be? I don't see nothing. I'm going back to bed."

He left the room with Jenny looking at the mirror. The door was closed, and she looked around the room. When her gaze returned to the mirror, there it was again, the soft glow, ever so faint in the glass.

"My goodness, what on earth is going on?" she said softly to herself.

Unable to come up with a reason for the phenomenon, Jenny crawled under the covers and tried to go to sleep. Every so often, she took a peek at the mirror. Nothing unusual happened and soon she fell asleep. As she drifted off, the whisperings started once more.

The sound of the voice almost roused Jenny, but not quite. The whisperings were only heard by the sleeping girl, and then only in her head. It was almost as if there was a direct communication between the voice and Jenny. Things said entered Jenny's subconscious mind and seemed like a dream. The voice appeared to be telling her of impending events, things that upset the young girl in her sleep.

Jenny woke with a gasp. A dream so vivid had frightened her terribly. In her dream, Jenny saw herself as if she were someone else. There was an unrecognizable figure attempting to pull her into a dark hole in the wall. The misty form was unknown to her, and she felt deathly afraid of it. She was sure that it meant her harm in some fashion.

Sleep for the rest of the night was not particularly restful. The voice continued throughout the night, and it became obvious that something was attempting to communicate with her subconsciously.

As the nights went by, the voice started to seem friendlier. She still could only faintly hear the voice whispering just as she was drifting off to sleep, and she wasn't sure of this at all. The soft glow was still there, but only she could see it.

At bedtime, she asked, "Bobby, come into my room and see if there is anything out of order here."

He walked in and when the door was closed with no lights on, he said, "Yeah, there is something odd here."

In anticipation of hearing that he actually saw something, she felt a bit of excitement come over her. "What do you see Bobby?"

"I see that it's dark in here and I'll trip on something if I move. What is it that you think I'm supposed to see?"

"Nothing, Bobby, I was just wondering is all." The disappointment was evident in her voice. "Thanks for coming in. You can go back to your own room now."

That night the voice in her sleep became a little more forceful. There was something that it wanted to communicate to Jenny. Her dreams became more upsetting and she woke in the middle of the night with a scream.

CHAPTER 11

Her mother entered the room. "Jenny, what is it? I heard you scream in your sleep. Are you having a nightmare?"

"Yes, I dreamt that there was a thing trying to drag me into the darkness. I don't know who or what it was. I'm frightened, Mother."

"Do you have any idea what is causing you to have these awful dreams?" Abigail asked.

"I have no idea." She wanted to say it started when she got the mirror but hadn't wanted to take the chance of having it removed from her room. It was a most unusual piece, and she wanted to keep it, despite the disturbing events that she suspected were being caused by it.

"Try not to worry about it anymore. Whatever it is that may be causing the dreams. I'm sure it is nothing that need concern you, so try to sleep, dear," Abigail said gently.

Jenny fell asleep again and didn't wake until morning. She got up and recalled the strange dream she had. In the light of day, it didn't seem as bad as it did in the middle of the night. At the breakfast table, Marcus read the morning paper. Studying the financial section, he wondered what the market would do in the near future.

Abigail poured him his morning coffee, to which he mumbled a cursory response. The children were given freshly cooked waffles and corn syrup. "Thanks, Mom, these smell so good. Can we go to the zoo today? School starts in two weeks, and we won't have the time to go after that," Bobby said.

"Yes that would be great, Mom," Jenny piped in.

"All right, but it will have to wait till this afternoon. I have a meeting at the church this morning. Marcus, do you have some money with you to pay our way in? I'll see if Colleen wants to go with us."

At the mention of Colleen's name, Marcus's attention was gotten. "What is this about Colleen?"

"I was asking if you have the money to pay our way into the zoo this afternoon. Colleen may be able to drive us."

"Oh, yes, I have extra money in my wallet. Here it is," he said, handing her a few bills.

A short time later, Marcus had gone to his office. Abigail got ready and asked, "Jenny, come to my room while I get ready, dear."

"What is it that you want, Mother?"

"Last night you had a bad dream. Is everything all right?"

"Yes, Mother, why do you ask?" Jenny queried in return.

"This is something that you haven't done before, and I find it a trifle concerning. Is there a problem, is something upsetting you?"

"I'm fine, Mother, no need to worry."

"Bobby said that you asked him if he saw anything in the mirror. What is that about?"

Thinking quickly, Jenny said, "Oh that, there was a reflection in the glass, and I wondered if he saw it too."

"All right, dear, but if there is anything bothering you, be sure to let me know."

"I will, Mother."

With this, she left her mother's room to go to the kitchen.

CHAPTER 12

Shortly after lunch, there was a ring of the doorbell, and Abigail answered it. "Come in Colleen. Would you like a cup of tea before we go to the zoo?"

"Yes, that would be lovely," the soft-spoken, perky, reddish-blonde-haired lady said.

In no time at all, the group parked the horse and buggy at the gated area outside the city zoo. Even outside the walls, there were sounds of large animals and the smells one would expect. The two ladies walked close together, arms linked, and chatted as the youngsters went from cage to cage looking, at the wild animals.

The monkeys swung around their cages, using the branches of trees to hang from. The elephants used the water in pools to douse themselves, so they could keep cool. There were zebras with their striped bodies and giraffes with those impossibly long necks and beautiful colors.

When Bobby and Jenny approached the leopard cage, the fierce cats acted very aggressively. The felines paced back and forth in the cage, obviously agitated. The same thing happened at all the big cat pens.

"Geez, what's the matter with them? They never acted

like that when we came here before," Bobby said as he headed to the next area.

Jenny stayed by the tiger pen as the cat paced back and forth, growling. Then, suddenly, it lunged toward the front of the cage as if attacking. With a shriek, Jenny jumped back and ran away. Only when she left did the huge feline finally settle down.

This is so curious, she thought as she looked back at the then-calm tiger. "The same thing happened whenever I approached the other cages with cats in them. Why would they act up when I'm close and then calm down when I leave?"

"Jenny, did you do something to make the tiger jump at you?" Abigail asked.

"No, Mother, I was just standing there, and it started acting crazy. I have no idea why."

The rest of the day was spent away from the big cat pens. None of the other animals reacted strangely to her presence. When they were on their way home, Jenny decided to go to the library to borrow a book on feline behavior. There was a city library a few streets away from her home. If they could get home early enough, she would try to go that day. Unfortunately, as it turned out, it had to wait until the following day, because Mrs. Williams had had to make a stop before driving back to their home.

After another disturbing night, Jenny asked her mother, "I need to go to the library this morning. I have my card ready and will use my bicycle to get there. Is that all right with you, Mother?"

"It will be fine as long as that is the only place you go and that you come straight home afterward." Looking closely at her, Abigail asked, "Is everything all right, dear? You look very tired lately."

Waiting a moment before she answered, Jenny said, "I

am a little tired, but I am sleeping enough. I'm not sure why this is, but I'm sure it will correct itself in due course, Mother." At the library, Jenny asked the attendant, "Could you tell me what row the books on feline behavior are placed?"

"Follow me please," the librarian said as she walked ahead of the polite young lady.

There were several to choose from. The librarian, whose name tag read, Alice Truman, helped Jenny choose two of the more informative ones and checked them out for her. Placing the rather large books in the basket hooked onto the front of the handlebars, Jenny rode home.

The rest of the morning was spent studying the information. Much of it was of little value to her. Halfway through the second book, Jenny found something of interest. As she worked her way through the paragraphs, she started to read aloud.

"'It has long been thought that cats have a sense humans don't have. In the days of the pharaohs, cats were thought to be able to see or connect with the spiritual realm. In the occult, cats are used as a medium, in order to contact the dead. Felines have been known to become very agitated when in the presence of a person thought to be in contact with an evil spirit. This has been difficult to prove, although there have been documented cases where many people were convinced of the validity of the accusations.'"

My goodness, can this possibly be true? I'm sure this is just fanciful and printed in the book in order to make things more interesting, she thought. There were, however, doubts running through her mind.

Bobby called from the hallway, "Mom says that you have to come down for lunch."

"I'll be there in a minute."

The rest of the day was not as pleasant for Jenny as it normally was. There were unsettling things flitting back and forth in her mind. She was starting to wonder if the mirror was behind her nightmares. If so, how could she deal with the problem and still keep it? *What is happening to me? Why did those animals react the way they did?*

"Maybe I should get a few books on the occult. Oh, boy, Mother would be so upset if she found out I had them in the house. I could always just read them at the library. Yes, that's what I'll do. Tomorrow, I'll think of a reason to be gone for a few hours."

Another bad night with more nightmares had Jenny waking up later than usual. She came down the stairs and almost tripped. Catching the banister at the last moment, she managed to prevent a fall down the long winding staircase. No one was within seeing distance so this went unnoticed by the family members. Her ankle, however, was a touch sore. By the time she reached the kitchen, most of the discomfort had worked itself out.

After breakfast, she asked, "Mother, I want to return the books to the library. I won't be very long."

"Why don't you take Bobby with you?"

Bobby, hearing this, decided immediately that the last place he wanted to go was a place filled with books and informed his mother, "Ahh, Mom, I don't feel like going there. School is gonna start soon, and I'll have to look at books all the time. I wanna play in the backyard on the swing. Okay, Mom?"

Abigail thought for a moment before answering. Looking at her daughter, she asked, "Is everything all right? You still look like you haven't been sleeping very well. Are you still having those nightmares?"

"I'm not sure what's wrong. I go to sleep and it's almost like there is someone in my room whispering to me.

I have these stupid dreams lately and I don't know how to make them stop."

"I think we need to have you see the doctor. I'll make an appointment this week. Be careful riding your bicycle to the library, dear."

CHAPTER 13

Finishing breakfast and brushing her teeth, Jenny was on her way. When she saw the librarian, she asked, "Could you please tell me where the books on the occult are, Miss Truman?"

"I'm not sure that you're old enough to be reading that type of book, young lady," she informed Jenny.

"My mother knows I'm here to do some research before school starts. I won't be taking them home. I just want to check on a few items of interest, and then I'll go home," she said, smiling at the older lady.

Although not totally convinced, Miss Truman showed Jenny where the books were shelved. Browsing the titles, Jenny waited until the lady left before picking out one labeled, *Communicating with Spirits*. Bringing it to the nearest table, Jenny started to read silently.

There are good and bad spirits that can have a devastating effect on people's lives. Bad spirits try to take control of the person they are in communication with. It is often difficult to tell which are which. By the time the attacked person realizes what they are dealing with, it is already too late. The animal kingdoms, especially cats, are very sensitive to bad spirits. By the time cats are af-fected by the presence, possession is already well under-way. There is very little information available on how to stop or reverse this taking over of the host.

My goodness, what am I to do? How can I find out if this is really happening to me?

Getting up, Jenny headed back to the row of books. Looking the titles over, she tried to see if any of the books indicated how to deal with an evil spirit. To her dismay, there were no books that were of any use to her. Going back to the table, she sat down and continued to explore the book she already had.

When she was finished with the book, she had only one suggestion offered to her. It was thought that a certain kind of priest could be of help in dealing with this type of issue. The church that she attended with her parents was a Baptist Church. There had been no mention of this church as a remedy for her ills.

Going home and into her room, she started to wonder if she was reacting to a nonexistent problem. This was all most likely an issue related to growing up. She had already felt adjustments in her body and was aware of subtle changes taking place. This must be what was happening to her. She almost laughed as she realized how silly she had been to think along these lines.

The rest of the day was much better as she had put out of her mind the disturbing thoughts that had dominated her those last few days. She even had a nice time playing with Bobby after supper. Soon it was bedtime and, after having a bath, she said her prayers and was tucked in by her mother.

Because she had had several nights that were not restful, she fell into a deep sleep quickly. There were little whisperings again, but she was already asleep before they started. The soft voice speaking to Jenny was not heard by anyone else in the household.

The voice continued through the night. It penetrated deeper and deeper. As it did this, Jenny lost control over her body. A few moments before three o'clock in the morning, Jenny got out of bed at the urgings of the voice in her head. She slowly walked toward the dresser with the mirror hung over it, totally unaware of this happening. Jenny walked closer and closer to the mirror. She was being drawn there by something unseen.

A few inches from the dresser, she stopped. As she stood in front of the mirror, the air grew cold. Jenny's long hair seemed to have a life of its own. To anyone watching, it would have seemed that there was a breeze in the room. However, this was not the case.

The familiar glow in the glass grew slightly brighter. From inside the mirror, a very inhuman thing slowly reached toward the girl. Taking hold of the dressing gown, it gently pulled the girl toward the glass. As she leaned forward, her hands bumped the dresser and a picture was knocked over, making quite a loud sound as it crashed to the floor. This was enough to break the hold on her, and she awakened.

Jenny screamed as she woke up with the feeling that she was about to be taken from this world, into another. This other world frightened her to no end. The sound of a door opening was heard in Jenny's room.

CHAPTER 14

Rushing across the hall and into her daughter's bedroom, Abigail asked. "Jenny, are you all right? What are you doing out of bed?"

"I don't know. All I know is that my hand for some reason hit the picture on the dresser, and when it fell on the floor, I woke up, freezing cold. It doesn't seem cold now."

"This is getting out of hand. I'll contact Doctor Spring in the morning and make an appointment for you as soon as possible. I'm sure he can get to the bottom of this. He was educated in England, and they're more advanced than we are."

Walking back to bed, Jenny lay down as her mother tucked her in and stroked her hair. Staying with her daughter for a time, Abigail worried that things may be more serious than they appeared to be. Looking around the room, in the shadowy light, her eyes came to rest on the dresser and mirror. *This all started shortly after these additions were purchased and moved into this room. Could it be that these items are the cause of my Jenny's nightmares? No, how could this be?* But the feeling persisted as she got up to go to her room.

As Abigail left the room, the soft glow that was in the glass returned. The voice though remained silent for the rest of the night. What had happened in this room, no one of this Earth could explain. This, of course, did not mean that there was no explanation.

CHAPTER 15

Morning came and, for Jenny, it was none too soon. Her nights were getting worse, not better. The day before, she thought that she had had it all figured out, but things were worse than ever. Waking up in the middle of the night, standing in front of the mirror, had shaken her up immensely.

Abigail called the doctor's office and said to the receptionist, "Hello, this is Abigail Weatherby calling. There is something terribly wrong with my Jenny, and I need an appointment as soon as absolutely possible." She listened to the voice on the other end of the phone and said, "Yes, we can be there in two hours. Thank you so much."

The visit to the doctor was made with the expectation that all would be resolved. As Jenny and her mother entered the examination room, Dr. Spring asked, "So what seems to be the problem, young lady?"

Abigail answered for her daughter, explaining what had been going on.

Looking directly at Jenny, he asked, "Can you tell if there have been any changes in your sleeping pattern?"

Jenny thought about telling him about the mirror and

dresser but decided not to. She had no interest in looking like a fanciful girl. Instead, she said, "There's something that is making me have nightmares. I'm not sure what it is. Maybe there is a rustling in the trees outside my window, or possibly there's a mouse in the walls."

"These are things that are outside my ability to control. They would have to be taken care of by your mother and father, I'm afraid. I could give you something to help you sleep, but I think you are too young to be taking things like that. This could actually be a detriment and create long-term concerns."

Abigail asked, "Then what can be done to help my Jenny?"

"The first thing that should be looked at is the noise Jenny is talking about. Second, if this persists, then maybe she should sleep in a different room for a while. It might change the dynamics and help her to relax. If none of this helps, I believe a psychiatrist may be in order. Other than this, I don't know if I can help you. I will give her a complete examination today, though. Would you be so kind as to leave this room while I do this?" Dr. Spring asked.

"Yes, of course, Doctor."

The exam took place with nothing new discovered. In the end, mother and daughter left the office with Bobby in tow.

"How come I had to wait so long, huh? I was getting really bored. They don't have nothing to play with there," Bobby complained, but he was ignored.

That evening Marcus was told, "It's important that we call someone in to see if we have a mouse problem in our home. Could you look outside Jenny's window to see if there is anything that might be brushing against the house? The doctor thinks one of these things may be responsible for her nightmares."

"If we had mice, I'm sure that we would have noticed long before now. As far as the noise by her window is concerned, I'll look right now."

Climbing the staircase, Marcus entered the room in question and walked to the window. He opened it and, sticking his head through the opening, studied the exterior surroundings. As far as he could tell there was nothing in the immediate area that accounted for the manufacture of any noise. The tree outside was nowhere near the house, so it couldn't be the problem.

"I've looked around and there is nothing outside the house to account for any noises," Marcus informed Abigail and Jenny. "I'll call the exterminators today and have them inspect the property for rodents, but I doubt there are any."

"Thank you, Father, I don't know why this is happening," Jenny said. In her mind, thoughts were going around that disturbed her. She suspected that the mirror was somehow responsible but was afraid to put these ideas into words.

These thoughts were put aside, as she had a difficult time coming to grips with the situation. How could a piece of glass and wood do any of this? The book said that a priest from a certain sect of the Catholic Church was required to correct this occurrence. Her hands trembled slightly as she pondered the dilemma. Maybe, she thought, it was time to go to Saint Andrews Church for a chat with the local priest.

The evening came to an end and it was bedtime. In Jenny's room, Abigail asked, "Do you want to sleep in the guest room tonight, dear?"

Jenny wanted to say yes, but there was a warm feeling in her which made her say, "That's all right, Mother, I think it will be fine." It was almost as if something had taken over her for a moment.

Sleep, despite her slight anxiety, came easily that night. *Are there things that are taking hold of me?* This was the last thought going through her head as she drifted off. The whisperings started again without her knowing or hearing it.

These continued through the night, growing in forcefulness. At three in the morning, Jenny was sound asleep, but for some unknown reason, she slid out from under the covers. Getting out of the bed, she slowly made her way over to the dresser. As she approached, something in the mirror moved toward her. There was a slight bump as she made contact with the front of the dresser.

This noise was just loud enough to wake her mother, who had fallen asleep in an armchair just outside her daughter's room. Opening the door, she gasped as she saw Jenny at the piece of furniture. Abigail did not see the change in the mirror.

As the door opened, whatever was coming out of the glass retreated quickly. There was anger within the glass. It wished to lash out, but only had control over the youngster that it desired. It knew all too well that patience was required. Over the centuries, it had had to wait for the right moment many times.

CHAPTER 16

Jenny, what are you doing out of bed?" Abigail whispered.

Her question was not heard, as her daughter turned and walked back to her bed. Getting under the covers, Jenny remained asleep as if nothing was amiss. Abigail stared at the girl, wondering what on earth was going on.

Memories of her own childhood came back to her. When Abigail was fourteen years old and going through physical changes, she too walked in her sleep. Those memories helped her to dismiss this episode as a normal part of life in this family. Tucking her daughter properly under the covers, she kissed her on the forehead and went to her own bed. The problem for her was solved, no real need to worry anymore.

As she lay down in her bed, Marcus murmured, rolled over, and continued to sleep soundly. Abigail felt she had figured out Jenny's sleeping issue. This would all end after Jenny went through the changes her body was adapting to.

CHAPTER 17

orning came and Jenny awakened with no recollection of getting up during the night. Coming to the kitchen table, she took her seat and prepared to dig into the pancakes her mother had placed before her. Pouring the syrup on, she slowly started eating. For some reason, she was not very hungry lately.

"How are you this morning, dear," Abigail asked.

"I'm fine, Mother. I slept well, but I'm still waking up tired. Maybe I'm starting to get sick. These pancakes taste a bit weird. Is this a new recipe?"

"No, this is the same way I always make them. Your taste buds may be a little off."

Marcus left for work and Abigail asked, "When would the two of you like to go shopping for your school things? I have time, late this afternoon when your father can drive us downtown. Or would you rather do it on Saturday morning, unless you're not up to it?" she said, looking at Jenny.

Finishing the pancakes, Jenny said, "I feel all right now, Mother. Let's do it today. There are a few things I would like to get, like pencils and a notebook. The ones I get at school never seem to write as nice as the ones you buy."

"I don't need nothing. Do I really have to go to school?" Bobby asked.

"Of course you do. First thing is that this is the law. The second reason is, you will one day take over your father's business, and you won't be able to if you don't have an education," Abigail pointed out.

"Oh, awright, I guess if I have to."

The things were bought and the shopping trip done. Bobby was happy because he managed to get his mother to buy him a piece of hard rock candy.

Jenny seemed to be distracted much of the time, and when asked about it, she said, "To tell you the truth, Mother, I really don't know why my mind isn't able to stay focused."

"It could be that your hormones are changing, and this is affecting your ability to concentrate," Abigail told her.

Abigail tucked her daughter in bed that evening. The two talked for a few minutes about the seasons of life.

"There will be many changes in your life as you grow up. Some of them will be more difficult than others. Just remember that I will always be there for you, Jenny."

"Thank you. Don't worry about me. I'm sure what I'm going through is perfectly normal, and it will pass soon enough. Goodnight, Mother."

CHAPTER 18

The lights were turned off, and Jenny immediately fell asleep. Soon after, the whisperings started. The voice again was directed only at Jenny. The clock downstairs ticked away, hour by hour. At three in the morning, Jenny stirred. The tone of the voice she heard in her subconscious had changed. It was no longer soft and suggesting, but rather forceful and commanding.

While she remained asleep, Jenny pulled the covers back. Swinging her legs over the side, she got out and stood beside the bed. Ever so quietly, she walked toward the dresser. As she approached it, a queer thing occurred within the glass of the mirror. It began with a slight bulging in the surface.

As Jenny came closer and closer to the dresser and the mirror, she reached to the side and moved a chair in front of the dresser. Getting on the chair, she raised her arms to almost shoulder height. Something in the mirror pushed at the glass, attempting to reach toward the girl and touch her hands. A mere few inches apart, a breakthrough was made. Slender, discolored, boney, blackish fingers extended from the glass to Jenny's outstretched hands.

Reaching past the girl's fingers, the apparition's hands closed around her wrists. Remaining asleep, Jenny was pulled toward the glass. Slowly, the boney hands, belonging to who knew what, pulled Jenny into the mirror.

There was no sound made as Jenny kneeled on the dresser and was pulled into the mirror. She disappeared from her world to a place beyond imagining. Darkness enfolded the young girl and, as she woke, a horrible scream escaped from her lips, but it was too late for Jenny, far too late.

CHAPTER 19

B obby, go wake your sister. It's not like her to sleep in this long," Abigail asked.

"Awright, Mother."

Running up the stairway, eager to get back to his breakfast, Bobby headed to his sister's room. Knocking before entering, he opened the door and peeked inside. Scanning the bed and then the rest of the room, he saw nothing. Walking to the closet, he expected to find her there, so he called out to announce his presence.

"Jenny, Mom says you have to come down to eat."

No answering reply forthcoming, he opened the closet door—empty. Speaking to himself, he said, "This is strange, where could she be? I got it, she's in the bathroom."

Leaving her room, he walked down the hall and knocked on the door to the washroom. No answer there either. Going to the head of the stairs, Bobby yelled, "Hey, Mom, I can't find her."

"What do you mean, you can't find her? She has to be somewhere upstairs."

"I looked everywhere. She isn't here," he insisted.

Abigail said, "Marcus, put down the paper and come

upstairs with me, I think something is wrong."

"I'm sure she is in one of the rooms. Where else could she possibly be?" he answered as he got up, following his wife.

The two entered Jenny's room and a search began. Marcus looked under the bed and in the closet, finding nothing. The search continued in the other rooms on the second level. The results were the same, and so the entire house was searched. No sign of Jenny was found anywhere.

Marcus, by that time very concerned, said, "Let's go back to her room and see if we can find any clues as to where she may be. Don't touch anything, though, just in case we have to contact the police."

Abigail, with a very worried look, frantically almost ran to her daughter's door. Once there, the two stood by the doorway and studied the bedroom. As their eyes drifted around the room, Abigail's eyes stopped at the dresser and the chair that was in front of it. "Marcus, look at the dresser. One of Jenny's photos has been knocked over again, and she would never leave the chair like that. She would never knowingly leave either thing like that. Look, there is a little scuff here at the front edge of the wood."

"Was her window open last night when she went to sleep?"

"Yes, it was. Why do you ask?" Abigail returned, as she wrung her hands in worry.

"I'm going to have a look at the window to see if someone came in through it and took our little girl," he said as the fear of disaster took hold of him. Going to the window, he studied the sill and the exterior wall and then the grounds near the house. Finding nothing, he turned to his wife and told her, "I think we have to call the police. I believe she has been taken."

At that, Abigail burst into tears. Marcus grabbed his wife as she started to collapse to the floor.

CHAPTER 20

Forty minutes after the call was made, the police arrived at the Weatherby home. As they came up the front walk, Marcus opened the door.

Abigail stepped forward, crying. "We think our daughter may have been taken from our home during the night."

"Can you fill me in on all the details, Mrs. Weatherby, while my men do a complete search of your home?" the sergeant asked.

Between sobs, she said, "We have already looked, but if that is what is needed, please do so."

The events of the previous evening and that morning were relayed to the policeman. When Abigail was finished, she was out of breath and her hands trembled.

"Is there anything unusual that you noticed today?" the sergeant asked.

"There are a few things in her room that were not as they should be. It's probably nothing, but it is out of the ordinary. Come, I'll show you," she said as she led the policeman to Jenny's room.

The three mounted the stairs and entered the bedroom. She showed him the chair, the knocked-over photo, and the scuff mark. "Jenny is very fastidious. She would never leave the picture like this, and as for the scuff mark, how would that happen? She never wears shoes in her room so where would the mark come from? Plus, this chair would never be left like this. Look at the rest of the bedroom. Everything is as neat as a pin."

"I have no explanation for the photo, the scuff mark, or the chair at this point. Mrs. Weatherby, has your daughter ever run away from home? Is it possible that she snuck out of the house last night and went to a friend's house?"

Marcus answered. "Our daughter has never done any such thing, and this is totally out of character for her. I think the alarm should be sent out. Maybe she has been kidnapped. Something has to be done. We're wasting time, while our daughter could be taken to who knows where."

"Let me and my men check this room and the grounds outside, and we'll see if anything can be discovered. If you would be so kind as to wait in the kitchen, we'll get on with it."

Even Bobby was questioned, with no positive results.

An hour went by with the parents fretting and worrying the entire time. Finally, the sergeant came into the room and informed the Weatherbys of their findings. "We have searched the entire property and every square inch of the home. We have found no trace of an intrusion into your home. There is nothing at this point that indicates your daughter was forcibly taken. This, of course, does not mean that it didn't occur as you said. It just means that, if she was taken, the perpetrator left absolutely no evidence behind."

"What are we to do? How will you proceed with this?" Marcus asked with a tear running down his cheek. Abigail was crying loudly as she suspected the worst.

"There will be an alert sent out, and we will use all our resources to find your Jenny. An officer will be left here, just in case there is a ransom demand. I'll get back to the station and get things started. If you hear anything, anything at all, be sure to inform me as soon as possible. Do you have a photograph of Jenny?" the sergeant asked.

Marcus got one from his office and gave it to him. With this, he quickly left, seeing himself out. He gathered his men, and they all went back to headquarters. The family was in a state of anxiety as they wondered where their little girl was.

CHAPTER 21

The day passed by slowly, with no sign of the missing girl. The evening came, and standing in the doorway of Jenny's room, Abigail looked around, just on the off chance that this had all been a horrible dream or joke. She cried quietly as she wondered where her little girl was.

Abigail recalled the conversation she had with Jenny the previous night. She told her girl that she would always be there for her. How quickly that had turned out to not be the truth. *Where is my girl? If this is a kidnapping for ransom, why haven't we been contacted?*

The smells in the room brought back too many memories for her to handle, so she turned and went to her bedroom. Abigail slept very little during the night. Marcus too, hardly slept, expecting a knock on the front door, or the ring of the telephone at any time. Even Bobby didn't sleep well, but he slept better than his parents.

Morning came, and it was evident that this household had a difficult night indeed. Breakfast was picked at as everyone waited for any kind of word that the situation had been resolved. Finally, unable to bear it any longer, they called the police station.

The sergeant answered the call. "I'm sorry, but there is no progress to report. Every station in New York has been notified and a description has been sent. So far we haven't heard anything in response to the case."

"What can we do? We can't just sit here and wait. Our girl is missing, and we feel helpless," Abigail shouted into the mouthpiece.

"I'm afraid that, for the moment, it's all you can do. We need you at your home in case someone attempts to contact you. We will get in touch with you if anything develops." With this, he hung up the phone.

The day passed. The next day came and went. The week slipped by, and still, nothing happened. The strain showed on the parents. It was obvious that they did not sleep. Friends came to lend their support, but in the end, nothing helped.

A month slowly drifted by, and it was assumed that the girl was gone. The police no longer thought the issue would turn out favorably.

Two months went by, then three, then six. Jenny's room was closed up and all hope for her return had been gone for some time. Jenny was never heard from again, and ten difficult years later, the home was sold as both parents were now deceased. Marcus and Abigail Weatherby never got over the loss of their daughter, and it had taken its toll on them. Bobby, without his older sister to guide and help him, was not fit to run the business his father had let slide since the disappearance of his daughter.

The contents of the home were put up for auction. One by one, the items were bid on.

The auctioneer sold one piece after another until he came to a dresser and mirror combination. Here, he said, "Next up for bids are a beautiful dresser and an exotic handcrafted piece with a very unique smoked glass mirror. Do I hear twenty dollars? Yes, I have twenty dollars from the young lady. Do I hear…"

CHAPTER 22

Margaret Louise Perkins was going to New York City on a visit to see Aunt Lucy, her father's sister. She was bringing her six-year-old twin boys, named Harold and Wayne. She came from a reasonably well to do family but was, unfortunately, a widow. The date was Saturday, June 28, 1922.

Her husband had died overseas during the Battle of Amiens in early August 1918. After his death, which took a long time to get over, she moved back home with her parents outside Davenport, Iowa. Daniel and Wilma Purdue lived on a successful horse ranch. Through excellent breeding practices, Daniel has raised many quality racehorses, which he sold for a good deal of money.

Margaret was a nice enough looking young woman, but some men considered her rather plain. Not that she was unattractive. She just wasn't what most men called pretty. Her disposition, however, was pleasant, and this made up for the other shortcomings. Slender of build and standing at five foot four, she didn't make a lasting impression on those she met. Brown hair and eyes completed the picture.

Life on the ranch had been good for the boys. The city

of Davenport was nice enough, but there were just too many people for Margaret to get used to. She had been raised on the ranch, but when they were married, Frederick had insisted they live in the city. It was a wife's duty to follow her husband. After all, he was the breadwinner.

After Frederick died overseas, Margaret had been lost for a time. When her father suggested that she and the boys move to the ranch, it seemed like the only reasonable thing to do. Living there, the boys were happy and growing so quickly. Life on the ranch was pleasant, and Margaret had the chance to spend time with the animals that she loved. Often times, she could be seen riding her favorite mare along the country roads.

Plans had been made to travel to New York City. Aunt Lucy had invited her and the boys to come for a visit. The tickets had been purchased and her father drove her and the children to Davenport. The New York Central Railroad train pulled into the station, and when the engineer sounded the loud whistle, it had startled her boys. The rumbling sound of the engine announced the train's arrival. The heavy locomotive sent vibrations through the floor they were standing on as it rolled to a stop.

People from all walks of life exited the passenger compartments. A large number of people were standing on the platform welcoming friends and relatives. The voices of happy people echoed through the air. Finally, when everyone had left the train, the conductor allowed the passengers to board. He checked the tickets held by each new person as they got on to the train.

Her boys had already been told what was expected of them, and Margaret was pleased that they were actually behaving. The two pieces of luggage were stowed and the three found their compartment. There was seating for six in the section. By the time the train began the jarring start of the trip, Margaret and the boys were joined by an elderly couple.

"Boys, we are going to be on this train for almost twenty hours, so I want you to behave. I have brought along some things to eat and plenty of water. If you get tired, just go to sleep."

"Mom, how fast are we going? Everything is moving so fast away from us," Harold asked.

When the older gentleman saw that Margaret wasn't quick to answer, he said, "We are traveling at almost thirty-five miles an hour. It is very fast indeed, isn't it?"

"Wow, it sure is fast," Harold replied.

The man smiled and went back to reading the *Davenport Daily*, a newspaper he had probably picked up at the station. The lady with him looked out the window as the scenery changed from city to country views.

After an hour of swaying and steady bumping, both lads were sound asleep. By the time they woke, almost half the trip was over. A visit to the washroom and both boys and their mother were ready for a bite to eat.

CHAPTER 23

When the train arrived in New York at ten in the morning, the three were more than eager to get off. Trying to keep the boys reined in had been quite a task for Margaret. The locomotive pulled the long line of cars into the railway yard before coming to a halt, with the boys looking out the windows at the unfamiliar sights.

"Is Aunt Lucy going to meet us here, Mommy?" Wayne asked.

"Yes, she is. Are you eager to see her? It has been quite some time since you saw her last."

"I guess so," he replied.

Entering the station and waiting for her luggage, Margaret looked for her aunt. "There she is, boys, the lady getting up from the bench on our right."

Both lads looked in the wrong direction. One looked to the left and the other straight ahead. Aunt Lucy was a lady in her late forties and slightly plump. At just over five feet tall with red hair, she was fairly easy to spot.

"Yoo-hoo, Margaret, here I am. It is so nice to see you. Hello, boys, come give auntie a hug," Lucy said. Which they did as Lucy gave each a big kiss on the cheek. Boys being boys, they both quickly wiped the cheeks off with their sleeves.

When the luggage had been unloaded, a cabby was hailed. The driver placed the pieces in the trunk of the car.

The ride to Aunt Lucy's home took twenty-five minutes, with the boys staring out the windows. They were now in the western section of the city, known as Cliffside Park, not too far from Union City.

The homes in this district were mostly three-bedroom, two-story red brick structures. Trees lined the streets with birds chirping as they flew here and there. A sense of community could be felt as people walking by smiled at Aunt Lucy. The boys saw a park with children playing in it nearby and, looking at auntie, Wayne asked, "Will we be allowed to play in the park?"

"Oh, my goodness, yes. We can go there tomorrow, right now it will be best if we get you all settled in. After all, it has been a long trip."

The boys were situated in their own room with two single beds in it. Taking her by the arm, Aunt Lucy led Margaret to another bedroom. "This will be your room while you're here, dear. Would you like me to make you a cup of tea?"

"Yes, that would really hit the spot, Auntie."

"Do you suppose the boys are hungry? I can make them and you a nice sandwich, if you like, dear," Lucy asked.

"Let me go ask them."

Margaret walked back to the other bedroom and found out that they were indeed hungry.

With the boys in tow, she seated them at the white painted kitchen table, while tea and sandwiches were being made. A glass of milk was poured for each of the boys.

While the lads ate their meal, the grownups got reacquainted. The two caught up on what had been going on in each other's life.

Aunt Lucy said, "By the way, your cousin, Jeffery, is looking forward to seeing you. He won't be here for a few days yet, though. He's working for New York Central Railway and is in some other state at the moment. As soon as he gets back, he said he would call."

"That will be nice. I haven't seen him for three years. How is he, has he got a girlfriend?"

"With him being out of town so much, he said that he hasn't had the time to meet anyone, but I keep hoping. I really would like to be a grandmother," Lucy said with a faraway look in her eyes. Bringing herself back to the present, she asked, "Come, why don't we go for a little stroll around the neighborhood?"

"That will be nice. I'm sure the boys are eager to have a little physical activity. What do you say, boys, want to go for a walk?"

Both at the same time said, "Yeah, let's go."

Once outside, the balmy, but slightly humid air, tussled Margaret's hair. Harold and Wayne both saw the park a short distance away and asked to go there first.

Aunt Lucy looked at her niece. "It is probably a good idea to let them run off a little of their excess energy, don't you think?"

"I agree. Otherwise, they will be running here and there. We won't be able to enjoy ourselves at all."

Off to the park, it was. In the central area of the park was a playground. Swings and slides occupied the lads for the next half hour. With much of their restlessness dissipated, they ran over to the fountain for a long drink.

"My goodness, you would almost think they were camels, the way they're filling up on water," Lucy said with a laugh.

Playtime finished, the group walked around the streets. Tall trees, planted years ago, lined the edges of the sidewalks and the center median of the streets. Trees alternated between maples and oaks, with a few crab apple and locust trees put in here and there to break things up a little.

The walk was slow and pleasant. The lads stayed close by as they no longer had an abundance of energy. On some of the tall wooden poles used to carry electricity to all the homes, papers were stapled. Many of these advertised services offered and items for sale. Margaret casually glanced at some of them as she passed.

There were several flyers advertising an auction to be held the following week. The date printed on the flyer was two days before she and her sons were due to leave on the train ride back to Davenport.

Listed at the bottom were a few of the items that would be auctioned. She stopped long enough to read the list, and the descriptions of two items piqued her interest. A dresser and an unusual mirror were two things that she could really use. Getting them back home was a concern, though.

"Is there something on the auction list that you're interested in?" Lucy asked her niece.

"Yes, I like the sound of the dresser and mirror. My dresser at home is falling apart, and I don't have a mirror in my bedroom. How to get them home would create a problem."

"Jeffery works for the railway and, because of that, he can bring it to Davenport free of charge. Would that help you, dear?" Lucy said, smiling at her niece.

"That would be wonderful. Is there a way to view the pieces beforehand, do you think, Auntie?"

"I do have a friend that knows the auctioneer hosting the event. I'll call Gertrude and see if she can arrange it for you."

CHAPTER 24

Lucy talked to Gertrude two days later and asked her for a favor. Gertrude contacted the auctioneer and received approval for Margaret to come and see the dresser and mirror Monday afternoon at one o'clock. The address was written down, and Lucy explained that because it was only four blocks from her home, it would be an easy walk.

The rest of the time, until she was due to see the pieces of furniture, was spent going to various places of interest in the massive city. The boys absolutely loved Coney Island, with its amusement parks. The rides were great fun for them. However, Margaret wasn't quite as thrilled about them as her sons were. Some of the rides were more than she could handle.

The cotton candy and caramel apples intrigued the two as well as the hotdogs and sodas. By the end of the day, the lads were so tired they fell asleep on the way home. The taxi driver's offer to carry the boys into the home was immediately accepted by the ladies.

The time in New York sped by ever so quickly. It had been one of the best vacations Margaret and the boys had had in quite some time. Before she knew it, Monday arrived and she and Aunt Lucy were walking down the street with the boys. Several times Margaret had to stop the boys from running too far ahead or out into the street. At Danvers Road, they turned left onto Barker and then to Fowler Road.

Soon the troupe entered a rather large building. The entrance led to a large open area, which had a great many chairs placed in neat rows. There was a platform with a podium on it for the auctioneer.

A pleasant older gentleman asked, "May I be of service ladies?"

Lucy took the lead. "We are here to see a dresser and separate mirror. My friend, Gertrude arranged it with the auctioneer."

"Oh, yes, Mister Ewen informed me that you would be coming to view the pieces. Please follow me," he replied as he walked to a door on the right-hand side of the large, high-ceilinged room.

Through the heavy door, they all went. The man led them past a number of items and finally stopped in front of a very nicely built dresser. The sturdy, ornate piece was made of a wood that was much darker than woods grown in North America. The mirror, which stood behind the dresser was pulled out and uncovered.

The mirror had smoked glass. The wood was very finely detailed and even darker than the dresser. It presented a striking work of art indeed. The beauty of the workmanship took Margaret by surprise. A warm feeling came over her as she lightly ran her fingers over the two items. Turning to the older man, she asked, "Can you tell me anything about these two pieces?"

He thought for a moment. "I believe that these items came from an estate in New York City. The people have passed away and, if I'm not mistaken, the daughter, whom these two items were purchased for, disappeared one night years ago. The son is still alive and is liquidating the contents of the home."

"Oh, dear, was the child ever found?" Margaret asked.

A sad look crossed the old man's face as he answered, "No, I don't believe she was ever located."

"I will return for the auction and would like to bid on these two pieces. Do you have any idea what would be a fair price to pay for them? My funds are limited, but I really would like to have them for my home in Davenport."

"My, what a coincidence. My son lives in Davenport. I think that you may get them with a bid of…say, twenty, to twenty-five dollars. Of course, you should start at five dollars, in order to size up your competition. I'll let Mister Ewen know the situation. He may be able to help you buy them at a decent price. Please don't tell anyone about this. If word got out that there is favoritism, we would be in big trouble."

"We won't tell a soul, I promise," Margaret said sincerely.

The walk home was pleasant because the weather was warm and sunny. The temperature was in the low eighties, and there were few clouds in the sky. The boys were having a great time and just loved Aunt Lucy who treated them wonderfully.

The day of the auction came, and Lucy had a neighbor look after Harold and Wayne. The two women got seats off to the left and five rows back from the podium. There were many empty seats as it was a weekday and most of the items up for auction were more for the average person. There were a number of high-end pieces on the block that day too, but they were of no interest to Margaret.

Several pieces were bid on and the prices seemed reasonable to the two ladies. In order to keep the interest of the patrons, items were mixed up, but followed a list. Almost halfway through, the dresser and mirror were brought out. There had been some discussion as to why these two were not being auctioned off separately.

The ones that had complained wanted either one or the other, not both. This worked in Margaret's favor as she did want both. The bidding began with Margaret opening at five dollars. Someone immediately countered with a ten dollar bid. She decided to wait for a moment, not wishing to appear too eager.

Another bid brought the price to fifteen dollars. The auctioneer rolled this number around and said "Going once."

Margaret raised her hand slightly, just high enough for the auctioneer to see it, but not the other bidder.

"I have a bid of twenty dollars." He looked around, and before a counter bid could be made, he said, "Sold, to the lady to my right." There was a groan from the other side of the room, and a rumble as a man complained that the set was sold too quickly. The next piece was brought out.

Margaret was happy at the turn of events. This had worked out better than she thought it would. Catching the auctioneer's eye, she gave him a quick smile. There was a slight grin in return as he started the bidding on the next item.

The money was paid and arrangements were made so Jeffery, her cousin, could have the newly acquired furniture picked up and shipped via train.

"Oh, thank you, Aunt Lucy, this has worked out just beautifully."

The two walked back home and retrieved the boys. Lunch was made and the rest of the day spent with the boys playing in the park, while the two ladies talked. The last two days of the vacation went by far too quickly. The ride to the train station was a little sad.

Aunt Lucy said, "I will miss having the three of you here. I'll have to see if I can come to Taylor Ridge for a trip to spend time with you and your parents. I've already contacted Daniel, and he will meet the train with the truck, in order to take your furniture to the farm."

"Thank you for everything, Auntie. Boys, give Aunt Lucy a hug."

This they did, and their aunt got tears in her eyes, knowing she wouldn't see them for some time.

CHAPTER 25

"How was your trip dear?" Margaret's mother asked.

"We had a wonderful time, Mother."

"Your father is talking to the conductor about having your things loaded onto the truck. Did you miss me, boys?" Wilma asked her grandchildren.

Having been warned ahead of time, the boys answered, "Yes, Grandmother, we did."

This brought a smile to Wilma's face, as she hugged the pair. She gave them each a kiss on the cheek, which they immediately wiped off.

The truck was loaded and the group headed for home. The dresser and mirror were brought into the house and then into Margaret's room. There were several hooks on the back of the mirror which would allow it to be hung sideways or up and down. The wire had been removed long ago, so the hooks were placed on to two heavy screws newly anchored into the wall. The dresser was then placed against the wall under the large looking glass.

Standing back, Margaret admired her new possessions. The smoked effect in the glass gave the mirror a unique look. The wood used to construct both items worked very well together. Looking around the room, which was situated on the opposite end of the home from her parent's bedroom, she liked what she saw.

A double set of French doors led to a small garden with seating area. This was very unusual for a farm property, but because their daughter lived with them, it was built there so she could spend time by herself. The doors and garden were added when Margaret moved back home after her husband died in that awful war overseas. Sometimes at night when she couldn't sleep, Margaret would sit in the boat swing in the moonlight. The summer nights were warm and she found a little peace in the garden.

Having to raise the two boys on her own had been difficult until her parents asked if she would like to move back home with them. Thank goodness she had had them to fall back on. Life on the farm was helping the boys grow into well-adjusted young males. This was mostly due to the influence of her father.

Most men she knew paid little if any attention to their young children. This was woman's work and, as the children grew up, they were thought of as being a cheap source of labor. Education was thought of as a necessary thing that may or may not be of use to a farmer.

The long trip on the train had taken its toll on both her and the boys. They were all in bed early that evening. As Margaret lay in bed and just as she started to drift off, there was a barely audible whispering in her room. The ever so soft voice didn't even register on her conscious mind. If she were to wake at that moment, she might not even remember hearing anything.

In the morning, she remembered nothing but did wake up a trifle anxious. Something was disturbing her, but she was unable to pin it down.

"Did you sleep all right, dear?" her mother asked.

"I slept right through the night, but I'm just a little tired for some reason."

"It's probably just because of the trip. I'm sure you will feel better tomorrow. The boys have already eaten and are in the barn with your father," Wilma informed her daughter.

Having had her breakfast, Margaret went to her room to prepare for the day ahead. On her way into the closet, she glimpsed a movement reflected in the newly acquired mirror. Turning, she saw nothing. To herself, she said, "I could have sworn that there was something reflected in the glass."

Looking around the room, she wondered if one of her sons was playing a trick on her. Finding nothing, she walked back to the closet. Just as she entered it, there it was again, a tiny movement reflected in the mirror. Determined, not to be taken in, she ignored what she suspected was a trick being played on her.

The rest of the day, she didn't re-enter her room. There were chores to do and supper to help with. She peeled the potatoes and chopped up an onion and a few carrots. The aroma of a roast that had been cooking for hours, and was almost ready, filled the air. This was her father's favorite meal. The cow, after a good number of years supplying milk, was supplying their meat. An arrangement with the butcher allowed for a practical division of the meat over a period of time.

The butcher deducted the weight that the Perkins family used from the records he kept. When they'd nearly used up all they had, a new cow would be brought in. The icebox in the Perkins home would have to be replaced one day in the near future, for one of those new-fangled refrigerators. At the moment, they were too costly and not dependable. But their friend, who sold these items in town, said they were getting better and better, and the cost was also coming down, due to new manufacturing processes.

In the barn, the chores were done and the males all came in to wash up and sit down for the evening meal. The boys were all excited.

"Mother, Grandpa let us help feed the cows and chickens," Harold said. "He said he'll teach us how to drive the tractor when we get a little older, isn't that right, Grandpa?"

"It sure is. You boys are growing up really fast, and one day you'll be running the farm. Isn't that right, Mother?" he said with a smile, revealing the teeth of a smoker.

Wilma smiled at her husband. "That's right, dear. Now, who's hungry?"

Both Harold and Wayne shouted out, "Me."

After supper was finished and the dishes were done, there was a knock on the door. Daniel being the closest to it answered it. Opening the heavy wooden door, he peered through the screen door and saw someone he didn't much care for.

"Hello, James, what is it that you want?"

"Hello, Mister Perkins, I've come to see Margaret."

"Why do you want to see my daughter?"

"There is a social this Saturday evening, and I thought she might want to go with me," James told him.

"Your wife died less than six months ago. Isn't it customary to wait at least a year before you start seeing another woman?"

"I'm sorry, but those are customs from the old days. This is nineteen twenty-two, you know, and things have changed," the young man said to the older farmer.

"I disagree with you. There are things that are right and things that are wrong. This is wrong," Daniel retorted, with a glare in his eye.

He didn't care for this all-too-forward young man in the least.

Margaret appeared beside her father at this moment. "What brings you over here, James? I'm sorry about Nancy dying of consumption not long ago. How are you and the girls doing?"

"We're getting along fine now, thank you for asking. I came over to ask you to the social on Saturday evening at the town hall."

"Thank you for asking, but it is a little soon for that. The people would be shocked if we went there together. There would be all kinds of talk and gossip. I'm sorry but I have to decline your offer."

Perplexed, James said, "I don't care what people think. They can just mind their own business. I don't think there is anything wrong with my asking you. I'm sure you'll have a perfectly pleasant time, so I'll ask you again, will you go to the social with me?"

Just a bit taken aback, Margaret said, "Please don't press the issue, James, *I* do care what people think, and this is improper. It's just far too early."

With an angry look on his face, James turned on his heels and stomped off the wooden porch. He cranked his well-worn automobile and drove away in a huff. At the crossroad stop sign, he drove right through it without even slowing down.

Daniel looked at his daughter. "My goodness, that young man has a temper. I heard that Nancy had complained of his abusive nature to the women folk at the church all the time."

"Yes, I heard the same thing. Nancy claimed he even struck her on a number of occasions. I don't like James, and I'm certain that if you hadn't been here, he would have tried to push his way into the house."

Deep in thought, Daniel thought that he would keep

his shotgun, the one he used to hunt geese with, handy. He'd, of course, have to warn the boys not to touch it. He had a feeling that this incident with James was not over.

The rest of the evening had the adults in the family slightly on edge. At eight o'clock Harold and Wayne were put to bed and tucked in by their grandmother. Margaret and her parents discussed the event that happened earlier. It was obvious that Daniel was upset with this incident.

He started the conversation by saying, "I doubt this is the last we'll see of James. I heard that once he had his sights on Nancy, he didn't let up until she agreed to marry him."

Wilma concurred. "I heard that too. When they were married, he got her pregnant and started drinking. Now he has three little girls, and I've heard he is looking for a mother for them."

Margaret sighed. "I, for one, certainly don't want him for a husband. Frederick was such a pleasant man, I couldn't bear to be with such a lout as James."

"If he comes here again, I'm going to go to the police station and put in a complaint," Daniel informed the lady folk.

Bedtime arrived and Margaret slipped under the covers. Just as she dozed off, the whispering started. If anyone else had been in the room, they would have heard nothing. The voice was for one person only, and in her subconscious alone.

At first, the voice was soothing and pleasant. This continued for several nights. Close to the end of the week, it began to become more assertive. It had an agenda and meant to fulfill a desire. It had been far too long in a state of hibernation. It did have company that it had acquired, one by one, but its needs had to be replenished.

Friday evening, after she had gone to bed, the voice

was interrupted by a knock on the French doors leading to the garden. There was an unpleasant young man peering through the glass. The entity was angry at being disturbed and wanted to lash out at the disturbance. Unfortunately, at that time, it could only handle one task at a time—Margaret.

Margaret awakened at the sound. In the glow of the moonlight, she saw a figure looking at her. It took a moment for her to recognize James. She shouted at the young man outside, "Leave me alone. What are you doing here?"

"I just want to talk to you," he answered. "I really like you and want you to come with me to the social tomorrow evening." There was a slur to his words, and it was evident that he had been drinking.

Hearing the rather loud voices, Daniel got out of bed. Grabbing the shotgun, he ran to the front door and confronted the drunken young man.

"What are you doing on my property, James? You've been drinking, haven't you?"

"I just wanted to talk to Margaret. There's nothing wrong with that," James said, still slurring his words.

"I want you off my property, and if you come back, I'll press charges against you, do you understand me?" Daniel shouted angrily.

"You can't stop me from seeing Margaret. I want to marry her. She'll come around, you'll see," he said as he turned away and staggered back to his poorly maintained vehicle. Driving off, he swerved back and forth on the road.

Through the glass, Daniel asked, "Are you all right, dear?"

"Yes, although he did startle me when he banged on the glass."

"I'm going to the police tomorrow morning and swear out a complaint. That boy is dangerous," he told his daughter.

"I think you're right, Father."

Margaret got back into bed and fretted about the persistence of the young man. That kind of attention she did not want. It took quite some time to fall asleep again. When she did, she had no idea that there was a dark brooding within the looking glass. It was as if the entity within the mirror had thought that, if only it had more strength, it would have handled the unwanted intruder and possibly captured two new companions at the same time. However that was not possible, so the work here would need to be hurried.

CHAPTER 26

The next morning after breakfast, the boys were asked to help their grandmother, while their mother and grandfather went to town. The ride into town was fairly quiet as each formulated what message they wanted to relay to the policeman.

Parking the truck on the road in front of the building which housed the police department, they entered. They were directed to the officer that handled these types of problems. After explaining what had been going on and giving a brief description of the person, the complaint was filed.

Officer Frank Benson recognized the name and said that he would have a word with the young man.

"What will happen if he doesn't stop harassing my daughter?"

"If that happens, a restraining order will have to be sworn out. If he doesn't comply with that, he will be arrested. I'm sure this will be enough to stop the unwanted attention, though."

On the way home, Margaret said, "Thank you, Dad, this whole affair frightens me. I don't know why James feels that he can do as he pleases."

"I don't either. You would think that he would know better. Maybe he has gotten away with this kind of behavior all his life and thinks it's normal."

Daniel took the boys around the farm as he fixed fences that had come loose from the wooden posts. In his apron, he carried fence pliers, a hammer, and U-shaped fence staples. Now and then, he found a staple on the ground where it had fallen. The animals bumping and pushing against the fence to get at the green grass on the other side had loosened the staples to the point where they sometimes came out of the wood.

The afternoon sun was warm and, as the three made their way along the fences, the two youngsters found little things to keep them occupied. A garter snake was spotted and the two chased after it to get a closer look. The way it slithered through the grasses fascinated the pair.

Their attention was held for only a short time as a mouse scurried away, only to be caught by a hawk. They watched gleefully as the bird of prey flew away with the rodent firmly held in its claws.

At supper, Wayne told the tale of the snake to his mother. When he was finished, Harold took over, going to great lengths to tell of the mouse and the fierce screeching hawk.

"You should have seen it, Mother, that mouse didn't stand a chance. That hawk was the biggest one we've ever seen." The story was told with great enthusiasm, and by the time he had finished, he was almost out of breath.

All in all, it had been a very exciting day for the boys. After they had a bath, both were soon sound asleep in their beds. Unfortunately for Margaret, that day had been full of worries. To make matters worse, James was spotted driving slowly by the house as the three adults were relaxing on the bench located on the front porch.

When he saw that he had been observed, he sped away.

Daniel shook his head. "My goodness, the young man is persistent. If this continues, I'll call Officer Benson and have him deal with James. This nonsense has to stop."

At bedtime, as she lay in bed, the whispers were heard again, just as Margaret fell asleep. The voice, which until then had been only suggestive, took on a more insistent quality. It did its work throughout the entire night.

There was a glow in the mirror, which, until then, had been very faint. Whatever was in this glass hanging on the wall was growing stronger. It was drawing strength from the sleeping form in the bed.

Outside the home, a poorly maintained vehicle stopped by the side of the road. The young man sitting behind the steering wheel let his thoughts run in directions that were not conducive to Margaret's happiness.

In the morning, Margaret awakened, feeling like she hadn't rested properly. She would have stayed in bed, but her sons were eager to start the day. Wearily, she got up and dressed. In the bathroom, she washed her face with cool water. This made her feel a little better.

At the kitchen table, Wilma looked at her daughter. "Did you have another bad night, dear? You look very tired this morning."

In response, Margaret said, "I actually slept right through the night. I don't know why I feel so tired."

Daniel looked up from the newspaper he was reading. "It's probably because of James. He drove by again this morning. I'm going to have to call Officer Benson. The complaint isn't working. That stupid young man doesn't take no for an answer, and I believe stronger measures will have to be taken."

Officer Benson watched as the father and daughter entered the station. He had a very good idea as to why they were there. The two saw the man they wanted to talk to and walked straight to his desk.

"Good morning, Mister Perkins, I take it that my warning to James Matthews has gone unheeded."

"That's right. He has driven slowly by our home several times staring at Margaret's bedroom. When he saw us watching him, he sped off. We want to file a restraining order against James. This has gone on long enough," Daniel said with obvious frustration.

"Yes, sir, it has. There's another way that this can be handled if you're of a mind."

"What way is that?" Margaret asked.

"Do you have any relatives that live away from here? If you do, you could go away for a while. This, of course, may only delay things, and won't fix the actual problem," the policeman said.

"I have an aunt in New York City, but to tell you the truth, I don't want to run from this stupid young man. If he bothers me anymore, I want him arrested. He needs to be stopped. If he isn't, he'll just turn his attention to someone else, and who knows how that will end?" Margaret said quite forcefully.

"I've got the paperwork here. Have a seat, and we'll get to it," Officer Benson said, reaching into a drawer.

Everything was filled in, and Officer Frank Benson headed toward the rundown home at the edge of town. The young man received the restraining order but was not happy. He was told of the consequences if he did not comply. This included driving by the Perkins home. Poorly dressed young girls ran around the overgrown yard in tattered clothes.

CHAPTER 27

A week went by with no sign of the rude young man driving by Margaret's home. However, in the middle of the night, James still parked his car on the side of the road, hoping to glimpse the object of his desires.

All the while, the entity in the mirror grew stronger and more forceful, draining energy from its unsuspecting host. The voice continued to enter the subconscious mind of the young lady in the bed, taking a deeper and deeper hold on her.

Two weeks later at the breakfast table, Wilma looked at her daughter with concern. "Margaret dear, I am worried. You look sicker with each passing day. I think you should see Doctor Walters today."

"I don't know what is going on, I sleep through the night and yet feel like I haven't even gone to bed at all. Maybe I *should* see the doctor."

The appointment was made and Daniel drove his daughter to see the family doctor who had delivered Margaret years ago. As they walked into the doctor's office, they ran into a few people that they'd known for quite some time. Saying hello, the people's eyes turned toward Margaret.

An elderly lady asked, "Margaret dear, are you feeling poorly? You do look quite under the weather."

"Yes, I do feel poorly. I'm not at all sure what the problem is. It started a few weeks ago and has been getting worse with each passing day."

A voice called out, "Margaret, the doctor will see you now."

Slightly unsteady on her feet, she walked to the examining room. The doctor asked the usual questions, "Why don't you tell me what the trouble is, Margaret? What is it that you feel? When did it start and have you been in contact with anyone who has exhibited these symptoms?"

"I get a full night's sleep every night, and yet I wake in the morning as if I haven't even gone to bed at all. It started about three and a half weeks ago. I was in New York City visiting my Aunt Lucy recently. I had my boys with me. I don't recall meeting anyone who was sick, and my boys are just fine, so I have no idea what is causing me to feel this way."

"I'll do a thorough examination, and we'll see what turns up."

Taking out his stethoscope, he started the exam. Her blood pressure was measured, and he inspected her throat. When he was finally finished, he said, "I have checked everything I can think of and have found nothing wrong with you. I'm at a loss as to what it can be. If you weren't sleeping, I could give you something for that, but you are. I will prescribe some special vitamins for you and see where that leads."

He wrote out a prescription which she could get filled next door at the drugstore. This taken care of, the two drove home. Trying to relax, Margaret went for a long walk around the farm. As she walked by the fence enclosing a pasture, a few of the cows came toward her and followed her around the field.

This took her mind off things as the nearest cow's tongue brushed her arm and lightly scratched her soft skin. A large cloud drifted across the sky in front of the sun and cooled her for a short time. The early summer weather was pleasant. She enjoyed this time of year very much.

Supper finished, the boys were put to bed. They wouldn't be starting school for quite a while yet. Both were eagerly awaiting this new event in their lives. Margaret was feeling very tired and decided to retire early herself. She went to sleep, totally unaware of the commanding voice. The entity in the mirror gained strength nightly as it drained the sleeping figure's energy. The time for action approached. The thing inside the looking glass was almost ready to take another victim soon, very soon.

On the road, later in the night, a car quietly pulled over to the side and parked. The figure of a young man could be seen in the moonlight as he cautiously made his way to the garden beside Margaret's bedroom.

CHAPTER 28

I just have to see her. They have no right to stop me from talking to Margaret. Why won't she marry me? I have needs and she can supply them for me. My girls need a new mother to replace Nancy. What the hell was wrong with her? I'll bet she got consumption on purpose. She didn't like me. What an ungrateful, stupid woman. I gave her a house and kids, what more did she want? I said I was sorry when I hit her. I was drunk. What is it she expected, when she wouldn't let me have my way with her after a night out with my friends," James muttered to himself. "The cop told me I'd be arrested if I go near Margaret. Well, they can't arrest me if they don't know I'm there, can they?" With this, he looked at the clock on the wall in his kitchen, seeing that it was two in the morning. The girls were sound asleep and wouldn't wake until morning. The oldest would be in school in a number of weeks. James wondered where he'd get the money for some clothes for his eldest to wear.

He started the car and drove toward Margaret's house. He thought she should jump at the chance to have a new husband. He could take his girls and live at the farm too.

There was plenty of room in that big house. He could even help the old man once in awhile, if he had to. "Why won't they co-operate with me?" he asked himself angrily.

He parked the car on the side of the road. Getting out, he walked unsteadily toward the garden outside what he knew to be Margaret's bedroom. Slowly, being careful not to make any noise, he snuck toward the French doors. When he felt safe, he leaned close to the glass. Looking through the window pane with anticipation, he saw the sleeping form of the girl he wanted.

Off to the side, he noticed a slight glow in the mirror on the wall above the dresser. There seemed to be some movement reflected in it. Suddenly, he saw something unholy in the glass of the mirror, and immediately there was a sensation of extreme pain in his head.

As fear took over, he screamed in agony, running away from the house. The swing in the garden wasn't even seen, and he hit the protruding upper support beam with his head. Falling to the ground, he cursed and tried to regain his footing. The fear in him was so great that he didn't even feel the gash on his forehead.

Stumbling off the farmer's property, James ran to the car. The lights had come on in the house, and the front door was opened. James didn't even see the man holding a shotgun in his hands as he sped away.

The only thing in James's mind was that he had to get away from there. He knew, without a doubt, that he would never return to that place. His hands were trembling uncontrollably, and he almost drove off the road into the ditch several times.

CHAPTER 29

A scream and then a crash awakened Daniel and his wife. Jumping out of bed, he grabbed his gun and headed for the front door. Over his shoulder, he shouted for Wilma to go check on Margaret and the boys.

Standing in the doorway, he saw what he believed was James behind the wheel of his car. The driving was erratic, and it was really a wonder the fool hadn't gone into the ditch. Quickly walking to his daughter's room, he went to see if she was all right. Margaret too had been awakened by the scream and was being comforted by her mother.

The boy's room was at the back of the house away from where the commotion had occurred, and Daniel saw that they were still asleep. Turning on a lantern, Daniel inspected the grounds outside Margaret's bedroom. He found that everything was in order until he inspected the boat swing. Here he saw that it had been moved and soon realized that the intruder had run into it. There was a substantial amount of blood on the gravel and he knew that James probably screamed because of the impact.

Daniel was fairly certain that it was James that he saw

in the speeding car, but he couldn't be positive of this. He'd call the police in the morning. If they talked to James and saw that he had a bad cut, it would prove that he had been there.

Immediately after breakfast, the police were contacted, and the same officer came by the farm to assess the situation. As he looked over the scene he said, "Going by the distance the swing has been moved, and the amount of blood on the gravel, the person who ran into it got cut badly. The height where the skin is on the swing indicates that he more than likely hit his head."

"I am fairly certain that it was James Matthews that I saw driving away," Daniel said angrily. "The restraining order hasn't stopped him from coming around."

With a look of frustration on his face, Frank Benson informed the farmer, "I'll go over to his house and see if he has any cuts on him. If he does, I'll take him in and the judge will deal with him. I'll call you to let you know how it turns out."

As the policeman drove away, there was a feeling of relief that came over the family. "I sure hope this puts an end to it. I am getting really tired of that nincompoop disrupting our lives," Daniel said.

The day went by rather slowly as the family waited for the call from the officer. At just after supper, the phone rang, and Daniel hoped that this was the news he'd been waiting for all day.

Lifting the earpiece off the forked holder, he leaned close to the mouthpiece. "Hello."

The voice in his ear said, "Hello, Mister Perkins, this is Officer Benson calling."

"Yes, did you take James Matthews into custody? He did have the cut on his head, right?"

There was a slight hesitation before he answered, then, "I'm afraid that we couldn't locate him. He and the girls were gone by the time we arrived. I'm sure he'll turn up soon enough. He is probably staying at some relative for a while."

"What do we do now?" Daniel asked.

"We have to wait till he comes back, which I am certain he will. Most of his possessions are still at the house, and he'll have to come back for them sooner or later. When he does, we'll bring him in and question him. I'm sorry to call you with this bad news, but don't worry. I doubt he'll come around your place again anytime soon."

Daniel took a deep breath and let it out slowly. "I hope you're right. This whole thing has gotten out of hand. Thanks for the call."

The rest of the evening was not as pleasant as the family had hoped it would be. With the youngsters in bed, Margaret retired too. It wasn't long before she fell sound asleep.

There was a foreboding atmosphere in the room. Whatever was in the room with her was not happy. There was an angry presence because of the intrusion made the previous night. The entity now pushed harder at the sleeping form under the covers.

Soon, Margaret, while deep in sleep, pushed the covers back and slowly got out of bed. She was subconsciously directed to walk toward the mirror. The intensity of the commands allowed for no other course of action. Whatever was controlling her movements had taken her over completely.

As she got close to the dresser, a pair of boney, discolored hands came out of the glass. They reached out to the girl, who now reached toward the mirror herself. All this was done without any conscious thought on Margaret's part.

There was a small chair in front of the dresser, which she stepped onto. Slowly, she was pulled toward the mirror, and moments later, this new victim was gone, just as many in the past. With newfound strength supplied by the newest addition to the stockpile, the entity focused on the lock on the French doors.

It took much expenditure of energy, but slowly the knob controlling the mechanism turned and the door was left unlocked. This task finished, the scene was set and a relief of sorts came over the presence in the finely crafted mirror.

Margaret woke up inside the mirror. When she saw the entity, she screamed in terror, feeding the inhabitant even more.

CHAPTER 30

Not wishing to disturb her daughter, Wilma allowed her to sleep in later that morning. By the time the clock struck ten, she decided it was time to check on Margaret. She was very concerned for her girl because her health was becoming so fragile, ever since she had come back from visiting Lucy. Whatever it was that she had contracted surely must have come from New York.

Then to make things worse, that lout of a young man had given the entire family cause to worry. Mumbling to herself, she said, "Who does he think he is? What on Earth would make him believe that a girl like Margaret would have any interest whatsoever in a useless individual like him?"

As she approached the door to Margaret's bedroom, she let the thoughts go. Grasping the doorknob, she turned it, opening the door. Looking inside, she became a little curious as to why the bed was empty. Thinking about it, she realized that her daughter could be either in the bathroom or on the swing outside the exterior doors.

She found the bathroom to be empty, so Wilma headed to the French doors and thought that this had to be where Margaret was because the lock was undone. Going outside, Wilma looked at the swing and, seeing that her daughter wasn't there, started to become concerned.

Turning and re-entering the bedroom, she noticed that Margaret's clothes were still folded neatly on the chair by the bed. Her hands started to tremble as she saw that a small bottle of perfume on the dresser had been knocked over. Margaret would never allow it to remain that way. Rushing out of the room and then to the back door, she ran to the barn. "Daniel, Daniel, are you here? I can't find Margaret."

His voice called back to her, "What do you mean you can't find her?"

"I've looked all over the house and she isn't there. I looked in the garden and there's no sign of her. The French doors in her room were unlocked."

"She isn't out here with me. I'm going to call the police," he said as he ran toward the house.

Wilma noticed the apprehension in Harold and Wayne's eyes and attempted to comfort them.

On the phone, Daniel talked to Officer Benson. "My daughter is missing. You need to come here immediately, please. I am afraid that maybe James might have come back last night and forced her to go with him."

The voice on the other end of the line remained calm. "I'll be there as fast as I can. Search all the places that Margaret may be, just in case she decided to take a walk." With this, the conversation ended.

A short time later, the police vehicle pulled into the driveway. Two officers got out and walked to the front door. It opened long before they got there. An in-depth search was performed, yielding no clues whatever. By the time the police were finished looking around, the whole family was close to being frantic.

All pertinent information had been given, and the policeman carefully studied the bedroom itself. Examining the exterior of the doors leading to the garden, the officer said, "There is no sign of forced entry here. You say that Margaret would never leave the bottle on her dresser on its side like that?"

"That's right. She takes great care of her things. She would not go willingly with anyone without telling us. She is a good mother and wouldn't even consider something like that," Wilma said, crying.

"She hasn't had any change of heart toward James, has she?" Benson asked.

"No, she is afraid of him," Daniel said. "We have to find that boy, now. Who knows what he will do if she rejects him again."

"We'll do that right now. You all stay here, just in case she comes back. If she does, call the station immediately," the sergeant said as they ran to the car.

The siren was turned on as they raced down the road toward the suspect's home. The wailing faded as the car disappeared in the distance.

"What will he do to our daughter, Daniel?" she asked, as the tears rolled down her cheeks.

"Grandpa, where is Mommy? Did she go somewhere without us?" Harold asked, with tears in his eyes too.

"The nice policeman is going to find her, don't you worry," Daniel said, not feeling at all sure of that statement.

The day passed very slowly for the family. There was absolutely nothing they could do to speed things up. Anguish overrode all her other feelings, as Wilma tried not to think the worst. Daniel did his best to keep the boys occupied but had a difficult time keeping his mind from thoughts of hurting the person he knew was responsible for his little girl's disappearance.

At four in the afternoon, the phone rang with Daniel

rushing to answer it, "Hello." He listened for a few moments and asked, "Did you find her with him?"

The voice on the other end explained the situation to him and hung up.

Daniel turned to his wife and relayed the information he had received. "Officer Benson says that James Matthews returned home a short time ago and has been apprehended. His daughters have been taken to a foster home for the time being. When he was asked about Margaret, he denied having taken her. He does admit that he was here the other night, but left when something frightened him."

"Are you telling me that Margaret hasn't been found?"

He lowered his head, looking at the floor. "At this point, they have no idea where she is. They questioned the girls, and they know nothing. A search is being done, but they really have no idea where to look. He said he will keep us informed. He also wants to send a special investigator here to do a thorough search to see if anything has been missed. He asked us not to go into her room or in the garden till their man arrives."

"What are we going to do, Daniel?"

He walked over and placed his arms around his wife in an attempt to console her. This was truly one of the worst days of their lives. The boys took things very hard indeed, standing by the front window, waiting for their mother to come home. No one got much sleep that night.

The investigator came the next morning and spent hours looking over every detail in and around the home. He questioned the parents of the missing young woman with no real results. He studied the mirror and dresser. He searched the grounds surrounding the home and took samples of the dried blood. In the end, he left without giving the farmer and his wife any new hope.

The days passed by as if time had almost stopped. A

week came and went with no new developments. James
had been questioned over and over. He desperately denied knowing anything about Margaret's disappearance.
The gash on his forehead was damning and this eventual-
ly led to this case going to trial.

No trace what so ever was found of Margaret Perkins.
Everyone involved knew without a doubt, that James was
guilty of the crime.

A jury had been chosen and a public defender as-
signed to defend James Matthews. In the courtroom, both
sides presented arguments. The defense's case was weak,
but there was no body, so James was still somewhat
hopeful.

Looking at them, the jury could see that the whole
procedure had been taking its toll on the family of the
missing girl. Both parents looked like they hadn't had a
decent night's sleep in quite some time. They pleaded
with the accused to tell them where their daughter was.
The judge, although sympathetic, banged his gavel for
quiet in the courtroom.

In the end, after all the evidence had been presented,
the judge ordered the jury into deliberation. Behind
closed doors, the jury argued back and forth for two days.
The question of guilt was not the issue debated. Everyone
knew without a doubt that he was guilty. The question
was whether or not it was premeditated and whether or
not the death sentence was warranted.

In the end, a decision was reached and the judge informed. The jury had been called back into the courtroom
and everyone attending waited anxiously for the verdict.
The defendant was asked to stand and the jury foreman
asked if the jury had reached a unanimous decision.

Standing in the jury box, the foreman said, "We have,
your honor."

"What is the verdict," the judge asked.

"We the jury find the defendant guilty of second-degree murder, your honor," he said loudly.

There was a cheer from everyone in the courtroom as the judge banged his gavel several times to restore order. When all was quiet, the defendant was asked to stand again.

In a very strong voice, the judge said, "James Matthews, you have been found guilty of the charge of second-degree murder. I hereby sentence you to life imprisonment, with no chance of parole for a minimum of twenty years. Do you have anything to say before sentence is carried out?"

Weeping, James said, "Yes, your honor, I wish to say, I know I was wrong to go to Margaret's home after being served with a restraining order, but I did not take her. I swear there was someone else there at the time. That is why I screamed and ran, hitting the swing with my head."

The people in the courtroom booed until the gavel was once more brought down. The court was dismissed by the judge. The verdict was welcomed by the Perkins, but it did little to relieve the anxiety they felt. Their daughter was gone and Margaret's children would have to be raised without a mother or father. The family wept together in the courtroom for a few minutes then returned to an unhappy home.

CHAPTER 31

The culprit, who they knew without a doubt was guilty, had been sent to prison. This did little to alleviate the pain and suffering the four individuals on the farm felt. The disappearance of Margaret left a hole that could not be filled.

The room with the mirror was closed up while the entity within bided its time. It knew one day it would be in a position to add to its collection of souls that kept it company in the darkness and fed its needs for energy. Despite attempting to reach out past the walls of the room, it was unable to draw anyone strongly enough to make them enter.

As always, time passed. Weeks turned into months, and then, months turned into years. The grandparents aged and the boys grew up to be good young men, helping to run the farm very well indeed.

Ten years later, when the boys were then in their late teens, Wilma looked at the door that had not been opened for a long time and asked the males sitting at the kitchen table, "Do you think we should decide what to do with the contents of the room?"

"I think we should sell anything of value and give the

rest away," Harold said. "I don't want a reminder here any longer, Grandma."

"I agree," Wayne said.

With the decision made, the room was cleared out and everything of little value given to the needy. An auction took care of the rest. Although a little sad, the family moved on, and Margaret's former bedroom was made into a sewing room.

James Mathews's girls were adopted by people who gave them a far better life than they would have had if they'd stayed with their father.

CHAPTER 32

Gary and Francine Sutherland were in Davenport to visit their son Andrew. With unemployment still affecting over twenty-two percent of the workforce in America, Andrew felt fortunate to have a low-paying job in a textiles factory. He had learned to do many different jobs in the factory. That was the only reason he was still there. Nineteen thirty-four proved to be a hard year.

Francine still sent little care packages to alleviate some of the hardships her boy endured. The dust bowl in the central states had driven many people to seek new lives in areas not affected by the drought.

She and Gary felt lucky to be living in a city located at the western tip of Lake Superior. This gave the city all the fresh water it required. Passing a post office bulletin board, Francine noticed the wanted posters. John Dillinger's face stared back at her. Bonnie and that funny looking Clyde were also there. She wondered why these people did the things they did.

There was a poster advertising an auction and a list of some of the things being offered. Thinking out loud, she said, "That mirror in the bedroom, that fell and broke, still has me wondering how it happened. I see here that there's one on this list. There is also a matching dresser too. I'll talk to Gary about it."

There was a soup kitchen not far ahead and she saw that there were quite a number of people waiting to get a meal, lined up at the door. Francine volunteered at the soup kitchen in her neighborhood in Duluth, trying to help the less fortunate. The people that came for the hot meals wanted to work, but there just weren't any jobs for them.

She felt lucky to be married to a man who had had the foresight to save much of the money he earned and kept it in a safe in the basement. There had been runs on banks and many had closed their doors since. The Sutherlands were not rich but were able to at least live comfortably.

She spied Gary walking toward her and motioned for him to look at the bulletin board, saying, "We should replace that mirror that broke at home when it fell from the wall. This one sounds like it would be a good one."

In a gravelly voice, Gary said, "It comes with a dresser as a set. We really don't need the dresser, I wonder if they will sell it separately."

Thinking for a moment, she replied, "We can go there and ask. If they won't do that, we won't bid higher than we think the mirror alone is worth. The description says that the two items are very unique."

"Good idea. You always were a woman after my own heart."

The day of the auction arrived and the older couple in their mid-sixties sat in their seats off to the side. Several items of interest had been bid on and sold at very low prices. Money being hard to come by those days kept the prices of most things down. This was the case even in stores selling new things.

When the mirror and dresser were brought onto the

platform, it was said to everyone attending that the pieces were going to be sold together, despite inquiries to have them sold separately.

Gary leaned over and whispered to her. "To tell you the truth dear, I'm not really fond of that mirror. I wouldn't care in the least if someone else buys it."

Francine closed her eyes, and it was almost as if there was a voice in her head saying she should bid on it. Looking Gary in the eye, she said, "I like it, and I want that mirror. I don't know why, but I just have this feeling. Please try to get it."

Knowing better than to argue with his wife about certain things, he decided on how he should play this game.

The auctioneer started the bidding at ten dollars. When no one signaled him, he was forced to lower it to five.

Gary nodded his head to inform the auctioneer. No matter what the man did, he couldn't get a higher bid, and it was sold to the couple for five dollars.

Arrangements were made, and the two pieces loaded on the train at the rail yard after being wrapped up to prevent damage. The visit had come to an end. As Gary and Francine hugged their boy, the train whistle blew, signaling the couple to board the train.

The train ride was pleasant enough as the car they were riding in swayed back and forth, but they were glad to be home once more. The new additions were brought to the house, and the men hired for the job had hung the eerie-looking glass and moved the dresser into the main bedroom down the hall from the spare bedroom. Francine now and then slept in the spare room when Gary's snoring became a nuisance.

Gary stood in the doorway of the bedroom, looking at the new additions. He said, "I still don't like the thing. It's an odd piece, despite the craftsmanship it took to make it. The dresser is nice enough, but that mirror gives me the willies."

"Ha, ha, ha, whatever do you mean? It's a beautiful work of art. I just love it. The effect the smoked glass has makes it look so exotic. Who wouldn't just love to own it? If you don't like it, you can always sleep in the spare room."

"Are you sure it's not because you want to be near that thing by yourself?" he said, laughing a little himself.

Francine looked at her husband. "You know me better than that."

In the backyard, Gary weeded the vegetable garden. This pastime kept him occupied and provided them with enough food for the entire winter. The cold storage kept things reasonably fresh and whatever wouldn't last long was canned.

There were things that he couldn't grow, but he bartered with neighbors for these, by using some of the surpluses from his garden. Looking things over, he saw that he would have far too many carrots, onions, and potatoes. What couldn't be used for bartering, Francine would take to the soup kitchen.

Times had been very difficult for many people all across the United States for years. Listening to the radio, he heard a story that the latest dust storm in the mid-west had blown for two days and removed much of the once fertile soil. "What on earth are these folks to do? I can't even imagine the hardships they must be facing," he muttered out loud.

"The Teamsters have gone on strike," the announcer said on the radio, which Gary had moved closer to the open window. "There is widespread support for the movement. The police have clashed with the picket lines, and many of the striking members have been injured. Where this will end, is anybody's guess."

Gary muttered to himself as he watered the garden, no longer hearing the radio. "This strike has been going on for almost six months, I wonder if it will ever end. It seems that support from all over the country is coming to Minneapolis. The politicians are really up in arms against the unions."

"Gary, it's time to come in for supper. Are you talking to yourself again?"

Looking around to make sure none of the neighbors had been watching him, he said, "No, of course not. I don't talk to myself." But he knew that was a little white lie.

The two said grace and thanked God for his mercy in providing for their needs and his supplying them with food. Meat portions were kept to a minimum, because of the high cost. What little pieces were cooked had been very much savored. Apple pie for dessert, with a slice of cheddar cheese, topped off the meal.

Sitting on the front porch in rocking chairs, the couple chatted with people of the area as they walked past. Many people took advantage of the lower temperatures by going out for an evening stroll. Information about family members was a topic of conversation between the ladies. Work and the ongoing teamsters strike the topic of choice for the men, with occasional sports figures being discussed. As the sun set, Gary and Francine went indoors and prepared for bed.

CHAPTER 33

Turning in, the pair felt the exertions of the day ooze out of their tired muscles. Sleep came quickly for both, and they fell into a deep state of slumber. There was some puzzlement going on in the mirror.

Up till now, the only presence it had detected had almost always been singular. For one of the first times, it sensed that there were two beings in the bed overlooked by the mirror. Unsure of how to proceed, it did nothing this night. Attempting to control two at the same time would require quite an expenditure of energy. Energy it did not have to waste.

It had been a long time since last it had the opportunity to develop a relationship with a soul. Because there were two, it would have to proceed slowly if it decided to attempt gaining both sources. It had been at rest for a considerable time and so waiting a little longer, concerned it not at all.

It did have the company of several guests, which, although they did not appreciate being there in the slightest, had no choice in the matter. The constant state of fear its guests felt fed the entity within. There was no escape for them, and they knew it.

"Good morning sleepy head. Do you plan to stay in bed all day?" Francine asked her husband.

"My goodness, I slept very well last night."

"Would you like me to make you bacon and eggs for breakfast?" she asked.

"Yes, please, I'm starving."

"I'll get it ready. Remember, we have a meeting tonight at the church. We're going to discuss ways of getting more donations from the city and people who are well off," Francine said as she walked to the kitchen.

As he got out of bed, Gary thought about the coming evening. With a look of concentration, he said, "To tell you the truth, I think the city people have their hands full just dealing with the Teamsters strike. The whole thing is really getting out of hand if you ask me." As he got dressed, he saw a slight movement in the mirror. By the time he turned to look directly at it, there, however, was nothing to see.

After breakfast, Francine cleaned the dishes and made a suggestion. "Why don't we go to the butcher this morning? I hear that he went out of town to the farmer he deals with and picked up a load of beef and pork."

"I don't know. The price is up to around twenty cents a pound for roasts. How do they expect anyone to be able to afford that?"

"It's partly due to that strike, but I hear he has gotten a good price on things from the farmer because the farmer himself had already butchered the animals and had no way to get it to the city. It might be worth investigating, Gary."

An hour later, they walked down the street going at a leisurely pace. Four blocks later and they were standing in line at the butcher's store. On the inside of the window, the prices of various meats were written.

Studying the list, the two made their decisions. Going

to the counter, having made their selections, they gave their order to Fred, a man they'd known for years. Seeing that it would be quite heavy for his patrons to carry back to their home, he told them, "I can have it delivered by my son if you'd like. I'm sure it will be quite difficult for you to carry it that far."

Smiling, Francine said, "That would be very nice, thank you."

"Do you have enough room in your refrigerator for all this?" Fred asked.

"Yes, we do, it's almost empty. This shipment of meat came at a good time," Gary answered in return.

The walk home was pleasant and Dwayne, the butcher's boy, made the delivery shortly after. Everything was put away, which left little room in the refrigerator.

Francine looked at Gary. "Sometimes when I look at all that we have, I feel a little guilty. There are so many that are going hungry, while we live quite nicely."

"That's why we donate our extras from the garden to the soup kitchen. It is the government's job to look after the needy too. It can't all be left up to the people. They should have had more control on the stock market. We wouldn't be in this mess now if they had."

"I suppose so. I'd like to know when it will end."

The meeting they attended that evening was not very productive. There were only a few answers to the problem of feeding the hungry. With wages in the last number of years having been cut in half, there just hadn't been enough to go around.

Bedtime came and the two fell asleep. In the mirror, a decision was made. The soft suggestions started being made to both sleeping occupants lying in the bed. The process would be slower, but the seeds had been planted.

Before getting under the covers, Gary again spotted a movement in the glass of the mirror. Looking around, he again saw nothing. He finally decided that his eyes were playing tricks on him and went to bed with Francine.

The older couple woke in the morning, not quite as well rested as usual. The difference was not noticeable, so the day went by much as any other day. Gary spent time in the garden. He had had to put up some netting in order to keep the birds away from the soft fruit ripening on his trees.

All the new weeds were removed and, when he was satisfied with things, he took care to water just enough to keep his plants healthy. There was no point in drowning anything. Francine called him in for lunch, and then they walked to the park. Sitting on the bench, the pair watched the local pigeons fly around looking for people willing to feed them.

Several of Gary's friends had built pigeon coops for their homing pigeons. They seemed to have great fun taking the birds far away and timing them to see how long it took the birds to get back to the coop.

Some of them had remarked on the fact that the birds often got back before the owners did. Maybe the phrase, as the crow flies, had something to do with it. Gary had thought about it but decided that it really wasn't a hobby he wanted to get into.

In the playground area, there were families with little children on swings and slides. Summertime was pleasant for the young ones. They hadn't, for the most part, had to endure the harshness of life. Although some did know that their parents had lost jobs and were having difficulty supporting their families.

"Gary, do you think that America will ever be the same? We have lost so much."

He thought for a moment before answering. "It certainly will be a long road back. I hear President Roosevelt has a plan, but I'm not sure it will work."

The conversation was interrupted when a man, who was obviously intoxicated, started shouting at his wife. He said some unpleasant things to the lady about infidelity and stormed off, leaving the lady crying. A young boy who was playing in a sandbox came running over to her, hugging her legs.

The mother and son left, with the woman keeping her head bowed, looking at the sidewalk, as she quickly walked away.

Francine watched the lady. "Gosh, how humiliating for her."

"That's what happens when someone is unfaithful. I'm sure I would feel the same way as the man did if you were to have an affair with another man."

"You needn't ever worry about something like that, dear," she said, looking after the disgraced woman. "I do feel sorry for her. Maybe there was a reason she did what she did. The husband didn't look like he was a very pleasant person."

Gary looked at Francine. "Till death do you part. If a person can't keep that promise, they shouldn't be getting married."

Knowing where this line of argument was going to go, Francine decided to stop talking. There had been times in her marriage when things were not as they were at present. Gary had mellowed with age, which was a good thing. When Gary was younger and ambitious, there had been a harsh side to him.

She thought back to the time when Gary had insisted that she host a dinner with some potential clients. That had been a first for her, and she was a bundle of nerves as the evening approached. There was no one to help her and she took a few minutes too long setting the dining room table. By the time she got back to the kitchen, the roast had been a trifle charred. In an effort to salvage it, she trimmed off the blackened portions. By the time it was set on the table, the kitchen had been aired out, and she thought everything was all right.

It became evident very quickly that Gary and the clients were not happy with the roast. The dinner turned out to be a huge failure, and the clients left without signing the contracts. Gary fumed as the guests were shown to the door.

That was the first time Gary had ever struck her. He blamed her for the lost contract and he had become abusive for the next several years. Their son Andrew never knew about the physical abuse. Gary took great care to keep this hidden from everyone.

Time passed and because he made a few good choices, Gary managed to not be adversely affected by the stock market crash. Because he had felt things were not right, he pulled all his money out of the markets and the banks just before everything fell apart.

Seeing the result that the crash had had on all their friends and neighbors, Gary's demeanor softened considerably. He had become a pleasant husband again, for the most part. Minor things surfaced now and then, like his remarks about the unfortunate young woman, but mostly he was a much more gentle man. During the worst of it, Francine had at one point considered leaving him, but was glad she'd stayed.

The walk home was made in silence. Supper that evening was a little subdued as old feelings resurfaced for Francine. My, how she wished they had not gone to the park. The look on the young woman's face brought back memories she thought were long gone.

Against her better judgment, she went to sleep in the same bed as her husband. It took some time for her to drift off. She almost got up to go to the spare bedroom when Gary started to snore, but she thought better of it.

As she finally relaxed, slumber took over and the whispering started. There was a soft glow in the glass of the mirror. If someone were to look through the window from outside, they would think that a soft light was on in the room, if they actually saw anything at all. The curtains closed over the window, however, prevented anyone from looking in.

The communication continued through the night. A change in the household had begun. The entity living in the glass meant to take full control over as short a period of time as possible. It had done this a few times in the past. It needed to draw from the energy of the unsuspecting sleepers before it could do what was necessary to gain another source of food. The thing fed on fear and, though it had a number of individuals already herded, the energy was dwindling. When the energy supply started to fade, hibernation of sorts became a necessity.

CHAPTER 34

The earlier captives' energy supply slowly diminished as it was used. As time wore on, a new source had to be obtained to keep its needs fulfilled. During the lean times when it was prevented from obtaining new food sources due to closed-up rooms, there were periods of hibernation. This allowed for little consumption of its energies. The fear of its captives did, however, sustain it.

Margaret, its latest source of food, was already showing signs of depletion. The constant state of fear over the years had worn her down. She was utterly defenseless against her captor. There was no escape for her. She would be trapped there forever, and she knew it. One by one, she saw the others slowly being drained. The ones she thought were the earliest captives seemed on the verge of disappearing. However, none had totally left yet. There was no contact between any of them in the darkness surrounding her. The loneliness was almost as bad as the utter fear she felt. With no way out, she longed for death.

CHAPTER 35

Two weeks passed as the work of the inhabitant in the mirror progressed. The two in bed were beginning to feel the adverse effects more and more. Each night things progressed further.

The morning came with the sounds of birds chirping outside the window, a sound that had lately started to irritate him. Not feeling himself at all, Gary got out of bed very tired and drained of energy. Looking over to the other side of the bed, he realized that his wife was already up. Washing his face he, felt a bit better but not much. Irritably, he got dressed, going to the kitchen, expecting to be served his breakfast.

To his surprise, Francine was not there. Looking throughout the home, he found her sitting in a rocker on the front porch with a cup of coffee in her hand. As he opened the screen door rather roughly, he startled his wife.

"Aren't you going to make my breakfast?" he asked rudely.

"I'm quite tired this morning. I just don't have the energy."

"Do you actually expect me to make my own?" he said, raising his voice.

Anger left over from past experiences and having a poor night's sleep caused her temper to flare, and she shouted back at her husband. "I just don't feel well."

"I don't either. You know I'm no good at making my own." He paused a moment. "Would it kill you?"

A neighbor next door had picked that moment to come out of her home just as he shouted this last statement. She was shocked at what she thought she had just heard. She had noticed a dramatic change in her neighbors lately. She had known them in years past when things had not been harmonious in the household and thought those times had come back.

Gary turned and walked back into the house, slamming the door. Francine, because of habits formed long ago, got up to make her husband's breakfast. As she entered the kitchen, she said, "I'm sorry, dear. I don't know what got into me. I had a long sleep last night but woke up feeling very poorly."

"It's all right, dear. I shouldn't have snapped at you. I feel rather drained too." With this, he hugged his wife and sat at the table.

As she made eggs and toast for her husband, she said, "Do you have any idea as to why we're both so weary?"

"No idea whatsoever. I'm sleeping just fine. I should be rested, but I'm not. Maybe we're coming down with something."

"That must be it," she replied.

Later in the morning, Gary tended his garden. There were only a few weeds to take care of. Looking closely, he found that something had deposited a slimy substance on the strings holding his tomato plants to the stakes. He replaced these and looked for the culprit.

On a half-eaten leaf, he found a large green caterpillar. He threw it to the ground and angrily stomped on it. Looking for more, he found another. Because of the weariness of his body, he overreacted and swore at it as he stomped on that one too. Waving his arms in the air, he went to the shed and pulled out a sprayer.

Carefully, he sprayed all of the plants. He muttered to himself angrily as he did this job, unaware that he was being watched. When he was all done, he put the sprayer away and headed for the house.

Francine had noted of the scene in the back yard. "What on earth were you carrying on about in the garden?"

"I found some caterpillars in the tomatoes. These pests have the potential of destroying the entire crop."

"You check the garden every day so it's very unlikely that much damage will be done," she said gently.

"You're right, of course. It must be because I'm so worn down."

"I feel the same way. It must be that we've picked up something, I'm sure. Maybe we should go see the doctor," she told her husband.

"That will cost money I don't want to spend if we don't have to. After all, we're not actually feeling sick, just a trifle under the weather."

"All right, dear, why don't we just rest for the remainder of the day? It will probably go away on its own," she said as she patted him on the back.

The rest of the day, Francine tried to keep out of Gary's way. She too felt short-tempered and knew they'd end up in a row if they remained in close proximity. She tried to reason out why this was happening but couldn't come up with any answers.

Because they were both tired, they ended up in bed early again. If their eyesight were a little better, they would probably have noticed little movements in the glass now and then. They fell asleep quickly and were out for the night. This was not to say that all was quiet in the bedroom. All through the night, the voice continued to softly talk to them. A slow control over the inhabitants of the room took place. As had happened many times in the past, the thing within the mirror was working to an end that was not conducive to the well being of those in the bed.

Morning came and found the older couple sleeping later than normal. Gary woke with a start and moaned. "Are you awake yet?" he asked the sleeping form beside him.

Francine woke with a groan too. "My goodness, we're in bed late this morning," she said as she looked at the alarm clock on the dresser.

"I feel more tired than I did yesterday," Gary said irritably.

"So do I, what on earth is going on? I am starting to think we should go to see the doctor. Please say you will too."

"Yes, you're right, we need to see him. We'll get up, have a quick bite to eat, and then go," he said, getting out of the bed.

In the doctor's office, they were called in individually. Doctor Adams asked, "So, Francine, what seems to be the problem?"

She explained the situation, and the doctor asked, "I know Gary snores. Do you think this might be aggravating the situation, and you're not actually falling into a deep sleep? That would explain the tiredness. Is he suffering the same symptoms?"

"I haven't been kept awake by it, but that does make sense. Yes, he has the same symptoms as I do, and he is quite irritable lately, but then again, so am I."

Doctor Adams thought for a moment. "Do you have a spare bedroom?"

"Yes."

"Why don't we have one of you sleep in it for the next week. If things improve, then we'll know that his snoring is causing the problem. You aren't the first person that has complained about this type of situation."

Francine nodded her head. "All right, Doctor, I'll give that a try."

The good doctor walked to the door and called Gary into the room. He asked a few questions and after receiving the answers, he made the same suggestion to him as he did to Francine.

The two headed for home and Gary asked, "Which one of us is going to sleep in the spare room."

"I don't like the mattress on that bed, but I will sleep there if you insist."

"No, no, I don't mind the mattress, so I'll sleep in the spare room. Maybe we should have tried that before we went to the doctor, it would have saved us some money," he said, frowning somewhat.

"Oh, for God's sake, why don't you stop worrying so much about that?"

They were almost in front of their home when he raised his arm in the air and shouted, "What do you think, money grows on trees?"

A curtain in the window of the neighbor's house moved as Gary looked in that direction. He lowered his arm, quickly walked up the steps of the porch, and unlocked the front door. He knew very well that he had been acting terrible toward his wife for the last week but seemed unable to stop himself. What must that woman Maureen next door think of him?

Inside, at the kitchen table, Gary sat and thought about how the past week had not gone well. He looked at his wife. "I'm sorry that this last while has not been the best. I think this thing we have is really affecting me a lot."

"Maybe sleeping in separate rooms will allow us both to get some proper rest," she said, trying to keep the waters from becoming turbulent again.

Lunch finished, he went into the backyard and inspected his vegetables. The tomatoes were free of caterpillars, but there were aphids on several of his other plants. Aggravated, he walked to the shed again and loaded the sprayer with the proper insecticide. As he sprayed he muttered loudly to himself. He was very disgruntled with this problem. It seemed much worse this year than it had in many.

Because he had just sprayed, he realized that if he watered the plants he would wash off all the spray. He tried to think of a way to water, only hitting the soil. He ended up turning the water on very low, so the stream didn't splash the plants.

In the end, he still splashed the plants and felt he had washed off much of the insecticide. In frustration, he threw the hose to the ground, walked to the house, turned off the tap, and sat on the step, fuming. He muttered to himself as he thought that things were getting out of his control.

That night, he went to the spare room, leaving the main one for his wife. He was in bed far earlier than normal. Francine also went to bed early herself, relieved to be sleeping alone.

Gary's night was restful as he slept by himself, away from the room with the mirror. Francine too slept through the night. However, she did not rest well at all.

In the morning, Gary was up before his wife and knocked on the door, waking up Francine.

"What do you want?" she said, drowsy from lack of rest.

"Did you not sleep well again dear?"

"No, I did not. I feel even worse than I did yesterday. Why did you wake me up?" she asked, obviously frustrated.

"Would you like to stay in bed awhile longer?"

"Yes."

He left the room not coming back until he heard her moving around. Opening the door, he asked, "Are you feeling better now?"

"No, not really, I don't have any idea what is going on here. Did you sleep all right?"

"As a matter of fact, I slept surprisingly well. I feel much better. I really wish you felt well too. I thought this should have cured the problem, sleeping in separate rooms," he said.

Francine got dressed and came to the kitchen. Looking around, she saw a bunch of dirty dishes and a few pans left on the stove. A look of intense anger crossed her face. Seeing this, Gary started cleaning things up. He feared that a war was brewing and really didn't think he had a chance of winning it.

Half an hour later, he had things tidied up enough to talk to his wife. "Is there anything I can do to help you, dear?"

"Yes, get out of the kitchen and leave me alone for a while."

Gary decided it would be in his best interest to go for a walk. Fifteen minutes later he sat in the park, wondering what was happening to them. Maybe if she slept longer, things would improve. He determined not to wake her the next morning. Making his own breakfast was something new for Gary, but it had become necessary.

Two hours later he walked in the front door. The house was quiet, and he saw that the bedroom door was closed. With his ear to the door, he listened. If he was not mistaken, there seemed to be a very soft voice coming from within. The sound, unfortunately, was so soft that he couldn't tell if it was Francine's or not. The only reason he heard anything was because he had been subjected to it too.

Fearing another tongue lashing, he decided not to open the door. Instead, he went to the back door and worked in the garden for the next three hours. When he was finished he went into the kitchen and saw her sitting at the table.

"Did you sleep all right, dear," he asked.

"I slept, but I don't feel any more rested. I'm not sure what to do. If things don't improve in the next week, I believe that I may visit my sister in Portland."

"I don't know if I can find anyone to look after the garden for an extended period of time," he answered.

"I didn't mean that you would be coming with me. I meant that I would be going alone. I need some time away. I need to rest. My sister only has one extra bedroom and your snoring will interfere with my sleep."

"I don't want you to go. I'm sure we can work out something here. How am I going to take care of the household without you?" he questioned.

"You will just have to manage. I've made up my mind."

With this, she got up and went out the front door, sitting on the porch. Her neighbor next door saw her and asked, "Is everything all right, Francine?"

"To tell you the truth, Maureen, I'm not feeling well. I'm tired all the time and the doctor suggested that Gary and I sleep in separate rooms for a while, because of his snoring. Even this isn't helping."

"What are you going to do to fix this thing? Are there any specialists that can help?"

"I just told Gary that I'm going to visit my sister, Emma, in Portland for an extended period. He isn't happy about that but has no choice. I'm going," Francine said emphatically.

"I saw him yelling at you several times lately. He isn't becoming abusive again, is he?"

"We've had words, but nothing has really gotten out of hand. I want to leave next week so if I'm not here, you'll know why. I think I'll go in and start arranging things."

The air in the Sutherland home was quite frosty for the rest of the day. Gary didn't want his wife to go away for any amount of time, and she wouldn't allow him to go with her. Francine wanted to leave at first opportunity. She felt that her health was deteriorating quickly and needed to do something drastic to correct the problem.

CHAPTER 36

Francine spent the rest of the afternoon getting things ready for the trip she intended to take. She called her sister and asked, "Hello, Anna, I'm not feeling very well and wondered if you would mind if I paid you a visit?" Silence for a moment, so she continued. "I'll be coming by myself. Gary isn't happy about this, but I need the time away. I don't know how long I'll stay, I just know that I need to get some rest, and I can't get it here." Anna agreed. With this taken care of, Francine said to Gary, "I'm going to the train station tomorrow to make the arrangements for the trip."

Taking a deep breath and letting it out with an audible sigh, he said, "I'll come with you and pay for the ticket."

She would prefer to go alone, but since Gary handled all the money, she had no choice. The rest of the day was not a pleasant one for either of them. Evening came and found Francine in bed before nine o'clock, where she fell asleep immediately.

Sensing that its quarry was planning to leave, there was a feeling of urgency in the glass hanging on the wall. Things were moving in a direction that the entity had not foreseen. The schedule would have to be accelerated. It went to work that night planting its control deeper, much deeper. The idea of gaining two new recruits had already been abandoned.

The morning found Francine asleep until ten o'clock. Waking up, she felt that things had gotten even worse for her. Being so tried, she feared that her life may be coming to an end. The urge to leave this home grew stronger with each passing day. It took an hour for Francine to get herself presentable enough to go to the train station.

After asking the ticket master a few questions, she got Gary to pay for a ticket on a train that would be leaving in three days. He tried to talk her into buying one for the following week, but it was a losing battle. The two had words about it, which raised a few eyebrows. The walk home was not a nice one. As they walked up the porch steps, Gary saw the neighbor watching them. He glared at the woman he considered a busybody.

The rest of the packing was done, and now the only thing stopping her from leaving was the train. It was all she could do to make supper that evening. She left the dishes for her husband to clean up and headed for bed once more.

That night was more intense than any other since the mirror had been moved to the home. Control deepened and Francine was losing a battle she didn't even know she was fighting. There was only one way to evade the impending event. There was only one person who could save her, and he didn't know he had any control over the situation.

In bed really early yet again, with only that night and the next one, before her trip started, Francine lay in bed, slipping into the clutches of an entity that needed her for a source of energy. Things were not quite ready and so there was a hastened attempt to move toward the moment of assimilation.

Morning came late for this home. Gary, in the garden, had a feeling of frustration and lashed out at the neighbor's cat that had the gall to come into his yard. His temper was not helping him, and he didn't know how to keep his wife from leaving.

Inside the home, the day couldn't go by fast enough. If it were possible, she would leave this very minute. The feeling of exhaustion was becoming more and more a part of her, and she just wanted it to stop. Going to her sister's she knew would help. She was not sure if she would come back or not. Gary controlled all the money, but this couldn't be allowed to stop her.

Sitting on the porch, Maureen chatted with her but it was mostly a one-sided conversation. She was very concerned for Francine. There was something terribly wrong there, and her suspicions immediately fell on Gary.

The day slipped by extremely slowly, especially for Francine. By eight o'clock, she was ready for bed. She set the time on the alarm clock, and walking over to the dresser, turned the alarm on and placed it on the edge. Putting it on the dresser would force her to get out of bed, in order to turn off the loud clanging of the bell.

Her bags were packed and the ticket was in her purse. This night couldn't pass by fast enough for her. She toyed with the idea of sleeping on the couch and leaving immediately after getting up. She had made a few sandwiches for the trip and had a glass bottle filled with tea. The idea of sleeping on the couch was dismissed because she had slept on it before and awakened with a sore back.

It took no time at all for Francine to fall asleep. Visions of getting away filled her head just before she drifted off. These were soon replaced by new thoughts.

Six hours after getting into bed, full control had been achieved. Francine stirred and, while she was still in a deep sleep, she slowly got out of bed. A chair had been placed on the floor in front of the dresser for putting on her face powder.

This was something Gary never allowed while he was sleeping in the room. She knew full well that doing this had been an act of rebellion on her part.

Slowly she closed the gap between her and the dresser. She no longer had a will of her own and had no idea of what was happening. Francine stopped directly in front of the chair and did as she was directed. She put one foot on the seat and then stood as she placed the other one on it. As she kneeled on the front of the dresser, a pair of boney, blue, bruised hands and then arms reached out toward her.

Taking her by her upper arms, Francine's helper drew her into the mirror. Pulling her knee closer for support, her foot hit the alarm clock. It fell off the dresser, bouncing on the wooden floor as she was pulled all the way into the mirror.

The mechanism was tripped and the alarm went off. The sound did not enter the glass, alerting, Francine because she was already in the mirror and didn't hear anything but her own screams. The sound of the alarm clock going off did, however, wake Gary. Still groggy from sleep, he entered the room, turning on the light.

Looking at the bed, he saw it was empty. Turning his head to look around the room, he had the idea that she must be in the bathroom, but that didn't make sense. Why was the alarm going off?

Picking the alarm clock off the floor, he shut off the incessant ringing.

He called out, "Francine, are you up?" Hearing no reply, he checked the rest of the house. Checking her bedroom again, he noticed that her luggage was still there, which caused him to be concerned.

Just in case, he looked out the front door and down the street, nothing. With no other options, Gary called the police station frantically.

An officer soon came to the home and, when he searched the home and saw the packed bag, belonging to the wife, he called his superior for assistance. A short time later there were several policemen in the home and the questions began. Unfortunately, Gary had few answers for them.

Half the neighborhood was awake because of the sirens that were on as the police had come to the home. An officer, seeing that the lights were on next door, questioned the woman that answered the knocking. It was plain to see that she was not a fan of Gary Sutherland.

Maureen relayed the things she had overheard and seen the past few weeks, ever since the older couple next door came back from visiting their son in Davenport. By the time she had finished, she had painted a pretty bleak picture of the situation next door.

The officer returned to the Sutherland home and informed his superior officer of his findings. Gary was asked to come to the station for some routine questioning. This questioning lasted for quite some time.

A thorough search of the property revealed absolutely nothing. The search was expanded and the train station checked. No one that was questioned remembered seeing Francine. Gary was warned not to leave the area without informing the police.

He called Anna informing her of the situation. Gary had a hard time getting her to see that he was not involved with his wife's disappearance. By the time she got off the phone, she was almost shouting at him.

Due to the conversation the officer had had with the neighbor, Gary was arrested on suspicion of murdering his wife. The fact that there was no body found complicated things, but in the end, Gary was tried by a jury.

The most damaging evidence had been provided by, Maureen Fischbach, the lady living next door. The day she went outside to her front porch and overheard Gary and Francine arguing, she swears she heard him threaten his wife, saying, "I'll kill you."

Gary tried to clarify the statement, by testifying to what he actually said, but no one believed him. Anna wrote a statement to the effect that her sister was coming to her home in order to get away from her husband, which was read in court by the prosecution.

In the end, this was enough to send Gary to prison. The sentence, because of circumstantial evidence, was reduced to five years, before he would be eligible for parole. It was a long five years for Gary.

Andrew, his son, was at the sentencing and, when he was allowed to visit his father, was instructed to sell the home and all its contents. The home ended up being sold for less than its true value, due to the rumors that a murder had been committed there.

The contents of the home were sent to auction. Most of the items fetched little in the way of funds. The main items of interest were the dresser and mirror, and even these went for a low price. The money that Gary had hidden in the house was given to Andrew to hold on to. These funds were depleted when an appeal was launched. The only one who benefited from the appeal was the attorney.

It took very little time for the money to disappear, and Gary remained in prison. His son Andrew wanted to believe in his father's innocence but had reservations, due to the testimony of the neighbor at the trial. He spoke to her months later and asked if it is possible that she may have misheard Mister Sutherland.

"I am certain that I heard your father threaten your mother, I'm so sorry," Maureen said to the grieving man.

He returned to Davenport, resigning himself to the fact that maybe his father did kill his mother. The only other possible explanation offered by his father seems fanciful at best. His father thought that there was something funny about the mirror, but really didn't know what it might be. Andrew toyed with the idea of keeping the dresser and mirror, but in the end, decided against it. In the back of his mind, he believed that the problems his parents had had started shortly after they bought the set. His father would be released in five years and maybe the two could begin a new relationship then. He had a difficult time making up his mind as to whether or not justice had been done.

CHAPTER 37

The thing in the mirror had a satisfied feeling. Things would have been even better had it managed to acquire two more souls for the energy supply it required, but this had seldom happened, so nothing had been lost.

Once again, it found itself being viewed by possible new sources of energy. Many looked, but most were discarded as unsuitable. The choice to influence an individual would have to be made soon. The time for a new owner approached quickly.

It thought back to a time long, long ago, a time when things were different when it had walked in the world. The life it led was outside the norm. During his time on earth, he took the lives of those he thought inferior. He took whatever he wanted, and there were few who could stop him.

As happened in life, all too soon age started taking its toll. Desperate for a continuance, he was approached by one who was more evil than he. A deal was struck, but the result was not what he had anticipated. He thought that he would continue to walk the earth forever, doing what he had always done.

The one he made the bargain with tricked him into the cursed dark mirror. Now he was a collector of souls for the evil one. When he had used all the energy with which the captives were able to supply him, they would make the final journey into the everlasting darkness. Even he was not eager to go there, so he continued capturing the unsuspecting. He had looked for an escape for centuries, to no avail. Maybe one day he would find it, but till then, the journey went on.

Again in an auction house, a potential new recruit had been found. A young woman with breeding was enticed by the thing within. The thought was placed in her mind that she simply had to have the set.

CHAPTER 38

The year was nineteen thirty-five. David Smith owned a furniture store in Rapid City, South Dakota. The town was nothing to write home about, but David grew up there. Not much happened there unless you counted the launching of a hot air balloon. This event had been a major thing in some people's lives there, but it didn't interest him in the slightest.

David was too busy trying to make a living to care about such things. His travels took him to many of the larger cities in the northern states. The trip so far had been a waste of time. Most of the items he found at the auctions weren't worth the time and effort to bring to Rapid City.

Times were hard for most folk, and it took something special to draw their interest. Because he was on the road much of the time, his wife had taken their daughter and moved back home with her parents on the east coast.

There had never been a real bond formed with his little girl, so he really didn't miss her or her mother. Besides, it was easy enough to find company for the night. He had found many women who were dissatisfied with the men they were married to and were eager enough to spend some time with him. He was a good-looking man and had a slick way about him. This had always helped him in business too.

After entering the auction house, he took a seat near the front in the middle of the room. David sat through the bidding on several pieces that mildly interested him. He made a low bid on two of the pieces, not really caring if he got them or not.

It was imperative to get things at a really decent price, or he couldn't make money on them.

There was a set of china that he might turn a profit on and so he went after it. He tried to play it cool by waiting to see who was interested and to see just how bad they wanted the set. In the end, he was the only one that wanted it and managed to get the set for a song.

Next, the auctioneer drew everyone's attention to a dresser and accompanying mirror of exotic design. He had already inspected the pieces and figured that if he could get them for twenty dollars or less, he should be able to make a few bucks on the resale.

The bidding started at five dollars and soon went to ten. "Ladies and gentlemen, you will not have a chance to purchase anything like these two beautiful, handcrafted items again in the near future."

This brought the bid to fourteen dollars and for a moment, David hesitated. He wanted the bidding to stop after his next offer. Raising his hand he signaled a bid of seventeen. In his mind, he thought this was high enough to deter any higher bids.

"Going once, going twice, sold to the gentleman on my left."

David smiled to himself as he was still paying less than he thought he would have to. At that moment, there was a shout from the back as a newcomer in a white suit, had just entered the room.

"I would like to make a bid on those pieces," he said loudly in a southern accent.

The auctioneer informed him, "I'm sorry, sir, but the bidding is closed on those items."

The man, who looked like he was very well to do, took in several deep breaths and lowered his shoulders, obviously very disappointed.

David seeing an opportunity got up and made his way over to the cashier to pay for the newly acquired items. Out of the corner of his eye, he saw the man walk toward him.

He stopped when he was about five feet away from David. "I wonder if I may speak to you for a moment, sir."

The man spoke in a very cultured manner, and David was immediately aware that he was dealing with a person belonging to high society.

When the two were out of earshot, the man explained why he wished to speak with David. "My name is Beauregard Covington, please allow me to inform you of the circumstances in which I find myself. I am here from Charleston, South Carolina, on business. Earlier this week, I viewed these two pieces with my wife. She fell in love with them and pleaded with me to purchase them. I was in a taxi from the hotel, when the vehicle broke down. By the time I acquired another taxi to bring me here, I arrived too late to bid on the items in question."

"That is unfortunate for you. But on the other hand, it did work out well for me. I should be able to turn a tidy profit from them in my store," David said, hoping that the man would take the bait.

"Am I to understand that you would consider making them available to me if we can reach a proper agreement on the price, sir?"

"I might be talked into selling them to you if the price

is right. In my exclusive store, I'm quite certain they will fetch a tidy sum," David said, thinking this was his lucky day.

"I know you paid seventeen dollars for the pair, a steal I might add. What would you be willing to let them go for, here and now?"

David thought for a moment. He knew this man had money, but like most people with money, it wasn't always easy to get them to part with it. He did have a good feeling about this, though. "I think that I would have no trouble getting…fifty dollars for them."

The man almost choked when he heard that price, saying, "I don't think that will be an easy sum to acquire, sir. I will offer you thirty, and that is a nice profit with no work involved."

David knew this man wanted them badly, so he decided to play this hard, saying, "forty-five dollars is a fair price in my estimation. I'm sure the missus would agree."

"You are a scoundrel, sir, using this line of argument to sway me," he said with a slight smile on his face. "I will give you forty dollars and no more. I would rather face the disappointment of my dear wife than to be taken advantage of any more than this."

Knowing he had reached the limit his new acquaintance would bear, David stuck out his hand and shook the Southern gentleman's. "You have a deal, my good man."

The money was exchanged and the cashier informed of the change in ownership. Beauregard made the arrangements to have the pieces wrapped and shipped to his home near the shores of the Atlantic Ocean in Charleston.

David walked out of the building very pleased with the deal he had just made. He was certain that he would never have made that much profit from the two items if he had taken them and sold them in his store. It had been a good day indeed.

CHAPTER 39

Beauregard headed back to the hotel,, knowing he had overpaid for the pieces, but he couldn't put a price on the happiness of his beautiful wife, Constance. She was in the room with an expectant look on her face when he entered. He smiled and she knew that he had gotten the object of her desires.

She knew she would be the envy of all her friends. The mirror, especially, was like no other she had ever seen. She was exceptionally happy. "Thank you so much, dear, I knew you would get them for me. How much did you have to pay for them?" she asked.

He didn't bother to tell her he got there too late and had to pay the buyer more than he thought they are worth, so he said, "The bidding went higher than I anticipated, and I had to pay forty dollars in order to get them for you."

"I'm sure they are worth every penny. Are you having them shipped to our home?"

"The pieces will be on the train tomorrow. I'll instruct the help to pick them up from the station and put them up in the bedroom."

Beauregard had a nasal problem caused by living in

close proximity to water. He was also ten years older than his wife and a very restless sleeper. This caused a problem in their relationship for the first year or two of their marriage. He now went to bed with her until the nasal problem started then moved to the spare room. The new sleeping arrangements had fixed the problem and both got a good night's sleep. This along, with a nice sized spending allowance, kept her happy.

Whenever he went on any business trips, Beauregard took Constance with him, and they did the town in style. The plantation was profitable enough to keep them in a lifestyle that she was used to. He realized that a woman such as Constance did not come with a cheap price tag.

"Are we still going to dinner with the mayor this evening?" she asked her husband.

Smiling pleasantly, he said, "Yes, we are, dear. Did you buy that dress you were looking at to wear tonight?"

"I did, and it looks absolutely fabulous on me. Thank you, dear, for being so understanding with me."

The evening out was everything Constance had hoped it would be.

The mayor's wife, although several years older than her, had been eager to hear about life in the South. "You must tell me about your plantation. I have heard stories, but never from someone who actually lived on one."

Constance turned up the charm. "Then you must come visit us in our home. I would love to have you and your husband stay with us. I'll give you the grand tour, and we can have a party with all the delicious dishes the South is known for."

"That would be simply marvelous, dear."

The evening passed and, before they knew it, the two were on their way home. It had been a wonderful trip, but it was nice to be back in Charleston. Her friends were eager to hear of her adventures up north and the new acquisitions. The help was sent to the rail yard to pick up the mirror and dresser.

Hours later, the dresser was placed where it would look the best, and the mirror had been turned sideways and hung on the wall. This would allow Constance to view herself better when trying on dresses. The two pieces were side by side and produced an interesting combination. The dresser was on one wall near the corner of the room, and the mirror on the wall at right angles to it, so she could turn to look at herself as she sat at the dresser.

CHAPTER 40

The first night together in the room, a connection was made, but just enough to make contact with the two lying in bed. Having acquired Francine a short time ago, a new source was not immediately required just then. The entity decided to postpone the assimilation. Who knew? Maybe the two might possibly be taken at the same time. This thought appealed very much to the occupant of the mirror.

CHAPTER 41

Beauregard walked around the plantation with his foreman. Albert, of colored persuasion, lived in a tiny home a hundred and fifty yards from the main house. Beyond this were the living quarters of the workers in Beauregard's employ. There was a time, many generations ago, when his great grandfather ran the plantation with the slaves he owned. Times had changed, though, and this was no longer the case.

The workers were now free to leave whenever they wished, but few did. They were treated reasonably well and received fair wages. They would never become wealthy but had enough to live on. The wages were kept low enough to prevent any from buying their own homes or properties.

As Beauregard and Albert surveyed the scene, a list of things to be taken care of was written down. Because the weather had been quite warm and humid, many things had become overgrown. There were a few things in need of repair, and Albert received instructions on how Beauregard wanted it done.

Albert told the workers what was required of them and then took the flatbed truck to pick up supplies. When he returned, he was asked to bring the Cadillac to the front of the traditional home.

The driveway circled in front of a large, screened in, elliptical shaped porch, surrounded on both sides by yellow roses and trees with Spanish moss hanging from the branches. The iron gates separated the property from the road that led to the beaches.

The city of Savannah was within easy driving distance from Charleston. That was where the lovely Constance had been raised by her well-to-do parents. Being accustomed to wealth, it took a man of status to win her heart. Beauregard filled the position quite well.

Coming from a long line of upper-class citizens, Beauregard was a man of influence and had considered running for office at one time. When he met his wife to be, he thought better of the plan and concentrated on the plantation, making certain that it remained a real source of income. Beauregard, having his hand in a number of other interests, kept the money flowing, despite the downturn in the economy.

The day was warm and so the top of the convertible Cadillac had been turned down. He would, of course, drive considerably slower than normal because Constance wouldn't want her hair to be messed up too much.

As the top was lowered, she came out of the home and walked down the stairway. In order to keep herself looking proper, she wore one of her elegant hats. Beauregard looked at her and admired the curves her slender waist created.

A leisurely drive and they were ready for lunch at the country club his family had been members of for many years. Several of the friends they were meeting had already been seated at a table overlooking the ocean. Only the elite were allowed in this facility. The prices were high, but more than worth it. The chef was top notch and, as they made up their minds as to what they would order, drinks were served by a well-dressed waiter.

Most of the males had the lobster and all the fare that went with it. The ladies, not wishing to avail themselves of such a messy meal, ordered lighter items from the menu.

Florence, one of Constance's best friends, asked, "Please do tell me about the mirror and dresser, you bought up north. Are they really as exquisite as I have heard?"

"Oh, yes, they are. You will have to come over and see them. Beauregard dear, can we have a party this coming Saturday evening? I really would like to show my friends the new pieces you purchased for me."

He looked at his wife with a smile. "Of course, my love, anything your heart desires."

A pleased look crossed her face as she and the other ladies decided on what to serve at the occasion. The ladies offered several suggestions and then debated the merits of each, finally deciding on what seemed to be the most popular.

The men took out cigars and discussed things of importance and how to take advantage of them. These men looked after each other and had made much money this way. A business opportunity had arisen, and it needed to be decided on how best to handle it.

A tract of desirable land had come on the market for back taxes. The four men would purchase it and divide it amongst themselves. One side of it bordered Beauregard's plantation and would increase the size of the estate by twenty five percent. He had had his eye on the property for years and was surprised that he hadn't heard about the owner's troubles. The owner was not a man of breeding, so had never traveled in this circle.

The next day the four paid the arrears and became the

new owners. A surveyor was hired and the severance application filled out shortly afterward. Five hundred acres was then in the possession of four different men. Much of the land was covered in mature loblolly pine trees. Two of the new owners had acquaintances in the lumber industry, which they all intended to take advantage of.

These trees produced wood that was used in the manufacture of doors. The industry heads were contacted and soon a bargain was struck to have the trees harvested. The idea was to remove all the trees and then plant cotton, which would be bought by the cotton mills.

A tidy profit would be made by all. The wealthy men would, of course, soon be wealthier. The former owner, already an old man, would never know how much money he could have made had he sold the timber. He died a pauper several years later. This mattered little to the four men, as they couldn't care less about the man.

The party was a success and, when the ladies saw the exotic mirror and dresser, now polished to a high sheen, they were suitably impressed. The smoky glass lent an eerie quality to the mirror and the dresser complemented it well. Standing back a few feet, the ladies were able to view themselves, top to bottom. A few offers were made to purchase the items, but they were politely turned down.

Life continued on a grand scale for Beauregard and Constance. While much of the rest of the country had fallen on hard times, there were those who seemed to prosper. The couple was happy and, one day, she realized that there were changes in her body, and after a doctor's appointment, Constance found that she was expecting a baby. She, at first, was not happy that she was with child, but, as the weeks went by, the idea grew on her. She realized that she was actually beginning to look forward to the birth of her baby.

Beauregard, on the other hand, was ecstatic, hoping that the baby was a boy, so the family name would be carried on. He had no brothers nor did his father. For a time, he thought that he might be the last Covington, the end of this line.

Constance had been in possession of the mirror for almost two months now. The couple slept together for the first hour at bedtime and then due to the nasal problem, Beauregard had been forced to move to the spare bedroom. It was either that or have an unhappy wife in the morning.

CHAPTER 42

At the three month mark, all was normal with the pregnancy. This was when it started, a soft whispering in the bedroom after the man left. A connection was made and there was a feeling of satisfaction within the mirror, two for the price of one.

The entity was in no great hurry, it had time. This was an opportunity that was different from those in the past. The only question was, how long to wait before acquisition should be attempted.

CHAPTER 43

Beauregard and Constance prepared the nursery for the baby, which if all went well, would arrive in less than six months. There was joy on the plantation which stemmed from the two happy parents to be. A celebration party was thrown in honor of the upcoming event.

Some of the guests were young ladies who had grown up with the mother to be. These young women were very happy for Constance and wished her all the best, at least most of them. There was one, Isabella, who, although putting in a valiant effort, had yet to achieve the result that Constance had. She was somewhat envious, and this had been noted by some of the guests. Isabella left the party early as her mood spiraled out of control, and rather than embarrass herself further, she thought it would be better to go home.

The festive atmosphere of the party returned with the exit of the angry Isabella. Her husband received a tongue lashing for his inability to perform as expected. This ended up being a long night for the hen-pecked young man.

The party broke up well before midnight, due to the condition of the hostess. Well wishes were expressed as the guests left. Constance headed for bed, with Beauregard staying up for a short time as he finished a brandy and his cigar on the elliptical front porch.

The air was warm and the screened-in area relatively free of mosquitoes. Relaxing on a lounger, he thought about how his life was about to change. With the coming of a baby, he knew his social life would have to adapt, at least for a while. When the child was a little older, they may be able to go out to parties and dinners a trifle more. The household staff would have to be added to by hiring a nanny, which would free them up to some degree.

Constance lay down in bed and wondered what had gotten into her friend, Isabella. The two of them had always been good friends, but that evening, Isabella was not a happy person. If only she could have a baby of her own, things would go back to the way they were.

As Constance drifted off, a now-familiar voice spoke to her subconscious mind. Her new friend helped Constance to fall into a deep sleep. The connection between the two grew as the entity within the mirror began to take over. There was a slight anxious trembling in her womb.

Four months along and significant changes were happening to the mother. Her appetite had grown and she was filling out, a bit more than she thought she should. It took a real effort on her part to control her eating habits. Being vain, in this instance, was an asset.

She stared into the mirror at her darkened figure and turned sideways. The abdomen was already starting to protrude and she looked at all the changes that were going on. She had had to buy new clothes that were meant for motherhood. She, however, was only half pleased with this new look. After the baby was born, she was determined to do everything she could to retrieve her figure.

Going to the bathroom, she looked into the mirror there, studying her face. Despite the sleep she got each night, there were dark circles under her eyes. She had managed to cover them up with makeup but was growing concerned that all might not be as it should.

At the breakfast table, she said, "Beauregard, I think I'll go to the doctor today. Although I sleep perfectly well, I feel fatigued and there are dark circles under my eyes."

"I've been meaning to ask you about that. Do you have any idea what might be causing this?"

"None at all. I should be well rested with all the sleep I'm getting. Could you be a dear and call for an appointment?" she asked as she ate her fruit salad.

Finishing his bacon and eggs as quickly as he could, he left the room to make the call. A short time later, he returned. "You have an appointment for one forty-five this afternoon. I have a few things to take care of this morning around the plantation, but if you need me for anything, send one of the help to collect me," he said as he affectionately kissed her cheek.

Beauregard found Albert and, after the usual discussions about the weather, they got to work surveying the plantation. They ended their walk looking over the newly planted fields. This was the area that he had acquired with his friends. The trees had all been harvested and the stumps removed using bulldozers.

The land had then been cleaned up and tractors used to plow it. The equipment on the tractors finished the job of turning the forest soil into fine earth, which was then planted with rows and rows of high yield cotton plants. In a couple of years, the harvests should start turning a real profit.

The last few years had seen cotton prices drop somewhat. This had been making it a less desirable enterprise to get in to. Beauregard had figured out two ways of getting around this. One, he had planted this new strain of cotton which yielded far more cotton per acre, and second, he obtained through auction a new style cotton picking machine. This would allow him to use the machine to replace the people used to pick the cotton. The cotton would be picked far faster and because it would be picked early, he could then fetch the highest price for the product.

Because of that train of thought, Beauregard began toying with the idea of getting into the textile business. In the end, he decided against it because of the worker dissent. Instead, he had an idea that maybe shipping the bales of cotton to the textile factories up north might possibly fetch higher prices.

By the time he and Albert were done, it was noon and time for lunch. The cook made him a sandwich and a drink, which he polished off in good time, hardly tasting what he ate. After cleaning up to rid himself of any accumulated dirt, he got ready to take Constance for her appointment.

The ride to the doctor was pleasant enough, but Constance, it was obvious, was worried that something might be wrong. In the examination room, she told Doctor Schmidt, "I'm a little concerned that there may be a problem. I sleep well and long, but in the morning I am starting to feel more and more drained as time goes by."

The doctor was from Germany and had been a great source of help during her earlier medical problems. He listened to her with interest. "Can you tell when this all began and exactly how do you feel different. I know you told me you feel drained and tired, but is there something or a particular part of your body that is more affected than other parts?"

"I just feel so tired. There is no pain or any symptoms

that I can point to that are worse than others."

He did an in-depth examination and found nothing of any consequence. "I believe that some blood work is in order. I find nothing wrong at this point, but the tests may indicate some underlying problem that is not obvious. The hospital has the facilities to do this, and I will have my nurse contact them for an appointment. You will be notified of the time."

Getting dressed, she asked, "Is there anything I can do in the meantime, Doctor?"

"Make sure you have a balanced diet, with plenty of fruits and vegetables. Keep consumption of pork, including ham, to a minimum, and keep your levels of salt down."

"Thank you. I will follow your instructions."

In the Cadillac with the top in place, she explained what the doctor had said, and they rode back to their home in silence. Constance spent the afternoon in a lounger on the porch, lying in the shade. Thinking about her time at the doctor's office and why she was there, she fell asleep. When she awoke hours later, she felt better than she had in a while.

Beauregard had been visiting his accountant and, when he came home, seeing that Constance was in the lounger, walked over, asking, "How are you feeling, my dear?"

"I fell asleep in the lounger and feel somewhat better, I must say. Maybe the fresh air is helping."

Smiling with a little relief, he said, "Maybe you should have more naps outside. You do look more rested. By the way, the accountant says we are in very good shape financially. Would you like to take a short holiday to New Orleans?"

"I'm not sure I'm up to it at the moment, but I think we should go anyway. In a few months, I won't be in any condition to travel. When would you like to go?"

"How about leaving this Thursday? We will be able to spend the weekend and a few days at the beginning of next week there," he said, smiling with anticipation.

It was quite obvious he wanted to go, so she said, "Yes, that will be lovely. I'll have the maid help me pack for the trip."

As he got up, over his shoulder, he said, "I'll make reservations at the Cornstalk Hotel on Bourbon Street."

Thursday arrived, and Constance was feeling slightly better than she had for a while. She had been napping outside in the afternoons, and this seemed to be helping. Gently, Beauregard helped his wife into the car and, at a nice leisurely pace, drove away. In order not to tax her too much with a long drive, he had already made plans to stop for the night in Atlanta.

Friday afternoon saw them arrive at the Cornstalk Hotel. A porter at the hotel helped them with their bags and the two were registered and taken to their room. The room turned out to be an elegant suite. The young man was tipped, and they were free to relax.

Opening the French doors, Beauregard stepped out onto the small narrow balcony. The scene below showed the famous French quarter of New Orleans a short way off. Bourbon Street a hundred yards away was filled with shops and people meandering down the sidewalks. Here and there, people played music, looking for a handout.

Constance came up beside him. "My, this is a gorgeous scene. I love the architecture and the beautiful trees along the street. I'm so glad you brought me here. I hear the restaurant downstairs is absolutely divine."

The evening meal, as Constance desired, was taken in the dining room of the hotel. Sitting at the table looking over the menu, Beauregard ordered a cocktail drink and Jambalaya for the main course. Constance had a lighter dinner, thinking the spices in the Jambalaya might be too much for her.

After the meal, the two walked arm in arm, down the street, enjoying the sights. That night, for one of the few times in quite a while, she slept well and woke in the morning feeling quite rejuvenated. Being in a chipper mood, she enjoyed a nice breakfast and then the two took a tour of New Orleans by horse and buggy.

The sights were exquisite and the architecture amazing. They were taken along the seawall and watched the seagulls flying over the saltwater, looking for food. The air coming off the ocean was balmy and had a pleasant fragrance to it. There were magnolias planted all around the city giving it a serene atmosphere. But, of course, the blooms had long since disappeared.

For lunch, Beauregard decided that the world famous barbecue ribs were in order. They were slightly messy, but this was nothing that some soap and water wouldn't take care of. Constance preferred a bowl of fruit, including mangoes, one of her favorites.

Two days passed as the couple enjoyed their time away. Looking across the table in the dining room of the hotel, he asked, "How are you feeling, my dear?"

"I believe that this time away is just what I needed. I feel so much better. Thank you for suggesting it."

"I want only the best for you, my love," he said, taking her hand in his.

Soon they were on their way home, a happy couple. The drive was leisurely and, again, they stayed overnight in Atlanta, not wishing to tax the mother-to-be. Once they were home, the maid unpacked their things and drew a bath for the lady of the house.

Constance enjoyed the bath for half an hour and dressed for a relaxing evening with her husband. By nine-thirty, she was ready for sleep. Preparing for bed as she crossed the room to go to the bathroom, she caught a slight movement reflected in the mirror.

Turning to look around the room, she expected to see her husband but soon realized that she was alone. *Funny, I could have sworn there was someone in the room with me*, she thought.

She walked to the mirror and looked to see what area of the room the reflection could have come from. By the time she was done, she was no farther ahead than she was when she first noticed the movement. *My eyes must be playing tricks on me.*

The occurrence was soon forgotten as the life within her made its own movement. This amazed her as she thought about how this had changed her life. She was awake for only a short time, as she pulled the covers over herself.

The voice started once more and plans were made by the uninvited guest in the room. The life within the form sleeping in the bed was being explored, and when this happened, the unborn felt agitated by the presence. Constance was totally unaware of anything wrong.

CHAPTER 44

The months went by quickly. The blood work had revealed nothing out of the ordinary and so was dismissed. The tired feeling had returned long ago but had been offset by naps taken in other areas of the house. The weather was cooling down little by little, but nothing like it did in the northern states.

The temperatures seldom went below forty degrees Fahrenheit in this area of the country. It hovered between sixty and sixty-five. Beauregard had been kept busy with the plantation and deals being made with his three close friends. Despite the fact that a depression was still happening around the world, there were opportunities for those with the resources and intelligence to take advantage of them.

Constance was not as cheery as she was before expecting the baby, but rallied after her naps in the afternoon. Neither suspected that anything could be seriously amiss. They both looked forward to the birth, but he was especially anxious to find out if he was going to be the father of a baby boy. Unfortunately, there was no way to find out ahead of time what the sex of the child would be.

Constance, now only two months away from the due

date, was getting quite uncomfortable. Her abdomen was starting to protrude considerably. *I wonder if I will ever look like I used to.* She had thoughts like that whenever she looked in the mirror. *Maybe I should stop looking at myself.*

That, of course, was not going to happen. Most attractive women found it impossible to walk by a mirror without looking into it. To make things worse, the mirror in her room was an extraordinarily beautiful one, and the reflection it cast was unlike any other.

At night, as the time approached, control tightened on the expectant mother. A decision was made to soon take over completely. In an effort to make sure that the subject's will was no longer her own, she was made to get out of bed and approach the looking glass. This attempt was not as successful as would be necessary when the time came to make the move. There was some resistance coming from within.

Efforts to deepen the connection were made over the next few weeks. The entity had underestimated the influence of motherhood. This had been the first attempt to seize total control over a subject in this condition.

The naps in the afternoon were becoming shorter and shorter as the baby became more and more active. Unable to do anything to fight off the invasion, the child fought back in the only way it knew how. It made things uncomfortable for the mother when she was not in her own bed. At night was when it too was being controlled to a degree by the thing in the mirror.

Another visit to the doctor shed no light on what was causing the baby to be so overactive during the waking time. The doctor was curious as to why this was only happening during the day and not at all during the night.

Beauregard thought about it. "It might be a good idea for Constance to spend the rest of the pregnancy at her parent's home. This way her mother, who has experienced the discomforts of carrying a baby four times, can be of assistance."

Although she thought this was a good idea, she said, "I would rather be in my own home."

Beauregard offered a compromise, which Constance liked much better. "Why don't you let me ask your mother to stay at our home for a time? This may well alleviate the pressure on you."

"Yes, I think that is a much better idea, thank you, dear."

The call was made, and the following week Beatrice was brought into the home. Beauregard had always gotten along well with his mother-in-law, despite the fact that he was ten years older than his wife and only thirteen years younger than his mother-in-law. Constance's siblings were living in Europe and had planned a visit well after the baby was born. Beauregard's and Beatrice's views of life were similar, and the fact that he could provide very well for her daughter was the icing on the cake. Both had always felt that money meant privilege. Both Beatrice and her husband came from old money, and her ancestry could be traced back to the founding fathers of the nation.

Beatrice considered moving into her daughter's room but soon thought better of it as she remembered what it was like when she was in that condition. She took one of the spare bedrooms. When Constance went to bed early each night, Beatrice read in her room so if there was a problem for Constance at that time, she would be able to hear her call.

The days slipped by and the grip tightened on the mother-to-be. With less than four weeks left to delivery, time was growing shorter and the discomfort grew for Constance. Beatrice explained that this was to be expected, but was nevertheless concerned about the dark circles under her daughter's eyes. These seemed to be more and more pronounced as the days went by.

"I can't fathom why you sleep so well at night, and yet look like you haven't slept at all. You say that you've seen Doctor Schmidt several times, and he has no diagnosis for this? When did this occurrence begin?"

Constance filled her mother in on the details. Beatrice could offer no advice or solution to the problem. Thinking for a time, an idea came to mind, so she said, "You know dear, I have heard that a priest dealt with a case where one of his parishioners had something similar to what is affecting you. I don't know the details, but have you considered maybe talking to Father Cortelli?"

"Oh, Mother, I hardly think that he'd be able to help me with this, after all, he isn't a physician, and I'm not consumed by an evil spirit."

"Since you put it that way, I do feel a little foolish suggesting it to you. I'm sure everything will be just fine once the baby is born, and your body goes back to normal. It may only be a hormonal change."

"I'm sure you're right. I'm happy that you're here to help me."

At night there were sounds in the bedroom, but the only one who heard them was Constance, and even she heard them only subconsciously. There was the soft glow in the mirror, but since she was asleep, no one saw it. Lately, there had been constant movement in the glass. A ghostly figure was moving and watching the sleeping form of the young woman in the bed.

In the morning, Beatrice walked into the room to see her daughter and was alarmed by how much the expectant mother's health seemed to have deteriorated. She caught a slight movement in the glass of the mirror and quickly looked around the room, expecting to see Beauregard, but the room was empty.

Looking closely at the glass, she saw nothing unusual and so walked to the bed. She had a hard time waking her daughter from the deep sleep. When she finally managed to rouse the girl, some of the color returned to Constance's face.

"I am very concerned for you, dear," she said. "I think you really need to be in the hospital for the rest of the pregnancy. Something is definitely wrong, and you should be where a doctor is close at hand."

"I think you may be right, Mother. I feel more drained with each passing day."

"I'll call our family doctor and make an appointment to see him as soon as possible," Beatrice told her.

There was more movement in the glass, but because the two females were in a discussion, neither noticed. The two left the room and went to the kitchen, where they discussed the matter with the father-to-be.

"If you feel that is the proper thing to do, then yes, by all means, Constance should be where she can be best-taken care of."

CHAPTER 45

Feeling the inevitable change coming, the entity in the mirror was angry. The interference that had been brought by the newest arrival in the home couldn't be tolerated. It desperately wanted to lash out like it did with the young man so long ago. Unfortunately, if the older figure in the home was frightened too badly, there would be the chance that the object of its desire would leave too.

If the young woman left to have the infant in another location, she would undoubtedly return at a later date. Then again, what if she didn't come back? The entity would have lost two energy sources. It wouldn't matter at all if the infant was inside the woman or not, the energy could still be taken from it too. It was just that the amount of energy it would be able to take from the tiny thing would be more after it was born.

A decision had to be made soon, as long as the woman remained there for at least one more night. If not, it would have to wait, and there was a chance of losing the source totally, which couldn't be allowed to occur. There was too much at stake.

CHAPTER 46

The doctor was called and while Beatrice was on the phone, she could be heard asking, "Is that right, Doctor? What can be done in the meantime? All right, we will be in your office in an hour." Turning around to face her daughter, she said, "It would appear that the hospital has a number of patients that have influenza. He is concerned about you being exposed to it. He wants you to come to his private office for a detailed examination. He will then decide whether or not to have you stay in a private clinic he owns. Unfortunately, you won't be able to be placed in it until tomorrow at the earliest. A patient recovering from surgery will be released in a day, possibly two."

Beauregard frowned. "I've heard about this influenza. I hear many people have died from it. I'm glad the doctor has a private clinic. Did he say whether or not there are people there with influenza?"

"He says they have not allowed anyone in the clinic who has been diagnosed with the illness. I think we should prepare to leave shortly, dear," Beatrice answered.

In her room upstairs, Constance got dressed and had a slight feeling of sorrow at the possibility of leaving her home for a time. She had no idea that this feeling was being placed in her by the entity within the mirror.

Beauregard drove to Doctor Allenby's office in an upscale area of town. They arrived five minutes before the time of the appointment. The receptionist took down the details and soon Constance and her mother were in the examination room.

The doctor asked many questions and then requested, "If you don't mind, Beatrice would you leave the room while I and the nurse perform a more in-depth exam?" When this was completed, he spoke with all three in his office. "I have not seen anyone in the past with the symptoms Constance has. It is my recommendation that she be admitted to the clinic as soon as possible. She needs proper care we can only provide here. We will run a number of tests to see what it is we are dealing with. At the moment, I am uncertain of what the problem is, but I intend to find out. Unfortunately, the earliest we can bring her in is tomorrow or the next day. It will all depend on the patient I have that is recovering from surgery."

"Thank you, Doctor Allenby. It's a relief to hear this," Beatrice said. "We will pack her clothes and wait for your call."

Beauregard shook the doctor's hand and expressed his appreciation too. The three left the office with Constance looking very uncomfortable. She did indeed look sick, and it was very evident that all three were extremely concerned about her health.

"Mother, I'm frightened. I feel worse with each passing day, and I am at a loss as to what can be done," Constance said as she cried softly.

"I'm sure Doctor Allenby will be able to figure it all out once you are in his care, dear."

For the first time, Beauregard was shaken too. He was

now sure that there was something seriously wrong with his wife and baby. Desperately he wanted both his child and wife to survive this ordeal. He wondered if something in his genes could have been responsible for this situation. Cautiously, he drove the automobile home.

Beatrice helped her daughter to pack her overnight case for her stay at the clinic. "I think I've packed everything that you will need. I can always come back and get anything we may have forgotten."

"Thank you, Mother. I think I'll lie down for a while."

"All right, dear, just call out if you need anything," Beatrice said and started to walk out of the room.

As she turned to the doorway, she noticed movement in the mirror again. *This is strange. Whatever can it be that is reflecting in the glass?* Seeing nothing, she closed the door.

CHAPTER 47

Inside the mirror, the entity knew that time was short and quickly got to work. It attempted to make the final preparations before it was too late and its quarry departed. If the victim was allowed to leave the following day, there was always the possibility that the forms in the bed might not return. Then where would it be?

Too much energy had been expended to allow that to happen. Things were not yet to the point where the young woman could be assimilated, but they were close. If only it had a little more time. Contact was made, and the work began in earnest.

CHAPTER 48

Constance lay in bed, asleep, but, once again, although a deep sleep, it was not a restful one.

Beatrice had a conversation in the kitchen with Beauregard. "I've packed her clothes for the clinic. I do hope they call soon. I fear Constance and the baby are in grave danger. I have never seen anything like this before."

"I don't know what I'd do if I lost her and the baby. They are my whole life. This house and my money mean little to me without them."

She rested her hand on his shoulder for support, knowing this situation had the potential to turn out badly. She suggested that he go outdoors in order to try to take his mind off the problem. "There is no point in you fretting in the house. Being outside might do you some good."

Two hours later, the phone rang and Beatrice answered it, saying, "Hello."

The voice on the other end said, "This is Doctor Allenby's office calling. I have a message for Constance Covington."

"I'm her mother, Beatrice. She is lying down. May I take the message?"

"Doctor Allenby has asked me to let you know that a room has become available and asks if she could be here tomorrow morning at nine please," the lady said.

"Yes, she will be there. Thank you so much," she said as she hung up the phone.

Going out the front door she looked for her son-in-law. She spotted Albert near a barn and called out to him. He came to her immediately and she asked, "Do you know where Beauregard is, Albert?"

"Yes, ma'am, shall I get him for you?"

"Please do."

Beauregard came to the house quickly, and Beatrice conveyed the news to him. A look of relief came to his face. "I am so happy to hear that. This is great. Finally, we will get some answers." He ran up the stairs and quietly entered his wife's room.

Looking straight to the bed, he failed to notice the glowing mirror. It quickly went back to normal without Beauregard seeing what was going on. "Are you awake dear?" he asked.

It took a moment for her to get her wits about her, and then she said groggily, "Yes, but I feel as tired as I did before I lay down."

"I'm sorry to disturb you, dear, but the doctor's office phoned and said you are to come in at nine tomorrow morning. Maybe they can figure out what's wrong."

"Thank goodness. I think I'll get up and sit in the living room. I don't know if it's my imagination or what, but I feel worse when I sleep here in my own bed."

"Here let me help you," he said as he took her gently by the arm. The thing in the mirror embedded a suggestion into her mind before she got out of the room.

Constance was brought to the living room and, with her protruding abdomen, she sat there uncomfortably. Beatrice made a cup of tea and brought it to her. "Maybe this will help your digestion. Can I have the cook make anything for you, dear?"

Constance took a deep breath before answering, "Just a biscuit will be fine, Mother."

It wasn't long before Constance fell asleep again. Her mother brought her a pillow and sheet, in an attempt to make her daughter more comfortable. The afternoon passed, and it was supper time. There was an aroma drifting around the home as the roast beef and potatoes were cooking. Constance woke up as the smell reminded her that she hadn't eaten much that day. Carefully, she got up and went to the washroom located on the main floor. When she was finished, she took a seat at the dining room table. Speaking to the cook, she said, "I would prefer just a small portion of everything, including the vegetables, Rose. I fear that there isn't a lot of room for food in me right now."

Rose gave a soft laugh and did as requested. The plate was placed on the table and the three dug in. There were moans of delight when they partook of the dinner. The three chatted about the events of the day and Constance staying at the clinic for a period of time. No one knew at the time how long the stay would be. The important thing was having both the mother and baby well taken care of.

By eight o'clock, Constance was ready for bed again. Beatrice made a suggestion. "Would you like to sleep in the living room tonight? I think it will be easier for you if you do. I'm sure Beauregard can have a bed brought down for you."

"I think your mother is right, dear," Beauregard agreed. "It will be better for you to sleep on the main level. It's no trouble to have the bed set up in the parlor."

Constance thought it over. There was a feeling drawing her upstairs. She didn't know why, but she wanted to sleep in her own bed. She realized it would be better if she slept downstairs, but the feeling was too strong to resist. She told the two, "Thank you, but I want to sleep in my own bed. Tomorrow, I'll be in the clinic, and who knows if the beds there are comfortable at all."

"If you are sure that's what you want, I'll help you up-stairs," Beauregard said as he got up.

After making a quick trip to the bathroom, Constance got into bed and was soon sound asleep. Both her mother and her husband stood over the sleeping form with concerned expressions. They left the room without noticing that a faint glow had appeared in the mirror.

Beatrice and her son-in-law went downstairs to talk, with him saying, "My goodness I really am concerned for Constance."

"As am I, she seems to becoming sicker with each passing day. I hope the clinic can find out what is wrong with her. It must be affecting the baby, whatever the problem is."

The conversation continued for an hour or so and then both retired to their bedrooms. Beatrice opened the door to her daughter's room just enough to see her asleep on the bed. Nothing appeared to be amiss, so she closed the door and retired for the night herself.

CHAPTER 49

Constance slept in bed, but because of the baby, she had a difficult time getting comfortable. She remained asleep but did not rest. Her mind was being taken over, and she no longer fully controlled her own body.

The soft voice emanating from glass spoke to Constance's subconscious mind. There was earnestness in the tone of the communication. Time was very short and a move had to be made that night or its chance could quite possibly slip away completely.

For several hours the clock ticked away the time. Deep in her mind, she fought for control, but it seemed to be a losing battle. As the hour approached three, involuntarily her arm pushed the covers aside. The baby inside her gave her more strength than her predecessors had in resisting the force in the room with her.

She and the baby fought back unconsciously as Constance was forced to get up out of the bed in her sleep. The steps toward the mirror were hesitant and jerky. The scene was like watching an inebriated sailor staggering out of a drinking establishment.

The fight continued as she got closer and closer to the glass. Her foot dragged across the floor, causing a soft sound to be heard within the room. Outside the room, the sound was ever so faint.

Beauregard being a light sleeper became restless, but not fully awake. He soon drifted back into the slumber of a worried man.

Constance and the baby kept up the subconscious fight but succumbed to the irresistible power in the room with her. Her feet continued to drag with each step and progress was slow but the inevitable end drew nearer and nearer.

Beauregard's sleep lightened to the point that he woke up. He listened for a sound in the night. He heard the soft, soft noise of something brushing against something. Having just roused, he wasn't sure if he actually heard anything.

Constance's forward movement caused her to brush against the chair in front of the dresser. There was a scuffing sound as the chair shifted on the wood floor. The child in her womb was kicking frantically, trying to influence its mother, but the mother was too deeply connected with the entity in the mirror. She was, at that point, standing in front of the mirror as the boney, darkened arms extended out of the glass. She slowly raised her arms in front of her too. As the two were inches apart, there was a sound in the room down the hall.

CHAPTER 50

In his bed, Beauregard fell into a light sleep. He was very concerned for his wife, and this prevented him from falling into a deep sleep. He roused occasionally for reasons he couldn't fathom. He thought he heard something, but the sound wasn't loud enough to be very audible.

He fell back into the restless slumber for a short time. Another soft noise, slightly louder awakened him enough to cause him to sit up in bed. He listened for a moment and then heard the soft brushing sound again.

Getting out of bed he turned on a light and put on a housecoat and slippers. Crossing the room, he placed his hand on the doorknob and twisted. There was a slight creak as he opened the door. There it was again, the same sound he believed he heard before. He thought that his wife had roused in order to go to the bathroom, so he was in no real hurry to barge in on her. He placed his ear to the door to listen.

The sound he heard was not what he expected to hear. Twisting the knob on the door to his wife's room and pushed it open.

CHAPTER 51

Her arms were seized by the entity and Constance's last chance to escape withered away. She was pulled into the mirror just as the door to her room started to swing open. By the time Beauregard stepped into the room, she and her baby were gone, disappearing into the mirror. Now that she was trapped inside the glass, she was no longer kept asleep.

What she now saw was beyond anything her worst nightmares could have imagined. The scream that came out of her mouth was inside the glass and couldn't be heard by those who stood outside it. Fear, unlike any ever experienced by Constance—the newest addition to those trapped in the mirror—took over her total being.

Beauregard, not seeing his wife in the bed, headed for the bathroom across the room. He knocked on the door and, when he received no answer, he opened it.

Having been awakened too, Beatrice walked into the bedrooms and asked, "Is everything all right?"

"I don't see Constance in here. Do you think she may have gone downstairs?"

Both went to the main level and a search was begun. Neither found Constance anywhere in the house. Panic started to take hold. Beauregard searched the entire house, finding no clues as to his wife's whereabouts.

He ran to Albert's quarters and had him wake all the workers. A search of the entire plantation was started, while Beatrice called the police. Half an hour later, three police officers arrived and were informed of the situation.

The bedroom was the first area to be investigated. A thorough study revealed that the only thing even slightly out of place was the chair in front of the dresser. The windows were checked and found to be unlocked, but being on the second floor, this caused no real concern.

The man in charge walked around the perimeter of the home, stopping under the window of the missing pregnant lady's room. He studied the soil to see if there were any depressions made by a ladder or some such device. He found nothing out of the ordinary.

The plantation workers started to come to the main house, revealing no new information. A search of the surrounding area was started, and the sergeant was called to the station to make a report. A missing person's report was made and an all-points bulletin sent out. A massive search was begun and continued for several days. No trace was found of the missing mother-to-be.

Beauregard was interrogated for hours, with no results, except for him losing his temper and almost striking out at the policeman questioning him. His lawyer put a stop to the interrogation, and the police attempted to look elsewhere but were stymied. There was no one else to question, except the young lady's mother, and that was seen as a dead end before it even started.

Over the course of the next few weeks, the plantation was searched in depth for signs of newly disturbed earth. There were several spots that had been dug up, but nothing was found.

Beatrice stayed with Beauregard for two weeks before

returning to her own husband who had come over to offer support now and then. She was a sad woman indeed.

Beauregard went into a deep depression as the time went by with no clues found as to what might have happened to his wife and baby. With Constance gone, Beauregard soon lost touch with his in-laws. With no wife or child, there was no longer a connection with Constance's family.

The bedroom was shut up and Beauregard became somewhat of a recluse. A few years later, he placed much of the home's contents into storage and put the plantation up for sale. The year was nineteen thirty-nine and the property fetched a poor price. There was a war erupting in Europe, and the world was being turned on its ear.

The mirror and dresser, along with many other things, remained in a locked storage facility for the next seven years, all but forgotten. The time passed slowly in the warehouse. The war which had brought many aspects of life in America to a virtual standstill finally came to an end and the economy once more began to stir.

The year was nineteen forty-six and the warehouse, which had been forgotten about, was sold to a developer. The contents were surveyed, and it had been decided that anything salvageable would be put on the auction block.

A long list was made of all the items to be let go. The auctioneer's people took care of all this and everything was packed up, loaded on a train, and sent to New York City. The prices to be had were far better in a large city. There were a great many things brought to be auctioned off to the highest bidder.

Long lists were sent out to all the major cities of all the things that were available. There were still many people with money and so, when the time came, the huge building was filled to capacity. The auction was done in stages. Furniture was done on one day, with jewelry and such on the next day, and machinery was auctioned off on the last.

People came ahead of time to view the items they were interested in. The site was a buzz of activity. The day arrived and the items brought out in quick succession, bid on, and removed.

There were only a few people interested in the odd mirror and dresser. Times and tastes had changed and so, as the bidding started, most people's attention was elsewhere.

CHAPTER 52

Many people walked through the area where rows and rows of used furniture were being made ready for auction. People from all walks of life poked and prodded, opened drawers and marked items for a better look. Businessmen looked for items to make money on or something for an office.

People who had lost everything in fires, or recently home from the war and needing furniture in an attempt to start over, were also there. There were even police officers looking to make certain that there wasn't any stolen merchandise among the legitimate items.

A number of folks stopped in front of an unusual mirror and dresser combination. A few were interested, but not enough to wait around long enough to be able to bid on them. There were so many things there, that it was difficult to narrow choices down to a small number of items.

The mirror searched for a suitable new owner as it touched minds in close proximity. There were a number of potentials. One was a man who had come back from the war overseas. His mind had been damaged while serving his country. Actually, it was already damaged before he went. It just got worse while he was over there.

This man heard voices now and then. The voices he heard weren't heard by others. He learned long ago while he was young, not to let others know about the voices in his head. Paul Rendell was alone in the world. He was the only child of parents who died while he was in the war in North Africa.

When he came home, he was able to take over his parent's home. It had been unoccupied for two years, except for a squatter, which the police had taken care of. There was a small sum of money that he had been left, and he had found a job at the local newspaper as a driver, delivering the newspapers.

Paul came to New York in order to fulfill his deceased father's wish to have his ashes spread in the lake in Central Park. He knew that it was probably against the law and so had done it in the middle of the night. When his family lived in the city, before the war, a trip to the park was made whenever possible.

While he emptied the urn into the water, he had almost been caught and so had had to run back to the cheap flop house he was staying at for the week. He tried to see a couple of old neighbors while he was there, but few of them still lived in the area, having moved on. Of course, due to his little problem, few of the neighbors had had much to do with him anyway.

During the war, while he was stationed in North Africa, his parents moved to Oklahoma City for a job his father had gotten. His father worked in the pesticide industry and died young because of it. His mother died soon afterward, long before Paul got back home.

Paul walked by the mirror and dresser and stopped in front of them. It was almost as if they were talking to him. This did not surprise him, because he heard voices often and knew they were only in his head. Looking around, he saw that no one else was paying any attention to the pieces of furniture so he knew there really weren't any voices. He had, in the past, learned to ignore these voices. It hadn't been easy, but knowing that they weren't real gave him the power to not be led by them like he had been when he was younger.

A feeling of well being came over Paul as he heard the soft pleasant voice saying he should buy the set. This was a new development with his hearing things. Normally there was little if any feeling accompanied by what he alone heard. Looking over the two pieces carefully, he noticed a tiny bit of damage. It appeared that while they were being moved by the workers, they were bumped against hard objects.

Paul had refinished a number of damaged pieces of furniture before and quickly saw that the marks were su-perficial. A decision was made, then and there, to make a bid on them when the time came the following morning. If all went well, he would have to make arrangements to have them shipped.

Paul went to the park for a last look around and to say goodbye to his father. He had thought about mixing his parent's ashes together but thought better of it. The two had not always gotten along too well. His mother had said on several occasions, when his dad wasn't there, that she would leave him if she had somewhere to go. With no relatives or real friends, she had no one to turn to. Paul had, for a long time, suspected that the curse he had had to live with all his life had been passed down to him by his father. His dad never admitted to having this con-dition, but Paul could tell by watching his father that he did indeed suffer from the ailment too.

The following day, Paul arrived early, eager to get things moving. He picked a spot off to the side to sit. He was one of the first and going by the itinerary, he knew he would have to wait quite some time for the things he wanted to come up for bidding.

Sitting there gave him time to think back on his years on Earth. His life had certainly not been an easy one. He always had trouble fitting in. During his school days, children made fun of him after they found him talking to himself.

Paul had learned his lesson quickly. At the first opportunity, he talked his parents into moving him to a new school. Living on the edge of two school districts allowed him to be transferred to the new school without a lot of fuss. Unfortunately for Paul, there were no treatments available to him. The family doctor never learned of the ailment and it had, up to then, remained a secret.

In the army, when he got drafted, he kept this a secret too, although it might have kept him home. The embarrassment involved with his voices kept him from informing the doctor that certified him acceptable as a recruit.

A series of items were auctioned off, but they were of no interest to him. He saw the mirror and dresser being moved on to the platform and the bidding started. A man on the other side of the room made a five-dollar bid. Someone else nearer to him raised the bid to seven dollars. It was bantered back and forth up to eleven dollars and stalled there.

"Going once, going twice…"

Up went Paul's hand, just high enough for the auctioneer to see it, but not his competitors.

"We have twelve dollars, do we have thirteen…going once, going twice…we have thirteen…. do we have fourteen… going once at fourteen…going twice—"

Paul's hand went up at the last instant.

"—we have fifteen…do we have sixteen…do we do have sixteen…sold to the young man to my right for fifteen dollars."

Paul breathed a huge sigh of relief as the other two bidders dropped out and he had the winning bid. He thought he had it at twelve dollars, but others knew how to play the game too and forced him to pay a little more than he had intended.

He paid the cashier in cash and informed them that he would make arrangements at the train station to have the pieces delivered to Oklahoma City. He received a bill of sale and all the information required for pickup by workers.

By the end of the day, all was taken care of, with the mirror packaged in cushioned cardboard and the dresser in a wooden box and then taken to the station. Paul was packed and ready to go once his purchases were loaded into a railway car. He had his ticket and boarded the train for the long ride home. He would have liked to have a sleeping berth, but saved his money and would attempt to sleep sitting up.

The whistle blew and the locomotive moved forward, causing the bump in each of the successive cars as the slack was taken up in the hookups. He was on his way home.

CHAPTER 53

The ride was a long one. Before he left the big city, Paul bought enough things from a local grocery store to keep him fed. Water in a jug kept him from getting thirsty, and some dry goods and fruit-filled his belly. Having been in the war taught him to eat what was available and not keep wishing for things he didn't have and couldn't attain.

He kept to himself, resisting attempts made by others to draw him into conversations. The people he was traveling with thought he was quite antisocial and quickly learned to leave him alone. No one realized that this was a safety mechanism Paul had had to learn the hard way. Even adults could be cruel if they were of a mind to, and Paul no longer took the chance of it happening again.

Whenever possible, he buried his head in a book or walked to the space between the rail cars and was buffeted by the wind, making conversation difficult. This suited him just fine.

As the train pulled into the station in Oklahoma City, he got his meager things together and prepared to disembark. As soon as he was off the train, he headed for the phone to call a mover in order to have his things transported to his home. He called several in an attempt to get the best price.

"Can you come to the train station now? I'm here and can help load it if necessary," he said to the man on the other end of the line.

The voice replied, "I can have a man there shortly. The name of my company is on the side of the truck so you'll have to signal him. Since you can help, that will make things much quicker and a bit cheaper for you."

It took an hour to have the furniture loaded onto the flatbed truck. When they were ready, he got into the truck with the man, thus saving transportation costs for himself. An hour and a half later and a bit of struggling, the things were in his house and the worker was paid.

The home Paul lived in was a very modest, small dwelling. There were three tiny bedrooms and one bathroom. The kitchen was located at the back of the house facing a small yard with a wire fence separating his property from the neighbors behind and to either side.

His mother had gotten along well enough with the people, but his father, like him, kept his distance and seldom got involved with them. The yard could use a mowing, and after he sharpened the blades on the push mower, he would cut it before it got too long. Once it reached a certain height, it became difficult to get it neat again.

Going to his bedroom, he looked at the dresser. Opening drawers he found a little dust and, taking a damp rag, he cleaned them all. Checking over the entire dresser he saw a number of scratches and set out to repair them, getting the things he needed from the workshop.

Once the dings and scratches were fixed, he polished the dresser until it looked almost new. Unpacking the mirror, he did the same to it. Looking at the back side, he looked for ways to hang it on the wall. Using a tape measure he decided where to place the heavy screws he'd require to hang it properly.

Using a pencil he put little marks where he intended to place the screws. Once they were secure in the wall studs, he lifted the heavy mirror and placed it on a blanket on the dresser. After a bit of juggling, he had the glass mounted on the wall.

Standing back, he checked to make sure it was level. Satisfied with the result, he cleaned the glass. His clothes were moved into the drawers, and he was a happy man— at least as happy as he ever got. Every now and then, his voices talked to him but he ignored them.

Having been gone for a while, he found that he was running low on supplies. This being the case, he walked to the store and replenished his refrigerator and dry goods. He still had three days off before he had to go back to work on Monday, so he thought he'd make the best of it.

Working at the local paper as a driver, he distributed the papers to all the local businesses and the paperboys who delivered them door to door. The job required him to get up at four in the morning. Having no friends to speak of, allowed him to get to bed by eight in the evening.

Being a rather unattractive young man had meant few girlfriends for Paul. As a matter of fact, he could count on one finger the number of girls he had had any kind of relationship with.

The girl was very homely and had her own problems, so the relationship didn't last very long. Paul had since resigned himself to the fact that he would probably be a bachelor the rest of his life.

Standing five-nine and weighing just under two hundred pounds gave him the strength to toss about the bundles of newspapers with little effort. It also prevented many from ridiculing him about his antisocial behavior.

A stern look was usually enough to turn away unwanted attention.

In his army days, many of the young men took advantage of cheap beer and alcohol. They would drink their sorrows away and, often in a drunken stupor, tried to get him to partake too. This he resisted.

"Come on, Paul, what's the matter with you? Do you hate having a good time? Here, have a drink on me," they would say.

A few times an individual would try to force him to drink, but when the unconscious man awoke, he knew better than to try that with Paul again.

Paul had had a few drinks only once. When he drank a few beers, the voices in his head got louder. The more he drank, the more insistent they became. At that point, he had no choice but to listen to them, it being impossible to ignore them. Alcohol, as it turned out, was not something with any benefits for him, so he stayed away from it.

There was one thing that he liked to do, and that was read. He liked adventure stories—stories about the prohibition and men like Al Capone and Lucky Luciano. *Tarzan of the Apes* and the *Grapes of Wrath* were books that had kept him entertained for hours. One of his favorites was the *Wizard of Oz*.

He made enough money to live comfortably, only because he owed nothing. His mom and dad left him the house and a little money, so he had few worries. He walked to work and drove the newspaper's vehicle to make all the deliveries. When the deliveries were made, he worked in the printing press area, keeping everyone supplied with materials.

Because he was so strong, the job was relatively easy for him. Paul seldom had a smile on his face, and because he was so strong and unapproachable, few people ever bothered him. He was a man that, for the most part, kept to himself. In the bathroom, he looked at the reflection as he stood there. His clothes were those of a worker. His face was anything but handsome and not the friendliest you saw around. His hair was black and his skin swarthy. He would not choose to look this way, but what could he do?

There was a rumble in his stomach, informing him that it was time for supper. Opening the refrigerator door, he peered inside. Not finding what he wanted, he looked in the freezer compartment door at the top. There was a piece of meat wrapped in wax paper. He would have liked to have had it, but it would take too long to thaw out, so another choice had to be made.

On the shelf in the lower section, he noticed a package of bacon. Along with a few eggs, he pulled out the bacon and prepared to fry it and then the eggs. He cut bread and placed it in a toaster that had hinged, flip up sides. Fifteen minutes later, he was at the table eating and washing it all down with a glass of milk.

The dishes were washed and put away. The time had come for a little radio, because his favorite broadcast, *Lights Out*, was about to begin. This thirty-minute broadcast was about mystery and murder and was very entertaining, helping to pass the time.

Turning up the sound, he heard, "Tonight's broadcast is titled, 'The Hangman.'"

Another voice came in at this point and started the story.

Paul had a routine he strictly followed. He was always in bed by eight and got up at four in the morning, whether or not he had to work the next day. Even when he had time off, he followed the routine. If he didn't, it was too hard to get up at four in the morning when he did have to go to work.

That night was no exception. Neighbors knew better

than to let their children play outdoors after eight in the evening. It had been made very clear to them that Paul would be very unhappy with them if he was awakened.

In bed, he thought about his recent trip to New York. He enjoyed the park, but little else. The train ride had been long and hot. The only other interesting thing was the auction, where he bought the dresser and mirror. He looked past his feet to where the mirror was hanging on the wall. It was an unusual-looking piece, and he wondered why he had the urge to buy it. It wasn't something he found particularly appealing, but there had been a voice in his head suggesting he procure it.

This voice hadn't been quite the same as the ones he had in his head most of the time. He could have resisted it but had gone along with it for once. He could ignore the voices when he wanted to, but chose not to this time, why?

As he drifted off, he fell into his usual deep sleep, not waking till his alarm went off. The hot bedroom had cooled off somewhat as a slight breeze had come in through the open window during the night. Thinking out loud, he said, "This is one of the good things about getting up early, it's nice and cool for a while before the sun comes up."

CHAPTER 54

With the morning of a new day started, Paul waited until he heard the neighborhood activities start outside. He went to the workshop to sharpen the blades on the push mower. This took half an hour and, when things were just right, he pushed the mower back and forth across the grass. The clipped blades flew behind the mower with each push. The smell of the cut grass filled the air with a pleasant aroma.

Halfway through the job, he saw the person next door standing on the other side of the fence. He really didn't want to talk, but the man was one of the few people Paul almost liked.

"Hello, Paul, how was your trip to the big city?"

Wiping the sweat from his brow with the handkerchief from his pocket, Paul said, "Morning, Arthur, the trip was fine."

"I see that you had some things delivered to the house. Did you buy them in New York?"

"Yes."

Arthur knew by hearing the short answers that Paul really didn't want to talk, but he couldn't keep his curiosity bottled up. "So what did you buy?"

Taking a deep breath, Paul said, "A dresser and a mirror."

Realizing he wouldn't get much more out of him, Arthur said, "Well, I won't keep you any longer," and walked away.

Going to the house, Paul got a drink of water from the tap and finished mowing the grass. After lunch, he decided to go to the library to see if there were any books he wanted to read. There were a number of them he wanted, but they always seemed to be out already.

That day, however, he was in luck. A double story written by Edwin Balmer and Philip Wylie was in. The book *When Worlds Collide and After Worlds Collide* was a story of adventure and possibilities. He had heard fantastic things about this book and its writers.

Immediately after signing it out, he headed for home to get started reading the long novel. The librarian said that if he required an extension, he would have to call ahead of time.

As soon as he got into his home, he sat down and opened the book. He read for two hours straight before he realized that he hadn't eaten for quite some time. He quickly prepared a sandwich and wolfed it down. After a glass of milk, he sat down and continued to read.

He absolutely loved the story. As news of the imminent disaster about to befall Earth spread, Paul found himself in the story. It was as if he was there with the people, reacting to the news of Earth's demise.

As the room started to get dark, he realized that it was past his bedtime. That Saturday had been one of his best. He almost felt that he was one of the characters in the novel. He found himself making plans as to what he would take on the desperate attempt to flee the impending doom of Planet Earth.

Getting into bed he almost forgot to set the alarm. It

didn't take long before he was asleep, dreaming of a time that was not the one he was living in. He and many others were making plans as to how to avoid being crushed by an incoming planet and its satellite.

There was a soft voice in the room that attempted to communicate with the form sleeping in the bed. This attempt was unsuccessful.

The alarm went off and, after Paul got out of bed, he had a quick shower. His mother had always gone to church on Sunday mornings, dragging him along with her. His father seldom went, except for Easter and Christmas. There was the occasional funeral and, once in a blue moon, a wedding to attend, but these no longer came about. Paul had no use for church or the busybodies there. They always asked too many questions.

A few chores around the house needed to be done, so Paul washed laundry and hung it outside to dry. He hadn't washed the sheets on his bed for two or three weeks, so they were also washed along with the clothes he would need for work the following morning. He ran washed clothes through the wringer on the top of the machine.

He remained very careful with that aspect of the job. He had seen his mother get her fingers pinched severely between the rubber rollers more than once. He could still hear the screams in his head and visualized her crying as she rubbed her fingers, trying to alleviate the pain. Everything was hung up and, as he finished hanging the sheets, he found that the things washed in the first load were already dried by the warm air. He could tell that it was going to be another hot day.

Taking them inside, he folded them and put them in the drawers of the new dresser. Looking at the mirror he said, "I still don't know why I bought you." There were voices speaking to him, but he had learned long ago how to walk away from them. At least he could walk away from them in his head.

A quick sandwich, a drink of water, and he was sitting in the chair on the back porch, opening the book. He heard a voice call out to him asking, "Hey, Paul, what are you reading?"

"It's a book from the library."

"What's it called?"

Feeling he was being pestered, he got up and walked inside without another word. Sitting in the overstuffed chair, he opened the book and was soon lost in the story again, the irritation on the back porch soon forgotten.

As it turned out, this was the best story he had ever read. The action and adventure were beyond anything he had experienced. The close call with the first passing of the alien planet had been survived and the building of a spaceship was started.

He was so engrossed in the story that the time absolutely flew by. Before he knew it, it was supper time, and while he was at it, he made his lunch for the next day at work. Placing his work clothes on the chair by the door, he settled in for a good night's sleep. It wasn't long before he drifted off with visions of a life he saw in the book.

The voice started right after Paul fell into a slumber. The entity in the mirror was not able to get through to the sleeper the way it had in the past. There was something dramatically different about this person. The sleeper had fought down things in his mind his whole life and had built up walls of self-protection. These barriers were difficult to get through. It took hours and hours to make the slightest headway into the mind of this troubled man.

The alarm went off, and Paul woke up ready for breakfast. Grabbing his lunch after putting away the dishes, he walked to the newspaper building. He was always the first there so he could load the truck by himself and be gone before most of the other workers arrived.

Driving around town on the deserted streets, he made his deliveries, all before seven in the morning. He stopped for a coffee and Danish and drove back to the building. Touring the work area, he saw what supplies were needed and hopped on a lift truck, bringing items to the stations. At ten o'clock, he took his lunch pail and sat down at his usual private spot.

The people he worked with seldom bothered him. He was well known for his reclusive ways and therefore left alone. Paul ate his lunch while he daydreamed about the novel he was reading at home. The smile on his face was noticed by others and commented on.

"Hey, Joe, what's up with Paul, he almost looks happy?"

"Beats me, Ben, we should leave him alone, though. This doesn't happen too often, and he'll get pissed if we disturb his happy mood. What do you think?"

"Yeah, we better leave that sleeping dog lie."

The rest of Paul's day went by quickly and, at two-thirty, he walked home. As soon as he walked through the door, he pulled the frozen slice of meat out of the freezer and let it start to thaw. He read for an hour and, seeing the meat was almost ready, he turned on the oven and seasoned the beef. Into the Pyrex ovenware the meat went and then into the oven.

The timer on the stove was set, and he peeled a few small potatoes, cut them up, and put them into a pan half-filled with water. Setting the pan on an element but not turning it on, he went back to reading. He couldn't stop himself. The book was just too good. If he had the time, he would probably read it twice while he had it.

The bell on the stove dinged, bringing Paul back to reality. Turning on the element, he checked the meat in the oven. Everything was cooking nicely, so he peeled a carrot to have with his supper. He didn't really care for the carrots, but his mother had ingrained in him long ago the necessity of having vegetables at least a few times a week.

Cleaning up after supper, he made his lunch again for work the following day. Because he had been sweating at work that day, he had a quick bath and returned to the book for another hour. This time he set the timer on the stove. He didn't want to get to bed late like he had the previous night. He remembered that he had been just a trifle tired at work that day. Not much, but just a little.

Lost in the story, the time flew by and the bell dinged before he knew it. This evening, he got into bed on time and was soon asleep.

CHAPTER 55

Again as soon as Paul fell asleep, the voice started to enter and influence the thought patterns of the sleeping mind. As it had the previous night, it had great difficulty working its way through the barriers. This was the first time it had run across this problem. Every time it had in the past attempted to make contact with someone, it was a simple matter. This strange mind was different though. There were things in this mind that didn't function as all the others had.

Trying to figure it out had been a slow process, and although the entity kept working at it, little progress was made. If too much force was used, the victim would be awakened and that would more than likely be the end of it for that night. The problem then would be that the sleeper might be alerted to its presence and that wouldn't do.

It, however in most instances, had almost infinite patience, and so the struggle continued.

CHAPTER 56

Waking up to the sound of the alarm, Paul went to the bathroom, washed up, and did his other things. Looking in the mirror, he noticed that he appeared to have not gotten enough rest.

"That's funny. I slept like a log last night, so why am I a bit tired?" he mumbled to himself. "Oh, well."

At work, everything went as it usually did. While he sat down and ate his lunch, he thought about the book he was reading, and a smile came over his face again. He wondered if something like that could possibly happen. Would he be able to work on the project taking place in the story?

The rest of the day was as every other day was. He liked his job and, as long as he was left alone, he got along with the other workers. He had been seen talking to himself on many occasions, and his fellow workers had commented on this. The one time that a person, who no longer worked for the paper, made fun of Paul about it, he was set straight in short order. Paul didn't say a word to the man. He just gave him a look, with eyes gone dead, that had scared the crap out of Gregory, and no one since then had had the nerve to say anything.

On his walk home from work, Paul stopped by the grocery store and picked up a bottle of milk, a chunk of liver, and a few apples. The items were put in the fridge, and he went to the backyard. He had a small garden in the corner of the property, which he watered and checked for insects.

All was as it should be and so, with an hour or so left before supper, he set the timer on the stove and sat in the shade on the back porch, making sure he didn't have company, and began to read again.

Lost in the story, once again, he read about the devastation taking place on the Earth. The closeness of the passing planets tore at the surface of the Earth with their gravitational attraction. He was captivated by the efforts of a group of people building a spaceship meant to take a few of the best off Earth to hopefully survive on a planet that would replace the Earth.

A movement in the back corner of his yard distracted him for a moment. A cat belonging to some unknown neighbor was lowering its hind end and about to leave a deposit Paul had no desire to clean up. Bending over, he picked up a stone placed there for this express purpose and hurled it at the feline. The stone hit the dirt right beside the cat, causing it to jump back over the fence and run away.

Looking at his watch, he saw that it was almost time for supper. He placed the bookmark in the novel and walked into the house. Peeling a potato and a carrot, he also chopped up part of an onion. He cooked the liver, onions, and potato as the aromas filled the small kitchen. The windows were open and a slight breeze carried the scents outside. This was one of his favorites, and he enjoyed the meal thoroughly.

There was a knock on the door, which surprised him. He had no friends to speak of, so it must be someone looking to sell him something he didn't need. Opening the door, he saw a man and a woman standing there with a bible in their hands.

"Good day, sir, have you heard the good news yet, sir?" With this, the man launched into a speech he had undoubtedly said many times.

Paul slammed the door shut and walked back to the kitchen to finish the dishes. "What the hell do these idiots bother me for?" he shouted out loud to no one in particular. "I heard all this stuff when I went to church with Mother. I don't need you people bothering me at home with this. I already know about Jesus and was baptized when I was a kid, so leave me alone."

Finally, he laughed. He shook his head and started reading again after setting the timer on the stove. Soon he was lost in the story again. He was being pulled into it and felt more alive at this moment than he had in quite some time.

For a moment, he wondered if he should try writing a book. This idea faded almost as fast as it came. He had no talent with this kind of thing and realized that it would take far more education than he had to take on this kind of challenge.

Bedtime arrived and he prepared his lunch and readied himself for sleep. As he lay down, with the curtains closed and the lights out, he noticed a faint movement in the mirror. Sitting up quickly, he stared at it, but there was nothing to see. "I'm sure I saw something reflected in the glass," he muttered.

He got up and searched the room, finding nothing. Puzzled, he climbed back into bed and was soon asleep. Not long after, the voice softly attempted to enter his subconscious mind. This time, it pushed a little harder. It worked at invading the host all night long. Little headway was made, but a tiny bit had been achieved.

Paul woke in the morning to the alarm. Getting out of bed, he felt more tired than he had the previous morning. He didn't feel bad but knew something wasn't right. This day at work was not quite as good as the one before.

He was anxious to end this day. That night he would go to bed an hour earlier and see if he could catch up on his rest. Reading was kept to a minimum and, by seven o'clock, he was in bed. He fell asleep in no time and as soon as he was, the voice began its difficult task of taking over the mind in the bed.

That night, a little more progress was made. The barriers were slowly being broken down. Why this task had been so difficult was a mystery to the entity in the mirror. It should have been much easier than this. By the time the alarm rang in the early morning hours, only a little more headway had been made.

Going to the bathroom, Paul looked at his reflection and saw a hint of dark under his eyes. Talking out loud again, he said, "I must be coming down with something."

He had forgotten to make his lunch and threw something together while he ate his breakfast. This had never happened before, and it concerned him. He wondered what was going on.

Maybe he should see the doctor. The trouble with this was that he would have to pay for it and didn't like throwing away money for nothing.

The day went by even slower than the one before and it was noticed by others that Paul was not quite himself. No one said anything for fear of being confronted by him, because he was a big man and strong as an ox. Many of the men had seen him carry things so heavy, that it required the effort of two men to do the same job.

As he walked up the sidewalk to his house, his neighbor Monty, asked him, "Is everything all right, Paul, you look a little sick?"

"Yeah, I'm fine," Paul said as he continued into the house.

With a feeling of concern, Monty watched him walk away. He and Paul didn't usually talk much, but he liked Paul's mother and so felt he should take an interest in the young man, despite the fact that it was hard to get more than one or two-word answers from him.

Inside, Paul sat on the kitchen chair for a minute and made a decision about supper. He had some extra money, and so, because he was a little tired, he went to a family restaurant few blocks away.

It took fifteen minutes to get there, with Paul not making eye contact with anyone.

Sitting in a window booth, he was approached by a waitress. "Would you like a menu?"

Paul looked up momentarily. "What is the special today?"

"We have a steak sandwich and French fries."

"Okay, I'll have that and a glass of cold water."

The waitress left and placed the order with the cook. Shortly after, she returned with a large glass of ice water.

Picking up the complimentary newspaper, he held it up in front of him and started looking it over. A story that had been on the front page was found two pages later. *Joan Croft, who suffered injuries in a tornado, was taken from the hospital, escorted by two men in military uniforms, and has yet to be found.*

He just finished the story when his order was brought to the table. Digging into the dinner, he was surprised at how good it tasted. All done, after paying for the meal, he walked back home feeling a bit better. The sun was still fairly high in the sky and the temperature was still in the high eighties. Fixing his lunch, he noticed the time was six o'clock. Setting the timer for an hour, he retired to the living room and began reading the book.

Once again, he found himself helping to build the spaceship that would take a select few to safety. The storms that were ravaging the Planet Earth, he, too, felt. The trembling of the soil and mountains almost shook the chair he was sitting in. The hour passed and the timer rang, telling him it was time to put the book down.

He was sorely tempted to keep reading as he turned off the timer. He sat back in the living room, but rested on the couch, intending to read for only a few more minutes. Instead, he fell asleep on the couch and stayed there for the night. He woke at three-thirty in the morning, startled that he had slept through the night on the couch, and felt great.

He got himself ready for work and arrived a little ahead of time. Loading the delivery vehicle up, he got on his way quickly. He made the entire drop-offs in good time and drove back to the newspaper building. He felt much better today and actually smiled now and then, but not at other people. That would have been out of character for Paul.

The day at work was done, and he walked home. Pulling a pork chop out of the freezer, he left it on a plate on the counter to thaw out. Going to the backyard, he weeded and then watered the garden, pleased that the plants were doing well. Inside, he turned on the oven and placed the seasoned meat in it. He peeled a potato, cut it up, and placed it in a pan of water on the stove. Then he set timer for half an hour and began to read once more.

It didn't take long before he was engrossed in the book. Along with the characters in the story, he fought for survival as the camp was attacked by desperate people from deserted cities wanting to take the spaceships to freedom.

The timer went off bringing him back to the present. He cooked the potatoes and opened a can of applesauce.

While washing the dishes, he noticed a puddle forming at his feet. Opening the cupboard door, he saw water dripping from the drain trap.

Using a mop, he cleaned up the water and knelt on the floor to inspect the problem. The upper clamp above the trap had come loose. While he had the pipes apart, he checked to make sure that the trap was clear of obstructions.

Once everything had been put back together, he tightened the clamp, using a pipe wrench. Satisfied with the job, he cleaned things up and put them away. He made his lunch for the next day, and after setting the timer again, sat down to continue with the book.

Going to bed at eight o'clock, he was sound asleep as soon as he lay down. The voice soon started and worked hard all night in its attempt to break down the barriers in the subject's mind. A battle of wills ensued with only a little ground being made against the sleeping form on the bed.

Paul woke up in the early morning hours as the alarm rang. He entered the bathroom in a state of tiredness again.

Looking at his reflection, he said, "What the hell is going on? I am more tired today than I was when I went to sleep last night."

This day at work, he was grumpy and yelled at one of his coworkers when the string on a bundle of newspapers came loose. An argument came close to fisticuffs between the two men.

The foreman intervened. "What's the problem, Paul? You look like you're not sleeping well. We can't have you exploding like this again, is that understood?"

Knowing he overreacted, Paul nodded. "I'm sorry, I don't know what's happening, I woke up exhausted this morning."

"All right, Paul, but try not to let it happen again. You know we don't allow fighting here."

Paul nodded again and walked away with his head hanging down, wondering what got into him. Things like a string coming loose had happened before without causing him to act the way he did. The rest of the day dragged slowly by, with Paul being careful while he did his job.

As he walked home he tripped when his foot hit the edge of the curb. He swore to himself, quickly looking around to see if anyone had noticed. There was no one nearby, so he continued his walk home.

Sitting at the kitchen table, he tried to work through the situation. Talking out loud, he said, "When did this all start? What can be causing me to wake up so tired?"

He pondered these questions and in the end, the only thing he knew was different than things had been was the fact that he had a new mirror and dresser. "How can these things be the source of my problems? It has to be something else."

As the afternoon progressed, he went into the bedroom and studied the mirror. After looking at it for a few moments, he could see nothing out of the ordinary. Thinking back to the day he first came across the two pieces of furniture, he remembered the feeling he got when he first saw them.

"Was it the voices in my head that I always hear or was it something else? Am I hearing things while I'm asleep? I can't put my finger on it, but something is going on. I can feel it."

He left the room determined to find out what was causing his ills. In an effort to locate the source of his dilemma, he would forego his reading. There were more important things to worry about. He wasn't really hungry today so he planned to have a sandwich for supper, instead of a full meal.

As he tended his garden, he pondered his options. "How can I figure out what is causing me to wake up so tired? I slept fine on the couch, maybe I should sleep there tonight." By the time he was finished in the garden, he had come to a decision. That night, he would sleep on the couch and the next night, which was Friday, he'd sleep in his bed. If his suspicions were right, he would have an answer by Saturday.

The evening passed and soon it was time for bed. Going into the bedroom to get changed and pick up his alarm clock, he almost changed his mind. There was something tugging at him at a level that he couldn't explain. He teetered back and forth, but, in the end, he got out of the room, managing to fight off the feeling.

Waking up the next morning, he felt so much better. That night, if he slept in the bedroom and woke up on Saturday tired again, he would have his answer. The day at work went much better than the previous one. Sitting down to eat his lunch, he relaxed and even smiled periodically. The man he had the argument with looked at Paul and wondered what was up with the antisocial co-worker. One day he was a miserable shit, and the next he seemed pleased with life.

The afternoon at the job went by quickly because he was busy. On his way home from work, Paul stopped by the butcher and picked up some sausage and ground beef. Going past the grocery store, he got a few apples and two bottles of milk, as well as a box of corn flakes.

By the time everything was put away, he was ready to start supper. Taking the ground beef, he made some meatballs and stuck them in the oven. He peeled and chopped a large potato and put it in a pan of water on the stove.

Paul looked out the window toward the garden and spied a red tomato and the greens of a row of carrots. A few rows over were a number of lettuce plants. Taking a small wicker basket, he walked over to the garden. The sun was shining down warmly on his face as he dug up a couple of carrots, broke off enough lettuce for a salad, and picked the juicy ripe tomato.

Being Friday meant he had a couple of days off, with another person filling in on his job on weekends. He planned to relax after supper and read the book he was almost halfway through. The dishes were done and, with nothing pressing, he sat down in the living room and read.

Lost in the story, he found himself on the trip off Earth preparing to land on the planet that had replaced the destroyed Earth. He was enjoying the story so much he almost read past his bedtime. As he got ready for bed, he felt happy about being able to sleep in his own bed. He didn't understand why, but he did.

CHAPTER 57

There was a feeling of anger in the mirror. The entity within felt it was being thwarted by the victim it had been attempting to control. No matter what it had done, progress had been slow. Headway had been made, but nowhere near what was required to bring in another energy source.

The other part of the dwelling, where the subject had spent the night, was too far away to do more than sense a presence. This had prevented advancement the previous evening. To make matters worse, the victim seemed to sense danger, or at least felt concerned.

Putting a pleasant feeling in the form's mind was easier than forcing the individual to do its bidding. As the quarry lay in bed, the entity prepared to launch a full-scale attack. Headway would have to be made soon. Otherwise, it could place the task at hand in jeopardy.

Soon the target was sleeping and a concentrated effort began.

CHAPTER 58

Paul brushed his teeth and, as usual, set his alarm for an hour later than he normally did during the work week. As he started to drift off, he thought of what the morning would bring. This soon was gone as he fell into a deep sleep.

The voice softly began to work on the subject. The force of the invading will built as the night continued. Slowly the wall began to crumble. Progress was finally made as the onslaught kept hammering at the protective shield that had been built up over a lifetime of adversity.

The resistance was still there but, by morning, significant inroads had been made. The road to takeover was well on its way by then. If more time were available, a real breakthrough might be imminent, but the alarm sounded, waking up the individual.

Paul's hand reached for the alarm but missed. He felt like he had worked several days straight as he staggered to the bathroom. Washing his face with cold water revived him a bit, but he knew he hadn't rested even close to enough that night. As he walked into his room, he was tempted to get back under the blankets and sleep some more.

He reached for the covers and stopped. The voice in his head tried to convince him to go to bed again. What stopped him from doing it was the fact that the voice was not the one he had been fighting all his life. The inner battle continued for several minutes. Because he had overcome this inner turmoil before, Paul won the battle and made his way to the kitchen.

The farther he got away from the bedroom, the less the voice was able to control him. A realization dawned on him as to what was happening. How he knew this, he could not fathom, but he knew, without a doubt, that if he slept in the bedroom anymore, he would be in trouble.

What the trouble was he didn't know, but whatever it was, it wouldn't be good for him. As he tried to solve the question, he decided that he had to take action as soon as he was able. This meant he must rest properly for a time. When he slept on the couch, he felt he was not in danger, at least not like he was when he was in his own bed.

He made a plan to try and sleep as far away from his room as he could. The place that was the greatest distance from his bedroom on the property was the work shed.

Having a few blankets in the hall closet, he proceeded to get them. As he got close to the bedroom door, he felt a slight pull on his emotions. It was like he felt happier when he was near his room. Shaking his head and gritting his teeth, he managed to fight off the feeling and quickly headed to the shed. It was already getting light outside, but no one was anywhere around. This prevented his being seen and having people wonder what on earth he might be up to.

Opening the door, Paul slipped inside and after moving a few things around, he had room enough to lie down and close his eyes. Despite his worry about what was happening to him, he was soon asleep.

CHAPTER 59

The entity within the mirror was angry at having not been able to finish the invasion of the victim's mind. Things were so close, if only the alarm had not awakened the sleeper, it may well have been able to work its way deep enough into the mind to break down the last of the resistance.

Even when the target came back into the room, it almost had him, so close and yet so far. One more night and the new source might possibly be his. From now on, it would attack at full strength whenever possible. The subject, of course, would have to be in the correct state of mind to be able to force him to do its bidding. The happy emotion seemed to work the best and so the plan of attack was made.

CHAPTER 60

Several hours after falling asleep, Paul woke up because of the sounds of birds on the roof of the shed as they chirped and flew back and forth. He got up stiffly, rubbing his aching muscles, relieving the soreness of being asleep on a hard wooden floor. The blankets kept him warm but offered little in the way of cushioning.

Despite the aches, he felt much improved. He was far more rested than he had been a few hours before. He walked to the back door and shook out the blankets. His neighbor was in his backyard and wanted to ask Paul why he slept in the shed, but he saw the scowl on Paul's face and decided it would not be in his best interest to converse with the man just then.

Putting the blankets away, Paul tried to figure out how he would proceed. He knew that the new voice in his head was coming from the mirror, or at least, he was fairly certain. He had learned to deal with the voice in his head long ago, but this new one was different. Although most of the time he didn't know it was there, he did know that it was affecting him adversely. If it wasn't, he wouldn't feel so depleted of energy.

"I need to get a few good nights' sleep in order to get my mental strength back. When I slept on the couch I seemed okay in the morning, but I'm not so sure it's going to be enough. Do I have to be farther away from it for a few days? No, the living room will be enough, I think." His mind made up, he continued in the kitchen preparing his lunch.

He spent the afternoon away from his house by going to a motion picture show. There were two movies playing. After looking at the posters, Paul chose the one with Humphrey Bogart and Lauren Bacall. *The Big Sleep* took his mind off his own troubles. He found the movie very entertaining and came out of the theater in better spirits.

The late afternoon sun was warm and pleasant, so he took a stroll through the park on his way home. On a soapbox at the entrance of the park, a man shouted out to whoever passed by about the return of the Lord. He shouted about the end of the world and that each person had to make a choice now. "Prepare yourself, or you will be doomed to purgatory," the man yelled.

Paul made a detour around the man and proceeded to walk away. An hour later, he was ready to go home and mentally got prepared to deal with whatever came his way. Tomorrow was a work day so after he ate, he made his lunch.

Although he was tired, he was apprehensive about sleeping. He considered sleeping in the shed again, but the soreness of his muscles deterred him from doing so. In the end, he pushed the couch as far away from the bedroom as he could.

Going to the bedroom, he picked up his pajamas and started to walk to the bathroom. While he was still in the bedroom the feeling that he was being foolish came over him. The comfort of the bed beckoned him to lie down on it. He could almost hear a voice calling out to him.

On the verge of staying, he realized that these were not his own thoughts. Fighting for control, he dealt with the thoughts as he always had with the voices that had plagued him for so long. It was not easy in his weakened mental state, but he finally rushed out of the room.

On the couch, the pull of the emotions was lessened a great deal. There, he could fight them off with little effort. A feeling of relief came over him as he picked up the book. Before he started reading, he set the alarm to wake him up in time to get up for work in the morning. The clothes he wore on Friday were in a hamper beside the kitchen. Instead of taking the chance of going into the bedroom and having to fight for control of his own body, he would wear the same clothes to work again.

Opening the book, Paul began to read. Although he got immersed in the story, the feeling of anxiety was in the back of his mind. There was a nervousness he felt and could not run from. Something was trying to get into his head, and he couldn't figure out exactly what it was. He put the book down as thoughts about the whole incident came rushing into his head.

The fight deep down inside, he knew, had been going on for a while, ever since he bought the two items. Actually, he knew it started when he went to see what was being auctioned in the New York City warehouse. That was when it began because now, that he thought about it, he realized that the feelings he had to buy the pieces were not his own.

Looking at the clock, he saw that it was after eight and that he should go to sleep, despite his anxiety of the situation. He didn't bother to brush his teeth, not wanting to go near the bedroom.

Pulling the covers over him he lay awake for the next fifteen minutes. One minute he was awake, and the next, he was sound asleep.

As he fell into a deeper and deeper sleep, a faint voice came into his mind. It did not have the strength it did when he slept in the bedroom, but it was there nevertheless. If he had been sleeping in the bedroom, Paul Rendell would then have been in the biggest trouble of his life. Even during the war in North Africa, he was not in this much peril.

The soft voice continued to beckon the man asleep on the couch. The entity in the mirror worked and worked all night long on its victim.

CHAPTER 61

The entity within the mirror fought as hard as it could, but the distance to its target was too far to allow it to grasp the mind with any real strength. The inroads that had been made so far allowed it to get only lightly into the mind of the form sleeping in the other room.

Would it have the time it needed to take over? It was a desperate time for both the entity and the man. The man knew he was in trouble and had taken steps to ensure his survival, but he had underestimated the resolve of his enemy.

All night long, a concentrated effort had been brought to bear on the sleeping man. The fight was ongoing, and the entity knew this might well be its last chance. It used all its will on the mind in the other room.

CHAPTER 62

Paul slept in the living room, unaware of the battle going on between his mind and the entity in the bedroom. It was touch and go, as the night progressed. The only thing that had saved him thus far was the distance between him and the mirror.

As morning approached, the difference between success and failure was minimal. When the alarm went off, the battle that night was concluded. By a narrow margin the winner of this fight was Paul, but only just. Another few hours and the end would have been different.

Paul got up off the couch, very weary. As he dressed, he almost staggered to the kitchen table. He knew that he was in no shape to go to work and picked up the phone in order that the newspaper could call in a substitute delivery man.

His boss could tell that his man was unable to come in just by listening to his voice over the phone. "Paul, take a couple of days off and get rested up. Let me know how you feel in a day or two."

"Thanks, Bill. I'm sorry to let you down."

"Don't you worry about it. See you in a few days."

Paul, for once, actually felt bad. Normally, he wouldn't care, but this episode was making him feel differently about his life. A relief came over him that he wouldn't have to deal with work and his troubles at home at the same time.

Thinking things over, he realized that he was not safe at home in his worn-down state. He had to put some distance between himself and the mirror. Going to the closet by the front door, he grabbed a bag and then ran to the bedroom, grabbing a few clothes as quickly as he could. He had what he needed and was almost out the bedroom door when the feeling of comfort came over him.

In his mind, the voice said, '*Why should I leave my room? I really do want to lie down on the bed and rest for just a minute.*'

The fight was on. Once again, the only thing that saved Paul was all those years of fighting the voice in his head. He managed to slip out of the room and down the hall. The farther he got away from the room, the stronger his need to escape became.

By the time he was at the front door, he was his own boss again. He locked the front door, ran to the sidewalk, and then down the street. It was five in the morning and, despite being exhausted, he made his way to the downtown area and found a hotel. The cool air felt good in his weary state.

He tried to book a room with the half-asleep clerk but found that he didn't have the cash to pay for the room.

The clerk said, "I'm sorry but you will have to have the money before you are allowed to take the room."

Paul was about to get angry, but instead, he asked, "Can I have the room and get the rest of the money from the bank down the street in a few hours?"

Looking at Paul and seeing he looked as tired as anyone he had ever seen, the clerk asked, "Do you have something of value I can hold until you get the money?"

Reaching into his pocket, Paul pulled out his father's old pocket watch, handing it to the desk clerk. "Will this do?"

"Yes, I'll write you out a receipt for it so you can collect it later."

After leaving instructions for a wakeup call, Paul went to the room and, feeling safe, fell immediately asleep. The sleep was restful and, when the call came from the front desk at ten, he felt a little better.

Getting up, he got dressed and made his way to the bank to get the funds necessary for a two-day stay and meals. After retrieving the watch, he ate in a nearby restaurant. As he sat, he tried to make plans on how to get out of the predicament he found himself in.

He realized that he had to be able to rest his mind and body before he could go back to the house and deal with whatever was trying to control him. After eating, Paul went back to the room and slept for several more hours.

By the end of the second day, he felt far stronger, having regained much of his lost energy reserve. It was three o'clock in the afternoon as he walked to his job and talked to his boss. "Would you mind if I borrowed the delivery truck for the rest of the day? I need to move something and have no other way to do it."

"I guess it will be all right. How are you feeling?"

"I'm a lot better. Whatever I had seems to have passed," Paul said. "Tomorrow morning, I'll be back to work on time. Thanks for letting me use the truck."

Bill watched Paul as he walked toward the truck thinking, *Something has changed in him. He seems more social than I've ever seen him.*

As he approached his home, a feeling of apprehension made his hands twitch. Even though he felt more able to deal with what he knew was an adversary, he also knew that if he let his guard down, he would again be in trouble.

Backing the truck close to the rear of the house, he parked it and walked to the shed and picked up the materials used to wrap the mirror for transport by the railway. There was a roll of string and a hammer he took with him too.

Steeling himself by taking a few deep breaths, he ran to the house and tried to stay focused on the task at hand. Quickly, he walked through the kitchen and down the hallway. Entering the bedroom, he threw the tarp on the floor, opening it as he laid it down.

Already he felt something in his mind attempting to gain the upper hand. A feeling of contentment was coming over him. He fought the feeling as he approached the mirror hanging on the wall. It took all his concentration to move the dresser away from the wall. Reaching for the mirror, he hesitated as he was having doubts about what it was he needed to do.

His hands were almost not his own as he fought for his life. The voice in his head was stronger than any voice he had ever had to deal with. If he couldn't gain the upper hand, he knew he was lost. Because he had fought the inner voices for so long, he mustered a last attack in order to move his hands. Grabbing the mirror, he lifted it off the screws in the wall.

In an effort to maintain his control, he dropped the mirror face down on the floor on top of the tarp. For some reason, this temporarily stopped the onslaught. As quickly as he could, he wrapped the tarp around it and tied it up with a string.

Standing it on edge he lifted it off the floor and, as fast as he could, carried it out of the house and threw it on the back of the truck.

With each step he had taken, the urge to stop had

grown stronger. Only fear of the consequences gave him the strength to run.

Paul ran down the street in order to put enough distance between him and the mirror to feel the invasion peter away. When he felt his mental strength return, he took a few deep breaths and ran back.

Without any wasted time, he jumped into the cab of the truck. Driving down the road and out of the city, Paul was under constant attack. By the time he was in the country, his resolve was beginning to weaken to the point he feared he might give in. His ability to fight off the attack was coming to an end.

Pulling off to the side of the road, he jumped out and ran as the gravel crunched loudly under his feet. Several hundred yards later, he was out of breath and no longer felt the presence of the voice in his head. Sitting on the side of the road, he tried to come up with a plan to get rid of the cursed thing on the back of the truck.

He had no idea what it was, but knew it must be taken away. He had been down this road before and knew there was a canyon not far from where he was. When his strength returned somewhat, he walked to within a hundred feet of the vehicle and prepared himself for the last part of the struggle. His insides felt all jittery from the battle he had been fighting. He hoped he had the resolve to finish the fight but was not at all certain.

Freezing his mind, he ran full tilt toward the truck. Starting it, he concentrated with everything he had, driving as fast as he could to the edge of a drop off in the canyon. He pulled over to the shoulder, parked the truck and ran to the back. The attack was so strong that he was again forced to run down the road again in order to escape its power.

It took at least fifteen minutes to get himself to the point where he felt he could take one last run at dealing with whatever had come into his life. He was more desperate to rid himself of this than he had anything in his life before. Up to that point, he knew he had just barely escaped what he was certain to be the most dangerous thing that had ever confronted him. Not even in the war as he was being shot at, did he feel so vulnerable.

In a last-ditch attempt, he steeled his resolve and worked his way back to the truck. The last hundred yards was covered at a dead run.

Reaching the back of the truck as it all began yet again, he took hold of the covered mirror and dragged it to the side nearest the drop-off. Losing his grip, he dropped it to the ground, as he felt the renewed efforts of the attack on his mind.

He took the hammer in his hand and lifted it above his head, as he strained to swing it. Desperately, he tried to take control of his body.

The ensuing battle of wills took its toll on the intended victim. The struggle went back and forth, with each momentarily gaining the upper hand. In a last-ditch attempt, Paul reached deep within, and the hammer came down striking the glass.

The control on his mind momentarily died off. Using this opportunity, Paul took hold of the mirror and threw it down the steep embankment. The tarp-covered mirror bounced down the incline, end over end.

Paul listened for the sound of breaking glass to reach his ears, but it didn't come. When the hammer struck the glass, there was no sound of it breaking either. When it finally reached the bottom of the deep gully, the mirror fell flat on the pebble-covered dirt.

As Paul sat on the side of the road, he no longer felt the invasion of his mind. Whatever was trying to take over him was gone for the moment. A feeling of great relief came over him. Inside, he felt that he had been given another chance at life. He intended to make the most of it.

Looking over the embankment, he saw the oiled tarp far below him. In an effort to destroy the thing that had plagued him these last few weeks, he picked up the largest rocks he could and rolled them down the hill in an effort to break the glass, once and for all.

His attempts to hit it did not prove successful. The only way he would be able to accomplish this, was to go down the steep hill and perform the task close up. This he was very reluctant to do, so he drove back home, parking the truck backward in the driveway. This way he could leave in the morning making minimal noise.

Going through his head were new thoughts he had never had before. *Why am I all of a sudden concerned about my neighbors and the guys at work? What the heck has happened to me? Can it be that the stinking mirror has changed something in me?*

On his way to the kitchen door at the back of the house, Paul saw his neighbor looking over at him. For some unknown reason, Paul stopped and asked, "Hi, Frank, how is it going?"

"I'm good, how are you? The other day you looked kind of under the weather. It seems that you've recovered."

"Yes, I feel a lot better, thank you. Why don't we have a beer on the weekend?" Paul said with a smile on his face. The voices that had plagued him all his life were finally silent.

Taken somewhat aback, Frank said, "That will be nice, look forward to it." He watched Paul enter his home, wondering what had caused this change in the man he had tried to befriend for years.

CHAPTER 63

Having suffered its first defeat ever, the mirror lay far down a gully. The battle of wills was touch and go for a considerable length of time. Puzzled, the entity wondered how the man was able to resist it. Now it lay far below a road and was unsure of its future.

The weather was dry and the oiled material surrounding it protected the mirror and frame from further damage. The ebony it was made from, being as hard as it was, had surprisingly sustained very little actual damage. The glass itself had not been harmed at all. This, of course, was no ordinary glass. Otherwise, it would have been shattered completely.

Two weeks went by as the mirror bided its time. All of a sudden, it felt a presence far away. Too far away to affect it in any way, but it was there, nevertheless. The presence stayed far away for quite some time then left, and it was alone once more.

CHAPTER 64

Simon Barnett worked for the Oklahoma Department of Roads. He had been traveling all the roads in the areas around the city for fourteen years. The job was not difficult but did force him to drive a lot. He spent a week or so, once a month, making his inspections. Road conditions were his main concern, but illegal dumping fell under his jurisdiction also.

He loved his job. He had had an accident when he was young, and it had left him with a limp that affected his gait somewhat but not terribly. This was the reason he was not drafted into the military during the war.

He married late in life at the age of twenty-eight. All his friends had found brides in their teens and early twenties. His limp was not a selling feature for most of the girls he met. Janet wasn't the best-looking woman around, and she was a bit headstrong, but she had been a good wife. They had two sons, aged thirteen and eleven, and owned a home on the outskirts of the city. There were times when he had tried to do things he didn't want her to know about. He was talked into going for a beer with the guys, and she knew about it without anyone telling her. When he asked how she knew, she said it just came into her head. How she knew these things, he had no idea. It was like she had a sixth sense.

On the road that day, he noticed that the gravel on the shoulder had been disturbed. Little ruts in the fine stones indicated that someone had stopped there and either had a flat tire or dumped something over the edge into the gully below. With his gimpy leg, it would be a chore to have to retrieve anything dumped in this spot. As he approached the edge, he hoped his suspicions were unfounded.

As he peered over the edge, his gaze made its way down the slope. When it reached the bottom, he noticed the tarp covered thing lying there. The distance to this garbage was close to a hundred feet. He did not have the tools with him to fish this newest trash out of the gully. He could have left it there, but Simon took his job seriously, and so he would make the effort to get it out.

Driving away, he thought about the best way to get the item or items out of the deep ravine. There was a hand-operated winch on the front of the truck which he could use to bring the thing up to the road. The trouble was he had to think of a way to prevent it from snagging on the rocks on the way up the slope.

He was not eager to make more than one trip down the steep embankment.

At the shop, there was a small skid with an upturned front end that he could use. Being curved up at the front would allow it to skim over most of the smaller rocks. If by chance it got stuck, he could lower it a bit and pull sideways on the cable, freeing the skid.

It was nine thirty in the morning, and it took an hour to get the skid and cables needed to lash the garbage to it. When he parked on the side of the road, he put warning markers a hundred feet each direction on the road.

Unloading the skid, he looked things over to determine which spot would offer the least resistance as he lowered the things down the slope. Putting on heavy work gloves, he hooked the steel cable to the skid and tied all the straps he'd require to it.

The skid was made of tubular steel in order to keep its weight down. He hooked the cable to the back end so the curved front went down first and wouldn't get stuck on anything on its descent, hopefully. Fifteen minutes later, the skid was at the bottom.

Unwinding an extra ten feet, in case he needed to move the contraption, he took a drink of water before heading down. Using the cable to prevent himself from slipping down the slope, Simon slowly worked his way to the bottom. "Geez, I sure hope I don't fall down here. I'm glad I told the foreman where I am, in case something happens."

Taking care not to step on anything loose, he got to the bottom near the debris. As he approached, a feeling of calm came over him. Walking over to the tarp, he lifted one end up and found that it wasn't as heavy as he had anticipated.

Lifting it up, he carried it over to the skid, setting it on the ground. Unhooking the cable, he pointed the unit uphill and reconnected the cable to the front. When he had the garbage strapped tightly to the skid, and as close to the back end as he could, he positioned the skid to follow the path of least resistance up the slope.

Using the cable, he pulled himself back to the top. By this time he was quite out of breath and thirsty. Sitting on the back of the truck he took a few minutes to recuperate. When he was ready, he started cranking the handle, tightening the cable. It took a fair amount of work to get the skid to the top. He had to let it back down a few feet and yank the cable sideways a couple of times in order to have the skid veer around a number of obstacles.

In the end, he had it pulled up and over the edge of the

slope. Unhooking the cable, he wound it up and secured it. Next, he untied the tarp, wrapped garbage. Simon loaded the skid back onto the truck and inspected the trash. He used his knife to cut the ropes and lifted the beat up tarp away from the contents.

To his surprise, he found the handcrafted, wooden-framed mirror. "Why would anyone throw something this nice into the gully?" he asked himself. "It surely must be worth something?"

Loading the smoked-glass mirror into the truck, he placed it so there was no chance of breaking it. The thought about why it hadn't smashed into a thousand pieces as it fell down the gully didn't even cross his mind. He felt good about finding this fine piece. He was looking forward to seeing the expression on his wife Janet's face when he showed her what he had found.

He wasn't far from his home and figured he might as well drop it off. If he didn't, there was always the chance that one of his supervisors would claim it. Driving carefully, he made it to his house in thirty minutes. The kids were in school and his wife was at some meeting or other, at the local church.

Simon placed the mirror in the garage and then headed back to the roads department facility to drop off the skid. If asked, he could always tell the person asking, that he took a bunch of refuse he found in the gully to the local dump.

He finished off the day, making his rounds inspecting the roads on the outskirts of the city. At four-thirty, he was done and headed for home. Pulling into the cracked driveway, he was greeted by his boys who were playing with a basketball. A homemade hoop had been attached to the garage over the door.

Because they were still fairly short, the hoop was lower than regulation height. Getting out of the family car, a nineteen thirty eight ford, he gave his boys, Burt and Grant, a pat on the head as he walked to the side door on the two-story clapboard home. The paint was peeling on parts of the wood around the doors and windows. It was a small home with one bathroom and three bedrooms, two of which were on the second floor. These rooms were where the boys slept.

The smell of supper reached his nostrils as he entered the home. "Hi, dear, I'm home," Simon shouted from the mudroom.

"Make sure you take off your dirty boots before you come into the kitchen," she said in return. The home might be slightly run down, but his wife kept it very clean.

Taking his boots off, he put slippers on and continued into the kitchen. "What's for supper dear."

Turning to give her husband a hug as he limped close to her, she said, "There was a special on pork chops, and I dug up a few potatoes from the garden. I made applesauce from the Spartan tree in the corner. I thought you would like that."

"It smells delightful, I can hardly wait. I'll change out of these clothes. I got a bit dirty today." With this, he left the room, going to the bedroom on the main floor.

The boys were called in for supper. "Wash your hands, boys, and be sure to use soap this time or you'll have to wash them again," Janet said sternly to her young lads. She loved them dearly but knew they'd try to get away with as much as they could.

Burt and Grant were almost the same height and looked a lot alike, but there were differences in them. Burt was just a little bigger boned than Grant. Grant's eyes were shaped slightly different and were lighter in color and his teeth had come in just a trifle crooked. The dentist wanted to put braces on them, but the cost was more than this family could afford. Besides, what difference could it make? Grant could chew his food just as well as anyone else. Neither of the boys was ever going to be a movie star. They were not ugly, but they didn't look like Clark Gable, that was for sure.

Janet and Simon had talked about having another child. She would have loved to have had a girl, but money being what it was, they just couldn't afford this. Besides, she was already thirty nine and not getting any younger. So time was running out for these kinds of thoughts.

Sitting at the table, the three males were served their meal, and the lady of the house sat down to join them.

Simon asked, "What kind of day did you have, dear?"

She finished chewing and, after swallowing, said, "I went to the church for the meeting concerning the congregational picnic this weekend. They asked me to bake a pie, and don't you boys touch it, do you hear me?"

"Yes, Mother," they said in unison.

"I must say this dinner is delicious. I really like the applesauce with the pork chops. Oh, by the way, I found something today that you might like. I'll bring it in after supper and you can tell me what you think," Simon said, smiling at his wife, knowing she would be quite impressed with his find.

Supper was done, with the boys helping by washing and drying the dishes. In order to save time, Simon took his wife's hand and led her to the garage. He opened the main door, and walking to the workbench, uncovered the mirror. He lifted it up, to move it into a better position, so she could have a good look at it.

As she looked at the mirror swinging toward her, she saw a movement in the glass. Instinctively, she backed away. Whatever showed itself in the smoked glass of the mirror upset her greatly. Without a doubt, she knew this was not good, and the shock of it caused her to scream. "Get that thing out of here, and get it out immediately. I don't want it here another minute," she shouted and ran to the house.

"My goodness, what on earth has gotten into her?" he said out loud. "I thought she'd love this mirror." He was totally unaware of what had just taken place. A careless movement by the entity, in eager anticipation because of the failed attempt it had just experienced, had created a problem.

A warm feeling toward the mirror came over Simon, and he felt compelled to go into the home and talk to his upset wife, to find out what was going on.

As he approached the mudroom door, she opened it and in a voice that indicated it would be a mistake to argue with her, she said, "Get that thing out of here and don't you dare ever bring it back, do you hear me?"

The glare in her eyes was something he had yet to see in her all the years of their marriage. Despite that fact that he wanted the mirror, he knew it would lead to big trouble for him if he didn't do as she had said, and so he did as instructed.

Walking back to the garage, he covered the piece and carried it to the car. It was too big to put inside, so he ended up resting the lower edge on the rear bumper and tying it down using a length of rope.

As he drove down the road, he tried to think where he could dispose of it. If he had the time, he was sure he would be able to sell it, but time was something he didn't have. Then a thought hit him, there was a used furniture store on Maple Street. Driving there, he found that the owner was just locking up as he pulled up to the curb. He beeped the horn to get the man's attention and got out of the car. "Hello, I'm glad I caught you here. I have a mirror that I think you might be interested in."

Simon untied it and removed the covering. The man examined the piece, noting the scratches. After studying it, he thought for a moment, knowing he could make money on this. He got a nice feeling when he looked at it. He had been in business long enough to know how to handle the situation. He hummed and hawed a bit then finally said, "The frame will require a bit of work to repair the marks in it, but I might be able to sell it. I'll give you seven dollars for it and not a penny more."

Feeling he had struck it rich, Simon said, "You have a deal." He stuck his hand out to seal the bargain.

The drive back home was more pleasant than the one going away. As he pulled into the driveway, Janet stood in the doorway, watching him as he got out of the car. "Well, did you get rid of it?"

"Yes, I did, dear, and you'll never guess what. I went to the used furniture store and sold it to the owner for seven dollars." Which he handed to her.

Her mood immediately softened when she received the money. "That is good news. We can really use the money."

"By the way, what was it that got you so riled up about that mirror?"

Taking a deep breath before answering, she told him, "It may sound strange, but I saw something in it, and I know it would have hurt our family. I don't know how to explain it, but the thing gave me the willies. It about scared me to death. I don't want to talk about it anymore." She turned and walked back into the house.

Simon knew better than to pursue this any farther. *At least this day hasn't been a total loss, we now have seven dollars we didn't have before,* he thought as he limped into the house.

CHAPTER 65

Two losses in a row was something that had never happened before. Being too anxious to proceed had turned out to be a mistake. It was a mistake that would not happen again, but all was not lost. It now had a chance to pick its next victim at leisure. The choice would have to be a wise one. A mind with few roadblocks would be chosen. There was no real hurry now, so the choice could be made when the right opportunity came around. The mood in the mirror was one of calm. *All things come to those who...*

CHAPTER 66

Manfred Holmes walked to his apartment down the road from the store he owned on Maple Street. He was a single man, at least he was now. He had been married to a woman that he took from another man years ago. That man was overseas fighting in France, helping to liberate Europe.

For a while, Manfred thought he had had it good, but that started going downhill when he found out she was cheating on him too. "What is it with these women? You can't trust any of them," he said to himself as he walked. "I was fairly good to her. I treated her as well as her first husband did."

He felt good about making the purchase involving the mirror. It wouldn't take much to get it into shape again. He had seen the wood it was made of only a few times before. He suspected that it was ebony, an exceptionally appealing wood found only in Africa. It was a material difficult to work with and even harder to get into the contour needed to form around the unique smoked glass mirror. He had never seen one like it before and had a hard time keeping himself under control as he inspected it.

Tomorrow, he would begin the minor repairs and thought he may have just the buyer for it. *Fix it first, and then contact Cornelius Donnay to see if he might be interested.* The two men had known each other for years and the mirror was right up Cornelius's alley. He would probably resell it himself to a customer with exotic tastes.

The evening was spent alone, but this was nothing new for Manfred. On the television, he had to adjust the rabbit ears several times to get rid enough of the snow on the screen to be able to see what was on it. He liked to watch *Truth or Consequences* and *Howdy Doody*, even though it was a kid's show.

He went to bed early that night. He wanted to get the newly acquired item into selling shape right away. He would do an in-depth repair on this piece. He thought that he'd better sand down the frame. He could then recoat it with a high-quality varnish. The glass portion appeared to be pristine so no work would be required on it.

Getting up early, he headed to the store. He was a slender man, thirty-seven years old, standing at just over six feet. His eyes were gray and his short cropped hair a reddish brown. As he passed the butcher shop, there was a knock on the window and he saw Melvin wave at him. Waving back and smiling, he continued on his way.

He had an hour and a half before he needed to open the store to the public. Going to the back of the building, he lifted the mirror onto the workbench face down. Loosening the fasteners he removed the frame, setting it on the floor. Gathering some protective materials, he wrapped the glass and placed it in a safe spot.

Putting the frame on the bench, he looked it over and decided on how best to go about the repairs. With a medium grit piece of sandpaper, he removed the original finish in no time at all. Switching to a fine grit, he finished the sanding job. After wiping down the wood, he made sure any depressions were clean and filled them with a wood filler of a type he had used in the past for high-end furniture.

Ten minutes before he had to open the front door, he stood back and inspected his work. Satisfied with the results, he thought about staining the wood in a complementary shade that would enhance its appeal, but, looking closely at the rich color already there, decided to forego the staining. He'd just touch up the repairs with the stain in order to blend it all together. The varnishing could be taken care of after closing up shop at the end of the day. He worked alone, so doing the job while the shop was open was out of the question.

During the day he had a number of sales and also made two other purchases. He, of course, only bought at a low cost and only when there was a good chance he could make money on the resale. His customers were usually happy with what they bought from the store, as he made all repairs that were needed to make their condition top notch.

Manfred had learned long ago not to try taking advantage of the people he dealt with—that was the ones he sold to, and the ones who sold to him. Much of his business came from repeat customers and word of mouth from them. He tried to be friendly with everyone and was on a first-name basis with many of them.

When the day was over and the store locked up, he went to the work area. Having had the entire day to think about it, he decided to use high-quality paint instead. Because the glass was dark, he was tempted to use a gold color to accent it. Unfortunately, he didn't have anything that looked right. In the end, he picked a light butter yellow. He was originally going to stain it a dark color and then varnish it, but thought this bold color with a varnish coat over it would lend a cultured feel to the piece.

The paint would require several hours to dry, being oil based, so finishing would have to wait until the next morning for the first coat of varnish. He was starving by the time he got home and quickly made a ham sandwich and had a beer to wash it down with. He would like a second beer but had found out the hard way that it easily led to a third and then a fourth.

He hadn't had any real problems with drinking himself, but had seen it happen to other people. Across the street from his apartment was a bar that frequently attracted drunks. Too many times he had been awakened late at night by yelling and shouting coming from intoxicated people.

In the morning, he was at the store early enough to put the first coat of varnish on the frame. Looking at it, he liked what he saw. At the end of the day, he would apply the second coat and then see how it looked in the morning. Maybe a third coat wouldn't be required.

The following morning, inspecting the frame, he found that a light sanding was needed and after doing that, he applied what he hoped would be the last coat. The day was a little slower, so he took a look at the mirror frame and was very pleased with the results.

When there were no customers in the store, Manfred called Mister Donnay, explaining the item he had found. The man, when he heard what Manfred had and the vivid description he was given, asked Manfred to send him a photograph of the mirror. He asked what the price was and agreed to purchase it if it lived up to his expectations.

CHAPTER 67

Cornelius Donnay lived in Denver, Colorado, and would require the piece to be sent if it met with his approval. He too, like Manfred, didn't want the mirror for himself. He wanted to sell it also, but only if he could acquire the piece for a price that still allowed him to make a few dollars. He had been quoted a figure, but as he had found in the past, everything was negotiable.

He had three people that might be interested in the mirror. If he played it right, he might be able to get a bidding war going. That would definitely raise the profit margin. In Denver, there were those who had money, and he hoped he could talk one of them into paying handsomely for what sounded like a unique item.

Then again, it wouldn't be the first time he got excited about nothing. He could drive to Oklahoma City, but it was almost seven hundred miles. A drive like that would eat up all the profits. Rail shipment was far easier and cheaper. Thoughts buzzed around in his head as he looked for easy ways to get the mirror to Denver—if he liked it, of course.

He came to a decision. After he received the picture and found that he wanted the mirror, he would see if any of his contacts were going to be passing through Oklahoma City. Maybe for a small fee, they'd bring it to Denver or nearby, saving him money in the bargain. *Yes*, he thought, *that may just work.*

CHAPTER 68

The day for Manfred was finished and the varnish on the frame almost dry. Bringing a lamp from the storefront, he inspected the job he had done. "Wow, this has turned out beautifully. I love the new look. Tomorrow morning, I'll put it together and use my Kodak camera to take the picture of it. I'm sure Cornelius will be pleased with it," he said, talking out loud.

On his way home to the apartment, he stopped at the local family restaurant on the corner. He ordered a hamburger with fries and ginger ale. Picking up a newspaper, he read the headlines and saw a story about Princess Elizabeth. It appeared that she was to marry the Duke of Edinburgh in the coming month. This was of no interest to him so he opened the paper to the sports page. He saw that the Yanks had clinched the pennant. He was surprised to see that the first four-engine jet airplane had been tested recently in Ohio.

After his supper, he headed for home and an early night in bed. In the morning, he was at the store early and put the frame back on the mirror. Bringing it into the store for a better light, he was surprised at just how nice it looked. If the profit margin wasn't as good as he hoped it would be, he might have considered keeping it.

The time to unlock the front door arrived, so he left the mirror where it was. As the day wore on, there was an inordinate amount of attention by customers interested in the mirror. Several people asked how much he wanted for it.

He told everyone that he already had a buyer for it, disappointing most of them.

He took the picture of the mirror and went to the photographer nearby to have it developed. The following day a well-dressed man entered the store after looking through the window. Having spied the mirror, he asked Manfred about it. The closer the man got to the mirror, the more he insisted that it be sold to him.

"I am sorry, sir, but I have another man who is very interested in it and is willing to pay a premium for it," Manfred told the gentleman.

Staring at the mirror as if he was captivated by it, the man asked, "How much is your buyer willing to pay for it?"

Caught off guard, Manfred told him a price five dollars higher than he had intended asking Cornelius for it. "Twenty five dollars," he said. This was indeed a high price for a mirror those days, but it was out of his mouth and too late to retract it.

The man thought it over. "I'll give you thirty dollars, cash."

The amount shocked Manfred, and before he could do anything to stop himself, he said, "Sold. You have just purchased yourself a beautiful mirror." Curious, Manfred asked, "Why do you want it so badly?"

Stopping for a moment, the man thought about it. "I actually can't give you a reason why. I looked at it and just had to have it. It is all quite peculiar, I must say. I have never done anything like this before. It is almost as if the mirror was speaking to me."

CHAPTER 69

After paying for the mirror, the customer made arrangements to have it shipped via rail to Houston, Texas. Sam Maters, the new owner of the mirror, left the store happy, but just a bit astounded as to why the mirror, all of a sudden, meant so much to him. It was all very strange.

Sam was an accountant with a small practice, on the outskirts of Houston. He didn't make a lot of money but did do all right. He had been in Oklahoma for a meeting with a number of others in the business. He was thirty-seven years old and married to a rather harsh woman. He often wondered why he married her in the first place. Her temperament showed itself before the wedding, but as many young men learned before him, a shotgun wedding was sometimes difficult to turn down. Except, it turned out that she wasn't pregnant at all. Sam's father-in-law was an influential man and had an overbearing personality. His daughter it seemed had inherited this trait.

The two had yet to conceive, and Martha held him to blame for this. She claimed he should try harder. How, he didn't know. Maybe this mirror would help ease the tension in the household, although he doubted that anything could do that, short of his demise, that was. He had often used a five letter word, starting with b, to describe her but never out loud. The price to pay for that infraction would be far too high.

Sam looked forward to these trips out of town. It allowed him a respite from trying times at home. A divorce would ruin him. His father-in-law would have seen to that. So Sam stayed married, knowing he would always be unhappy, but also knowing the alternative was even worse.

He bought his ticket for travel on the same train the mirror was being shipped on. The distance was four hundred and fifty miles and, leaving late that day, would get him home in the morning. The ride, as it turned out, was uneventful and saw him back in Houston by mid-morning. He made arrangements to have the mirror delivered to his house and grabbed a taxi for himself. He had a car but had decided to take the train that time. The cost was about the same, and he could relax on the train, arriving at his destination rested.

Walking in the front door, he received the greeting he expected. A cold-hearted woman could not give what she didn't have. The chill in the air was as it always was. Unpacking his suitcase, he had a shower to wash off the traveling aches.

By the time he was finished, the door knocker sounded. Sam answered the door and saw that the mirror had been delivered. Having the men bring it inside, he paid the bill and called out, "Martha, can you come to the hallway, please? I have something for you I think you'll like."

From the kitchen area, her harsh voice sounded. "What is it you want? I'm busy."

"I picked up something pretty impressive in Oklahoma City. Please come here and have a look."

"Fine."

Sam began unwrapping the present and had it uncovered by the time she came. As soon as she saw it, she stopped with her mouth hanging open. "That is a nice mirror. It will go well in my room in the dressing area. Get someone to bring it to the bedroom and mount it. I doubt you can handle that." She turned on her heel and walked away.

He knew she was pleased with the gift, despite the fact that she didn't have the manners to say thanks. He had a neighbor, Ed, who did handyman work. Taking the chance of his being home, Sam walked next door.

Knocking on the door, he was pleasantly surprised when Ed answered the door. "Do you have time to do a job of hanging a large mirror in Martha's bedroom, Ed?"

"Yes, I do. How large a mirror is it?"

Having measured it when he bought the mirror, Sam said, "Forty four inches wide, by thirty three high. It is quite heavy. I'm sure it must weigh close to forty pounds."

"I have just the hangers for it. There are brackets on the back, aren't there?"

"There are, I checked," Sam informed his neighbor.

An hour later, after Ed and Sam held the mirror up in a number of different spots in Martha's room, it was secured to the wall and Ed got paid. Martha had a nice feeling come over her as she looked at her reflection. It was almost as if she saw herself in a better light. Maybe the smoked glass had an altering effect on what she saw.

That night at supper she made a meal that was one of Sam's favorites, and although she didn't actually say it, he knew she was pleased with him. There were even hints about a possible union later that night.

Martha however, ended up going to bed early, feigning a headache. In reality, she was already feeling the pull of the mirror. Looking at it, she felt warmth come over her. This, of course, was a bit alien, as she had very little warmth in her toward anything.

Once she was in bed, sleep came quickly. Soon after, the soft voice entered her subconscious mind. Progress was made rather quickly. There was something about this mind and its harshness which made intrusion easier than it had been for most.

In the morning, Martha woke, a little the worse for wear. Sam knew immediately that he should stay out of her way that day. Martha snapped at him at every opportunity, and so he headed to his office without having breakfast.

The next day was the same as her mood became worse. During the night, the voice penetrated deeper, and despite the fact that she slept all the way through, she woke up tired. By the end of a week, dark circles were starting to show under her eyes.

Martha went to her father, Orville Cromwell, a local councilman. He was a harsh man when it came to dealing with people he didn't like. This might have been one of the reasons Martha was the way she was.

Looking at his daughter, somewhat concerned, he asked, "What's wrong, dear? You look like you're sick. Is that no-good husband of yours treating you badly?"

"No, he's the same as he always is, the little worm. I still don't know why I married him."

"Then what's wrong?"

"I don't know, Daddy. I go to bed, sleep the whole night, and wake up exhausted."

Her father was quiet for a moment, thinking the situation over. "I think you'd better see our doctor and have some tests done. For all we know, Sam might have given you some kind of poison."

"Oh, Father, he wouldn't have the nerve to do something like that. He's such a spineless jellyfish, he'd take it himself first."

"I'm not so sure about that. You remember the Andersons? He did that to his wife and almost got away with it. You'd better go to the doctor, just to be sure. Once you're dead, it will be too late," he said, putting his arm around her shoulders.

"All right, Daddy, if you think that's best. I'll make the appointment as soon as I get home."

When she got home, she did just that and then lay down for a nap in her bed. *What is it that I've picked up? Did that no-good husband of mine bring home some disease? If he did, he'll pay for it. But then' again, he did bring home that lovely mirror for me.*

CHAPTER 70

Sam finished off with a client and sat behind his desk, trying to figure things out. Thinking about it, he had various things go through his mind, *What is going on with Martha? She is always difficult, but she's gotten a lot worse lately. Those bags under her eyes are new, and she doesn't look good, not that she ever did. Maybe I should make an excuse to go on another trip. Where can I go that will take longer than normal?*

Not coming up with any good ideas, Sam got back to work. By lunch, he had caught up with most of his jobs and went for a light lunch at the corner restaurant. Not having breakfast had left him famished and slightly piqued. Looking out the window as he ate, his thoughts went downhill quickly as he saw his father-in-law approaching.

Orville spotted him through the window and headed for the door. The expression on his face was not a pleasant one, but then again it hardly ever was. Walking in, he sat across the table from Sam and asked, "What is going on with Martha. She looks terrible. Are you behind it?"

"What are you talking about, am I behind what?"

"She was feeling fine until you got home from your

so-called business trip. What are you up to, Sam?" Orville said with a snarl.

"I have no idea what's going on with Martha. Stop accusing me of doing something, and stop making a scene in public. I have a business down the street to worry about."

Orville looked across the table at the bewildered younger man and decided to cool his temper. In a milder voice, he asked, "What do you think is happening to my daughter then?"

"I have no idea. She was fine one day and the next she wasn't. Why, I don't know. She probably should go see the doctor."

"That's just what she is doing," Orville said, looking for a reaction. Seeing none, he thought, it might be possible Sam wasn't causing his daughter's troubles. With this, he left without saying goodbye.

Sam sat there, wondering what on earth was going on and why his father-in-law disliked him so much. Back at his office, he finished the day and headed for home. Once there, he wished he'd stayed at the office.

As he took his jacket off, Martha said, "I feel awful. Were you in contact with some sick people in Oklahoma? I'm sure I got this, whatever it is, from you."

"If you got it from me, I'd be sick too, wouldn't I?"

"You're probably just a carrier. You make other people sick, without getting sick yourself. That must be what's going on here," she said, almost shrieking.

"Why don't you go to the doctor and see what's wrong? Maybe he can help you."

"I'm going tomorrow, not that it will do any good."

"Your father came to see me today. He almost accused me of poisoning you. What's going on?"

"Are you poisoning me?"

"Of course not, why would I do that?"

She just looked at him distastefully and walked away, heading toward her room.

Sam made his own supper that night. An unpleasant marriage was becoming more difficult all the time. *How bad can this get and where will it end?*

CHAPTER 71

Martha washed up and prepared for bed, various thoughts entering her mind. *It seems the only place I feel good is here in the bedroom. I'm sure I feel so awful because of something Sam brought back with him from Oklahoma. Why did I marry that man? He is only a mediocre provider and even less of a husband. I should have listened to father.*

As she got into bed, her mood lightened and soon she was asleep. A few minutes later, the soft voice began to speak to her subconscious mind again. The voice continued all through the night. Slowly but surely, control of the sleeping form took place. For some reason, this mind was easier than most for the entity in the mirror to take over.

It sensed that the mean-spirited mind was very unhappy with its life. That would soon change if things kept progressing the way they were. A new energy source would build its power to control its own destiny. Possibly freedom from the cage it had been in for so long. The deal made long ago had trapped it in this mirror. This was not the life, if it could be called that, that it thought would be the result of the bargain made so long ago.

Always, it looked for an escape, but so far, that had been elusive. Most of the souls that had so far been captured had little belief in an afterlife. This was what made them of use. Once, a follower of Jesus came on the scene. No matter what was tried, or how hard it tried to take over the sleeping person, there was a barrier that was extremely difficult to break down, almost as hard as the troubled mind, recently lost.

Ever since then, the minds of people that had been prodded into purchasing the mirror had been searched for this belief. Atheists were the best targets to go after. Unless a special one came along.

The target's energy was drained as it was taken over. Martha, totally unaware of the ensuing battle, lost ground steadily. By morning, she was more tired than she had been the previous day. Rebuilding the energy level required an intake of food, and so she was given a subtle urge for just that.

CHAPTER 72

S am was up by seven-thirty in the morning and debated on whether or not to see how his wife was doing. Remembering how she had reacted to his homecoming the day before, he realized that would be a mistake. Making his own breakfast, he sat at the kitchen table, having eggs and toast with his coffee. He normally didn't cook much, and as a result, the taste of the meal before him was not what he had hoped for.

Washing up the dishes quietly, he walked to Martha's bedroom and placed his ear to the door. He heard the regular breathing of his wife. He was tempted to open the door a crack to make sure everything was all right, but he was afraid of waking her. Better to play it safe.

Not wanting a repeat of the chastising, he left the house as early as he could. He was in the office before Martha woke. The morning went by slowly. There were only two clients, giving him little to do. Martha, he knew had an appointment that morning, but he didn't know the time.

Picking up the phone, he dialed the number and listened as it rang and rang on the other end. Mumbling, he said out loud, "She must already be gone. I sure hope the doctor figures out what is going on with her. Maybe I can get in touch with Bernard in Jackson, Mississippi. He was at the convention in Oklahoma City, and he mentioned a large get together of businesses that are looking for new accountants."

Dialing the number on the card given him earlier, he waited for an answer. The person on the end of the line identified himself as Bernard Ames.

"Hi, Bernard, this is Sam Maters in Houston."

"I remember you, what can I do for you?"

Sam thought of how to broach the subject and figured he might as well come straight to the point. "You mentioned a convention of businessmen meeting in Jackson soon. When will that be and would I be able to attend and make my pitch. I could use the extra work."

"I still have your card, so why don't I register you the same time I do mine. The event starts Monday next week. Can you make it by then?"

"Yes, I'll change my work schedule and be there Sunday. That gives me two days to get ready before I take the train out. Thanks, Bernard, I appreciate it."

"Glad to help Sam, see you Monday, here's the address to go to." Bernard had Sam write down the instructions.

Calling the clients he had appointments with while he would be gone, Sam had them come in that week, thus eliminating the need for times later. If he had to, he would then be able to stay in Jackson longer if some people he met wanted his services.

He was not looking forward to going home that day, but the afternoon had passed and he had no legitimate reason not to. As he walked in the front door, Martha was waiting for him. "I went to see Doctor Benson today. He did a bunch of tests and took some samples. He can't find anything yet, but anything unusual will be found in the samples. If by chance you've put something in my food, you'll go to jail for the rest of your life. Daddy will make sure of that, you hear?"

He stood there for a minute, stunned. When he got his wits about him, he asked, "Why would you think I've done something to you? I'm not that stupid. Why would I want to? I love you. That's why I married you in the first place. My goodness, Martha, where have you gotten this notion from?"

"You don't love me. If you did, you would be a better provider than you are. Why can't you make more money and buy a bigger house? My father says you are just a useless bum, and I've wasted the best years of my life being with you," Martha said, raising her voice each time she started a new sentence.

"I'm trying to do something about that. I'm going to a business convention next week to drum up more work. If I make a few contacts, I'll be able to make a lot more money."

"Oh, sure, leave me alone when I'm sick. Thanks a lot for thinking of me. You don't care at all."

"But, Martha, you said you wanted me to make more money. This is the only way to do it. I have to meet new people in order to drum up more business."

Martha was no longer listening as she had already spun on her heel and was walking back to her room. She closed the door with a loud slam. Sam walked to the kitchen, dropping his briefcase in the hall near the small table.

In the kitchen, he saw a number of dishes in the sink and when he approached the stove, felt the heat from a recently used element rising above it. This meant she had already eaten and so he probably wouldn't see her for the rest of the evening. He decided he should make his own dinner and then wash all the dishes when he was done.

The evening went by very slowly. Several times he approached Martha's door to see how she was but had been afraid to knock. If she was asleep and he woke her up, there would be hell to pay. In the end, he went to bed himself not waking until morning.

CHAPTER 73

After telling Sam off, Martha felt better. How dare he leave her when she was so sick? "I hate that man. I should have married Rick Felton. I'm sure he would have asked if I had worked at him harder. At least he's been successful and has made a small fortune as a store owner."

Martha fumed for the next hour, just waiting for Sam to knock on the door, so she could rip a strip out of him again. It seemed that was about the only thing he was good for. Maybe it would be better if he did go away next week. At least she'd have the house to herself then.

Getting tired again, she lay down on the bed and was soon asleep. It didn't take too long before her mind was once again invaded. The control was strengthened during the night and it wouldn't be too much longer before the subject was ready for the taking.

This mind was going to be a nice addition. There was a quality there that would bring with it a large amount of energy. If it could acquire a few more like that one, it might have a chance of escaping the mirror, once and for all.

With its mind made up, there would be a concentrated

effort made to bring in as many sources as possible by reaching out a trifle farther and making contact with those minds. If the people nearby were given a pleasure nudge that was strong enough, a man and wife team might be influenced enough to be the next targets. A pair of children would work quite well too. This, of course, could only happen if the circumstances were right, but maybe, just maybe.

CHAPTER 74

Getting up in the morning, Sam made breakfast for himself and Martha. He ate his first and placed hers on a tray. Knocking on her door, he entered as she woke up. Again, she was not in a mood conducive to harmony.

"What do you want? Why did you wake me? Can't you understand that I'm not feeling well?" she said rather nastily.

"I thought you might like to have some breakfast in bed, dear," he replied sheepishly.

"I don't feel like eating. I'm not hungry. Get out," she screamed.

Leaving the room, he wondered if he should call the doctor and explain to him what was going on. On his drive to the office, he decided that he would call him.

Sam was quite disturbed by his wife's behavior and needed some help understanding what was going on.

As soon as he sat at his desk, there was a knock on the door and a client came in.

It took over an hour to deal with the small business-man and get him out the door. Opening a drawer in his desk, he pulled out the book that had all the phone numbers he had collected over a long period of time.

Scrolling down the list, he found the number he was looking for. Dialing, he waited for someone to answer.

"Hello, Doctor Benson's office," a female voice said.

"This is Sam Maters, Martha Maters' husband. I'd like to speak with the doctor please, it's rather important."

"One moment, I'll see if the doctor is available."

Sam waited for a short time, drumming his fingers on the desktop. In a minute or two, the familiar voice said, "Hello, Sam, how may I help you?"

Hesitating for a second, Sam answered, "To tell you the truth, Doctor, I am quite concerned about Martha. She is feeling very bad and getting worse with each passing day. This morning she actually screamed at me for bringing her breakfast. She has accused me of poisoning her. I have no idea why she would think such a thing, and it is disturbing me greatly."

"I was wondering that myself. She mentioned that when she came for an examination. I have sent samples of everything to the lab and should hear back the middle of next week."

"Oh, next week? I will be out of town starting Monday and will be gone most of the week by the looks of it. Business is a little slow here, and I need to see if I can get a few more clients at a businessman's meeting in Jackson, Mississippi. The way she is behaving, I think it best if I'm not around her too much, she's so angry."

"Yes, she did appear to be very irritated with you. I told her she had to be mistaken, but she was quite adamant. I'm sure she will see the folly in it when we have the results of the tests. Is there anything else I can do for you, Sam?"

"No, I just wish she would get better. It's been quite difficult for the past while. Thank you, Doctor Benson."

"Have a good day Sam."

Hanging up the phone, Sam leaned back in his chair and thought things over. He was sure that his wife caught something while he was away. There was an incubation period while a bug took effect in a person. So this had to be how it came about. If he had it, he would have started feeling bad before now.

The phone rang and when he lifted the receiver he heard a familiar voice. "Hi, Sam, it's Bernard Ames, I just wanted to let you know that you have been registered, and I've booked you a room in the same hotel the convention is being held."

"That's great news, thanks, Bernard. I should arrive there Sunday evening. I'm going to take the train to Jackson."

"All my friends call me Bernie, so why don't you? We can meet up at the hotel and have a few drinks in the lounge. Here is the address," he said, reading it to him. "See you Monday morning, Sam."

On his way home from the office, Sam stopped by the train station and bought the ticket for early Sunday morning. "You will have to arrive at the station before seven in the morning sir," the clerk informed him.

Sam was not looking forward to seeing Martha that day. When he got home, he breathed a sigh of relief when he saw there was a note on the kitchen table. Picking it up he saw his wife's handwriting and began to read.

Do not disturb me this evening, I have already eaten and am going to stay in my room. I do not wish to see you as I am feeling sicker all the time. If you bother me, I will move in with Father until I find out what is wrong with me. Heed this warning. Martha.

Thinking this over, he was tempted to knock on her door, just so she would move to her father's home. He had had about enough of this marriage. Unfortunately, she was far too vindictive, and even if she left, she would make sure he paid a high price for his freedom.

Her father would then ruin his business just for spite. Sam had never really gotten along with the arrogant man. It still surprised him the way the old man thought his daughter was such a fine catch, and that Sam was so unworthy of her.

The evening went by quickly and he used the time alone to pack a suitcase. The following day was Friday and because the situation was so tense in the home, he planned to change his ticket on the train for one that left on Saturday morning.

He slept fairly well that night, having made up his mind to get to Jackson ahead of time. The stress was taking its toll on him, and he was looking forward to getting away. In the morning, he left as fast as he could, taking his suitcase with him.

He left a note indicating his plans and headed for the office.

By mid-morning he had some free time and headed for the train station. His ticket was exchanged for one leaving at seven o'clock Saturday morning. Back at the office, he phoned the hotel he was staying at and managed to get the room a day earlier too.

As the day neared an end, he was dreading going home and made a quick call to his home. The phone rang and rang before Martha finally picked it up. "Yes, who is this?"

"It's me, Martha. I just called to see how you're doing."

"How do you think I'm doing? I feel awful, why did you call and wake me up? What's wrong with you?"

"I was concerned about you, what do you think?" Sam replied, knowing he wasn't anymore. All he wanted was to test the winds to see if coming home was a good idea or not.

"I'll be in my room, so don't bother me when you get home, do you hear me?" she said as her voice grew louder.

"I think I'll stay at the office tonight. I'm leaving for Jackson, first thing tomorrow morning, to drum up more business. I hope you feel better."

"It's just like you to leave me here all alone. You've never cared about me. I should never have married you," she shouted and slammed down the phone.

Getting off the phone, he was stunned by what had just happened.

One minute she told him to stay away from her, and when he told her he wouldn't be home, respecting her wishes, she twisted it around to make it look like he was abandoning her.

Luckily, there was a couch in the office, with a blanket and pillow in the closet. He hadn't used them for quite some time, so he took the blanket outside and shook it vigorously, getting the dust-out. He went to the local diner and ate his evening meal there as he thought about the direction his life was going.

Things had been growing ever more difficult over the last number of years. He wondered how he could get out of this terrible situation. Every idea he came up with left him broke and ruined.

After an hour at the eatery, he headed back to the office. Making the couch ready for sleep, he set the travel alarm. Changing into his night clothes, he brushed his teeth and then climbed under the covers.

Without having to concern himself with Martha, he fell into a deep slumber. When the alarm woke him at five thirty in the morning, he got up and changed. It took a few minutes to work the stiffness out of his muscles. A quick shave and he was off to the restaurant for a coffee and toast.

Six forty-five found him at the train station waiting to board. He carried his suitcase on and stowed it in the luggage rack. When the train pulled away, he felt as if his troubles were being left behind. Closing his eyes, a smile formed on his face, as the station disappeared in the distance.

CHAPTER 75

Martha sat in the living room wondering how things had gone so wrong. She had never felt as bad as she did then. Her appetite was diminished, but she still managed to eat a half-ways decent supper. That louse of a husband of hers had put her in this predicament, and when she got the results of her tests back, she would see him in prison if there were any suspicions that he had indeed poisoned her.

It had been a long day. She was already thinking about heading to bed, and it was only seven thirty. She forced herself to stay up till eight thirty by reading a book. As she read, she found her eyes starting to close. When her head fell forward, she was jarred awake.

"Enough of this, the only place I feel even remotely well is in bed, so why am I torturing myself?" she said out loud.

In the bathroom, she washed her face with warm water and went to her room. Changing into her nightgown, she looked at herself in the mirror. The mirror was the only thing that no-good man had ever gotten her.

"My, how terrible I look. Five years ago, I was a fairly attractive young woman. Why did I waste the best years of my life being married to Sam? I think that when he comes back from his stupid trip, which I'm sure will be a waste of time, I'll leave him and move back home with Daddy," she said forlornly.

Getting into bed she was awake for only a few minutes. Soon after falling asleep, the voice gently entered her mind and began the process of preparing it for the trip into a new realm.

CHAPTER 76

The ride on the train was pleasant. A young mother with her eight-year-old son sat in the seat facing him.

The lad looked at Sam. "Hey, mister, how come you're smiling when your eyes are closed?"

"Billy, don't bother the man," the mother said.

Looking at the boy, Sam cocked his head to the right. "That's all right, ma'am, I don't mind." Turning to look at the boy, he said, "I'm relieved to be going on a trip to Jackson."

"How come, didn't you like it in Houston? We're going to Jackson too, we live there," Billy said, shifting his gaze out the window.

Billy lost interest when the train traveled over a river far below. Sam introduced himself to Billy's mother.

She replied, "My name is Eleanor and you've already met my son Billy. Are you going to Jackson for a vacation?"

"No, actually, I'm going to a conference of businessmen. I'm an accountant and looking to drum up some extra work."

The two chatted for most of the trip. Sam got the feeling that if he hadn't been married, the two would have hit it off quite well. Too bad he'd made such a bad mistake marrying Martha. Before the trip ended, Sam wrote down where Eleanor lived. His wedding band had been left at the office. There was no particular reason for this, except that he wanted to feel released from the burden for the next week.

Checking into the hotel, Sam unpacked his suitcase. It was, by then, late evening, and he decided to go to bed early. The night spent on the couch was a little shorter than he was used to, so he was a bit tired.

The following day was Sunday and he met up with Bernard and his wife Frederica. He had lunch and supper with the couple. Bernard asked, "Does the little lady mind you going on these trips, Sam?"

Not wishing to reveal too much personal information he says, "No not really, she knows this has to be done in order to get ahead."

Frederica piped in with, "She must be an understanding woman. I don't like it at all when Bernard is gone."

At which Sam chuckled, not knowing what else to do.

The day was over and Sam thanked Frederica and Bernard. "It has been very nice of you to have me over for the day. I enjoyed myself very much, thank you."

With a smile on her face, she said, "You are most welcome. We had a nice time too."

Sam went to bed rather early again, wanting to be fresh the next morning. He had taken his clothes and hung them in the closet so any wrinkles would be removed.

CHAPTER 77

Saturday morning, Martha found the note Sam left, reading it aloud. "'I have decided to leave for Jackson, early. You seem to be more out of sorts than usual so I thought that I would leave you alone. Hope you feel better soon, Sam.'" She crumpled the note and tossed it in the garbage in disgust.

She rested most of the day, not leaving the house at all. Weariness made the day very long, and she was almost happy to be alone. Whatever was going on was draining all her energy. Having several small meals during the day made her feel a little better. In the evening she got to bed early again. The voice in her mind was close to being ready to bring the new addition home.

After a long night, Martha got up feeling as fatigued as she ever had. Looking in the bathroom mirror, she saw someone she barely recognized. Her face had lost its rosy complexion, and all that remained was a pale, baggy-eyed ghost looking back at her.

Washing up and vigorously rubbing her face brought back some of the color, but she knew she was very sick. Later in the day, she called her father, who had been widowed years ago. "I don't feel well, Daddy."

"I'm sorry to hear that, dear. Where is that husband of yours? Is he bothering to take care of you?"

Taking a deep breath and letting most of it out, she said, "He left me a note that I found yesterday morning, saying that he went to Jackson, looking to get more business at a convention."

"It figures he'd do something like that. What a useless excuse for a husband he turned out to be. I'd come over to see you but I have people coming over in an hour. Do you want me to call Doctor Benson in the morning to see if he has the results of the tests back yet?"

"Yes, please, Daddy, I feel so terrible. I wish this was all over with. All I want to do is sleep."

"I'll come over in the morning, dear. Maybe you should consider moving back home till you feel better. What do you think?"

"Why don't we discuss it tomorrow? It does sound like a good idea, though."

"All right, dear, see you tomorrow."

Looking around, Martha noticed the home was a little messy. While she had the time, she tidied things up. Each time she got near her bedroom, she felt a little less ill. *I wonder why this is*, she thought. The closer she got, the better she felt.

CHAPTER 78

The time was at hand. The subject was very nearly ready and one or two more nights would be enough to conclude the latest acquisition. There was almost a feeling of excitement in the mirror. After a few failures, a success would elevate its reserves. This latest addition would bring it to a point where its level of power would be almost enough to make a break with this cursed life in the mirror. One or two more strong personalities and it would have enough of a reserve to break free of the containment.

How many centuries had it been? The feeling of being let loose on the world again brought a thrill. The carnage it would be able to unleash would be absolutely wonderful. It would go to one of those third world countries and reap its vengeance for having been tricked into the mirror for so long.

Yes, the day could soon be there.

CHAPTER 79

Late afternoon came and after a light meal, Martha looked out the window of her living room. There were a number of large maple trees lining the sides of the street in front of the home. The sidewalk was cracked and lifted here and there.

Most of the homes in the neighborhood could use a coat of paint. Why would Sam bring her to a part of town where the less affluent lived? Her father had always made enough money to live in the well-to-do areas. She had grown up in nice homes, at least until she had married that man.

Maybe if she had stayed home longer, she would have met a boy from a prosperous family and been able to live a life of luxury. Instead, she was forced to live here with the nobodies.

Maybe it's not too late to change things. Divorce is frowned upon, but widows are cast in a better light. This thought, however, was cast aside as quickly as it came. She knew that, as much as she disliked Sam, she could never bring herself to take this course of action. Even though she suspected that he may well be behind her feeling so ill. *Of course, if he went to prison, I would be looked down on too as being married to an attempted murderer.*

Tired of having her imagination run away with her, she turned around and walked toward the bedroom. She was tired and wanted the day to be over with. Tomorrow, her father would call the doctor and she might move out of this house. Sam could go to hell for all she cared.

Crawling under the covers, Martha fell asleep, and it all began again. Picking up thoughts from her mind, the entity knew of her plans for the next day. Time once again was short, but it was close to success and so worked hard to accomplish its task before dawn arrived.

All through the night, Martha was attacked at the deepest levels that could be penetrated. Feverishly the entity broke down the last of the barriers that were between it and complete takeover. Martha had no idea of what was going on. The last several years of her life had been spent building a hatred for the man she had so foolishly married. This hatred was what was proving to be her downfall.

As morning closed in, the entity gave one last hard push and the meager defenses fell. Martha, in her sleep, pushed the covers back and slowly swung her legs out of bed. Getting up, she approached the mirror that had been hung sideways on the wall. This was done so she would be able to view herself, head to toe.

In a deep sleep, she was totally unaware that she was out of bed and walking toward the mirror. The hard glass surface became fluidly soft. As she approached, the boney old-man's hands, discolored and repulsive, reached out to Martha. Closer and closer she came to the mirror. Her hands lifted away from her sides and were grasped. There was no longer any chance of turning back.

Into the mirror Martha was drawn and disappeared as the glass once more became solid. There was no sound in the house, but inside the mirror, the horror of what had just taken place dawned on the now-screaming Martha. The entity was very satisfied with the new addition to its stores.

CHAPTER 80

In the morning, Orville woke and after the usual routine was done, he placed a call to Martha. The phone rang and rang, without his daughter answering. "Must still be asleep, I'll try again later," he said, out loud. Thoughts of Sam ran through his mind and started to irritate him. He had to stop himself because, otherwise, his mood would be detected by the people he needed to contact, and he didn't feel like having to explain himself.

He made the other calls and set up a few meetings, one with the mayor of the city. At eleven o'clock, he tried once more to call his daughter. As before, there was no answer, and he was growing concerned. Putting on his coat, he drove over to Martha's home and knocked on the door.

There was no answer and so he walked around the outside of the home, looking through the windows and knocking to see if there was any movement inside. When he saw nothing, he started becoming alarmed and searched under the planters near the front door to see if a key might be there for emergencies.

Finding one, he unlocked the front door, calling out loudly, "Martha, are you here?"

With no reply, he walked through the house calling out her name as he went. When he had searched every room and found nothing, he determined what plan of action should be followed.

Seeing the bed had been slept in, but not made, he realized that something had to have happened to his little girl. Martha would never have left her bed in that condition. Going to the phone in the kitchen, he dialed the number of Doctor Benson, just in case Martha had required an ambulance.

The receptionist at the doctor's office knew nothing about the whereabouts of Martha and said she would have heard if she had been taken to the hospital. Next, he phoned the police station and informed a Detective Barkley of the circumstances.

"It is too early in the case to start an inquiry in a missing person's case," Orville was told.

When it was brought to light just who Orville was, a different tone had been taken and the detective said, "I'll be right there, Mister Cromwell, don't touch or disturb anything please."

Twenty minutes later, the detective walked up to the front door. The two men shook hands and the policeman asked, "Do you know the whereabouts of your daughter's husband?"

"Martha said he left her a note saying that he was going to Jackson, Mississippi, Saturday morning."

"Let's see if we can find the note."

The search began and ended at the garbage container under the sink, where the crumpled note was found.

"It will be easy enough to verify his whereabouts if we determine when your daughter was last here. You said you spoke to her here yesterday afternoon?"

"Yes, I told her I would be coming here this morning. She has been feeling ill ever since her husband Sam got back from a trip to Oklahoma City. She suspected him of poisoning her and had Doctor Benson do some tests to see if indeed this might be possible. The test results haven't come in yet, so we don't know for sure if it is true or not."

"Do you have any idea where in Jackson, this Sam is staying?" Detective Barkley asked as he looked for clues as to what had happened.

"I have no idea where exactly he may be, but I do remember Martha mentioning that he was going to attend a businessman's convention, hoping to drum up some new clients. His last name is, Mater."

"I'll use the phone here to call in the information and have someone start checking out the possibilities."

This he did and took one last stroll around the premises. When he entered the bedroom again, he studied the mirror. "This is an unusual piece. Where did your daughter obtain it?"

"Sam picked it up on his last trip. Is it of any importance?"

"I doubt it. It's just so different than any I've ever seen before." With this, the two men left the house, locking the front door.

Orville was told not to go into the home again and asked if he would mind surrendering the key in case the police needed to go in again. Orville handed the key over and the two parted company. A few of the neighbors were standing outside their homes watching the scene, but no one said anything. When they were questioned, no new information came to light.

CHAPTER 81

The detective went to the station and found out where Sam Maters was staying through a trial-and-error procedure. He did this by calling a number of hotels and asking if there was a businessman's convention there. When he got a hit, he asked if there was a Sam Maters booked at the hotel. When the answer was affirmative, a message had been left for him to call the detective at first opportunity.

Tuesday morning, Sam called back. "Why did you need to contact me here?" he asked.

After telling Sam about the disappearance of his wife, the detective asked, "We would like to know where you have been since Saturday afternoon until Monday morning, sir."

"I got to the hotel Saturday evening and went to bed soon after. Sunday, I spent most of the day with a friend and his wife, till evening, and Monday, all day, I attended a conference here at the hotel. Why are you asking me these questions? Am I a suspect?"

"I'm just trying to eliminate as many people from the list as I can. May I have the names of your friends to corroborate your story, Mister Maters?"

Sam gave the name and the phone number of his friend and asked, "Do you have any idea what may have happened?"

"Not at the present time, but I'll keep you informed."

"I'll take the first train back to Houston and let you know when I arrive," Sam told the policeman.

"That's a good idea. I'll see you when you get here."

Sam took the next train back and called the detective when he got home. "I'm here at my house, did you want to see me?"

"You weren't supposed to enter the home. Were there no signs on the front door?"

"No, there was nothing indicating that I wasn't to enter my own home. Why?" Sam asked, a little perturbed.

"I'll meet you there shortly, please don't touch anything."

Leaving his suitcase in the kitchen, Sam went into the fridge and pulled out a bottle of beer and the fixings of a sandwich. By the time the detective arrived, he was finished and had the dishes washed and put away. He was getting a bit tired of always being told what to do and felt a bit resentful.

The interview with the policeman went well enough once it was established that he was genuinely concerned about what had happened to his wife. "No, Martha and I are not getting along well, but it doesn't mean I don't love her. We are just going through a rough patch, but who doesn't? My father-in-law has never approved of me. He seems to think that if you don't make a lot of money, you just don't measure up as a husband."

This seemed to hit a soft spot with Detective Barkley, and his attitude toward Sam lightened up considerably.

"Do you have any idea where your wife could be, Mister Maters?"

With a sigh, Sam answered slowly, "I know she hasn't

been feeling well for the last while, and she has been to see the doctor, but other than that, I have no idea where she could possibly be."

"Is it possible that there could be another man?"

"To tell you the truth, it really wouldn't surprise me at all. She has been a difficult woman and never satisfied with anything I ever did. I do have to leave town quite often, so yes, it is entirely feasible that there is another man." At this thought, his face took on a sad look as he contemplated the idea that Martha actually might be with another man.

The two walked around the house and checked to see if anything was missing. When they found that the luggage was all still there and all her clothes were too, the logical conclusion was that she hadn't run off with some other man. Not unless she decided to buy all new clothes.

When the detective left, Sam went into Martha's bedroom and looked for signs that might have been missed. He looked at his reflection in the mirror he had thought would make his wife happy. He saw a man who should be really upset, but after the initial shock, he found that he was almost relieved at the thought that she may well have left him. A nice feeling came over him.

Leaving the room, he closed the door. As soon as he was in the hall, the feeling left and suddenly his mind was his own again. He planned never to enter the room again. The memories he had in his wife's room were not in the slightest bit happy.

In the kitchen, he had another beer as the phone rang. Lifting the handpiece and bringing it to his ear, he was not happy when he found out that it was his father-in-law on the other end.

"Where is my daughter, Sam? What have you done with her?"

"What on earth are you talking about? I was out of

town when she decided to leave. The police have already checked my alibi and know I'm not guilty of anything," Sam said defensively.

"The test results will be back tomorrow, and then we'll see if you are or not. You could have hired somebody to hurt Martha. If you have, I'll see to it that you spend the rest of your life in prison, do you hear me?" Orville shouted as he slammed down the phone.

"What the heck is with that man? Where does he get these stupid ideas from?" Sam said while he wondered just how far the crazy man would go in his efforts to attack him.

If, by chance, Martha was not found, Sam thought he would have to move to some other city in order to get peace. Maybe the following day would be better. The old man did say the results of the tests would be in then. Then and there, Sam decided to call the doctor's office and ask to have the results made known to him as soon as they arrived. Yes, that was what he would do. He was certain that if the results turned out to be negative, the old man would tell him they were positive. That man would twist things around if Sam didn't find out for himself.

That was not a good night for Sam. He slept very restlessly and almost thought he heard a voice as he drifted off. In the morning, he woke a little the worse for wear. When he knew the office was open, Sam phoned and asked to speak with Doctor Benson. A moment later he asked, "Doctor, have the results of Martha's tests come in yet?"

"As a matter of fact, they have. They all came back negative, Sam. Have you heard from Martha?"

"No, Doctor, no one has heard from or seen her for days now. Did she mention anything at all to you about wanting to leave?"

"Not a word. I do hope that you find out what is going

on with her. Please let me know if you do, Sam."

"I will, Doctor, thank you for your concern."

The day went by and Sam had another call from his father-in-law. This call went no better than the last one did. The old man accused Sam of wrongdoing again and once more slammed the phone down in anger.

"I have had enough of this. He knows the results came back negative, and still he accuses me of having something to do with her disappearance. It would serve him right if she came back, letting everyone know I had nothing to do with any of it. I think, for now, I'd better take a room at one of the hotels downtown. I'll let Detective Barkley know in the morning."

Going to his room, he quickly packed a suitcase and left for the Astoria Hotel. He booked a room when he got there and unpacked his suitcase. That night he slept better, and in the morning after a nice breakfast, he called the policeman.

"Why have you moved to the hotel, Mister Maters?"

"My father in law keeps calling and accusing me of being behind Martha's disappearance. The tests the doctor had done all came back negative, but the old man still calls to harass me."

"I'll have a word with him as soon as we finish talking, Mister Maters. I don't care if he is a councilman, he has no right to badger you like that. Have a good day."

Sam went to the office, thinking it might be a bad idea, but sitting in the room wasn't appealing either. The phone only rang when a client needed some information. The old man didn't call that day. Maybe the warning he got from the cop did some good after all.

The rest of the week went by with no new developments in the case. Sam moved back into the house but felt ill at ease there. It was almost as if Martha's spirit was still there. When he drifted off, he heard a faint soft voice in the distance, barely audible, and it frightened him enough to wake him up. Maybe there was someone outside whispering just loud enough for him to be able to hear it. Unable to sleep well that night, he went to the living room couch and sat there, finally falling asleep, not waking till morning.

Whatever it was that he heard last night, he didn't like it, so he called a long-time friend, Jerry Rodman, and asked if he could bunk at his house for a while. Soon he was packed and out of the house yet again. In his office, Sam waited for Jerry to finish work before going to his house.

"Hey, buddy, what's going on? I heard your wife is missing," Jerry asked.

With a look of despair, Sam filled in his friend as to what had been happening, including his father-in-law problem. "When this is all over, I think I might put the house up for sale and move to some other town," Sam confessed. "Orville has too many contacts in this city, and he has already threatened to ruin me."

"I don't know how the man can be allowed to get away with something like that. I guess he feels he can do whatever he wants because of his position," Jerry said with a disgusted look.

The two chatted for a while and Sam was shown to the spare bedroom. "You stay as long as you need to. When the wife gets back from visiting her mother, next week, we'll start getting some decent meals. I can't cook worth beans," Jerry said, laughing.

While Sam was in bed, he wrote on a sheet of paper things he needed to do in the next few days. The first thing to do was to call his lawyer and advise him of Orville Cromwell's activities. Since the house was in his name only, he wondered if he could sell it while his wife was missing. He had no intention of cutting her out of the proceeds from the sale and would have Barton Finch draw up a paper to that effect. The paper would then be sent to Orville.

Martha's clothes would be delivered to her father's house by someone else. He had absolutely no intention of dealing with the man again if he could avoid it. He would take whatever furniture he needed and donate the rest to charity.

The next day while he was in the office and free from clients, he called the lawyer and found out that he could indeed sell the home, as long as the police no longer required it for investigative reasons.

Getting Detective Barkley on the phone, Sam asked him, "Is there any reason why I can't put the house up for sale. I find that I can't sleep there. With Martha's father threatening me for some time, I think it's best if I leave town. The man has told me that he will ruin my business, so I don't see the point in staying here."

"We've made an in-depth investigation and found nothing, so I see no reason why you can't put it up for sale. I talked to Mister Cromwell and told him he has to desist from harassing you. Has he called you since?"

"No, he hasn't, thank you for taking care of this. I have no doubt, though, that he will follow through with his promise to ruin my business. This is one of the reasons I want to move. The other is the fact that I hear voices when I'm trying to sleep while I'm in the house. It's probably just my imagination, but it is quite unnerving."

"You're not the first person to tell me this. I spoke with Doctor Benson and he assures me that there is nothing that concerns him in the results he got back from the lab. You are no longer regarded as a suspect in this investigation, Mister Maters. Good luck to you. I will be in touch with you if there are any developments. Please give me your contact information if you do leave the area."

CHAPTER 82

Sam called the real estate office after the house was put in order. An agent was found and, when contacted, he said, "Because of the time of year, early September isn't the best time of the year to sell a home because children have already been enrolled in schools and parents are reluctant to move at this time. There is interest for your type of home, and young families are buying houses in your price range, so who knows?"

The sign was put on the lawn and the waiting began. Sam didn't like intruding on Jerry and his wife Elli, so he moved what he needed to his office and screened off the living area, making the office quite small. He showered and washed his clothes at a neighborhood center and conducted most of his dwindling business in client's homes. It seemed that Orville had kept his promise to interfere with Sam's accounting business.

Three weeks after the home was put up for sale, the agent came to the office with an offer. It was a fairly reasonable one, so Sam signed the papers without arguing about the price. With a very short closing date, he soon had to empty the home of its contents.

A quick trip to Jackson and he found a rental property suitable for his needs. Space being at a premium, he took only what he needed and the rest was given to the local Goodwill. Sam liked the look of the mirror, but it brought back memories he would sooner forget. The piece along with all of Martha's other belongings were given to the charity. He had intended to send her things to her father, but because of Orville's behavior, Sam felt no need to be generous. He would keep all the money from the sale, but hold back a portion of it, it case Martha ever did show up.

The day for the move came, and seeing to it that everything was loaded on the train, he started his drive to Jackson. With a new life on the horizon, there was a feeling of freedom from a past he was eager to forget.

In an out of the way diner, as he opened his wallet to pay the bill for his lunch, he saw a piece of paper he had put there, what seemed a long time ago. In the car, he sat and read the note. Written on it was the address of the pleasant young lady and the boy he met on the train on his way to Jackson.

A smile crossed his lips and he decided that once he was settled, he would contact her and see where it all led. Life, it seemed, was finally looking a little brighter for Sam. He took the wedding band off his finger, and after taking one last look at it, threw it out the window of the car as he drove. This he felt was the final break he needed to be free of a most unpleasant burden. Even the air blowing in the open window seemed to smell better.

CHAPTER 83

The doors to the Goodwill store in Houston were opened and a new shipment of donations brought in. There was only one person handling things at the time. The man in charge was Farley Watson, a retired Catholic Priest.

As Farley had not made a lot of money in his life being a priest in a church on the other side of town, his belongings were meager, and he led a simple life. A month before, an uncle he barely knew, living on a small ranch outside of Cody, Wyoming, had passed away. A letter from a solicitor in Cody informed Farley that, because there were no other relatives, he had inherited the ranch and all that went with it. Farley had never been to Wyoming and although he would miss being in Houston, he had made arrangements to begin a new life on the ranch.

Farley had just turned sixty-six, and even though he could have continued as a priest for many years, he had become somewhat disillusioned. The world he knew had been disrupted by the things going on in the church. The lack of any willingness by the bishop to initiate changes caused Farley many hours of lost sleep. Nineteen forty-nine hadn't been the best year he had ever had.

A change of lifestyle was in order, and he was eager to move away. There was enough cash inherited with the ranch to allow for a reasonably comfortable retirement. It could not have come at a better time. One more week and he would be on his way. A new replacement was due to come in later that week.

Farley looked over the items that came in and began sorting them, according to the usefulness and section they belonged in. After an hour's work, he came across an item wrapped neatly in a burlap cloth. Untying the twine, he exposed a beautiful smoked-glass mirror.

Immediately, there was a tug from within him somewhere. He felt that the mirror was an item that he should make use of in his new home. Farley couldn't understand why it was happening. It was almost like a feeling of divine intervention, almost.

For a moment, he sat in a chair near the mirror and wondered about this compelling feeling. It was strange and he was hard-pressed to explain it. He had some doubts as to whether or not he should follow the urge that had so suddenly come over him.

It took quite an effort mentally to pull back and put the mirror away for the time being. He would have to pray about this. Even though he was somewhat disillusioned, a lifetime of being in the priesthood had left its mark.

There were a few people that came in for a helping hand, leaving Farley with a sense of purpose. Many people had fallen on hard times and were in need. He felt that he would miss this aspect of his life, but knew that he could always volunteer in his new community.

Later in the day, after having a light lunch and prayer, he walked to where he had placed the mirror and uncovered it. This time when he looked at it, there was little of that initial feeling in him. He liked the mirror, but it was then more an appreciation for the workmanship than of wanting it as a possible possession.

For the rest of the day, he thought about what his course of action should be concerning the mirror in the back of the building. An hour before closing, a man and his family came to the store driving an old flatbed truck, in need of help.

He was a kind, pleasant man, and when he was given the things he required, showed a real appreciation for the help given him and his family. Because of this, Farley asked the man for a favor.

"I was wondering if you could help me take an item to my home near here. I have no way of carrying it that far and would really appreciate it."

Being grateful for what he had gotten, the man replied, "I would be most happy to help you. We can load it onto the truck and we'll take it to your place straight away."

The mirror, already retied, was loaded on the back of the truck and the store locked up. A five-minute drive and two minutes work and the mirror had been moved into the house and put away. The rest of the week went by pleasantly, with the new man, who had come to replace Farley shown the ropes. All preparations were made for the move to the ranch.

The day arrived, and Farley was on the train, with his few possessions stored. The ride would be a long one, but he was looking forward to the new life. He watched from the train window as the scenery changed with each state they passed through.

CHAPTER 84

The train ride to Cody was long and tiring for Farley. There was little to do, and his muscles grew stiff from inactivity. When he finally arrived in town, his things were unloaded from the train and a man had been hired to deliver them and Farley to the ranch. First, Farley had to look up the lawyer, in order to pick up the keys and sign some papers. He passed a saloon and a saddler store, before he located the lawyer's office, just off the main street.

This took almost an hour and by the time a few groceries were picked up, the lawyer had already called the power company and had the electricity turned back on. When Farley and Joe, the man hired to take his things to the ranch, got there, it was late afternoon.

Unlocking the front door, Farley found that the lawyer, as promised, had had the place cleaned and tidied up. The refrigerator was already running and cold, with anything that could have spoiled long since removed. The cupboards had everything in place and the beds had been aired and the linen washed and folded on top of the dresser.

Farley's few things were unloaded and brought into

the small but quite adequate home, with the mirror and a few boxes stored in one of the sheds. He would do an inspection of the property and its outbuildings the next day. At that point, he was tired and wanted to rest.

With a few things in the refrigerator, he tested the stove and was happy to see it worked fine. The pots and pans were all clean, so he made a quick supper. After this, the bed was made up and again he was pleased when he saw the mattress had no stains and was in good shape. After preparing it, he got himself ready for sleep. Being in an isolated location, the night was far quieter than he was used to. More quiet, except for the howling of the coyotes, which had unnerved him at first.

In the morning, however, he felt fairly well rested, sleeping in later than he was used to. After breakfast, he toured the outbuildings. There was a garage, in which, to his surprise, he found an automobile several years old but in excellent condition. He looked at the manual in the small glove compartment and noted that the vehicle had been built in nineteen thirty-nine. It didn't look as though it had been driven much over the years. Farley didn't know much about cars, but he checked the oil and found that it was reasonably clean. The gasoline tank was full and the coupe looked ready to drive.

There was a shed that housed a tractor with various implements. One of which was a front-end loader. He would have to get someone to show him how to use it because this was all new to him. A workshop inspection finished the tour.

In the house, he ran across the survey of the property that the lawyer gave him, and so he sat at the kitchen table to study it. He found out that the ranch was of a nice size. It totaled two hundred and seventy acres. This was not large for a ranch but gave him plenty of room to roam.

The back side of the property bordered a state park, where there were many trails and a few campsites. None of the campsites, according to the map he viewed, were close to the property, so he probably wouldn't have any intruders showing up anytime soon. .

He'd have to do a walk around soon to familiarize himself with his surroundings. Having driven cars for years, he thought he'd take a look at the tractor and see if he could operate it. Walking to the shed, he spotted a number of crows perched on the roof and nearby trees. As he passed, they cawed loudly.

Opening the door caused the birds to take flight, with them cawing even louder and the sound of flapping of wings filled the air, as they flew away. The bright sunlight illuminated the interior nicely. First, he checked the fuel tank and found it full. Against the far wall, he noticed a fuel pump handle, connected to a tank behind another wall. This must be where fuel for the tractor was stored. When he took a close look at the tank, he saw a gauge on top of the tank registering a three-quarter full level. Lifting the handle, he sniffed the open end and was pleased to note that it was gasoline and not diesel fuel. It would supply fuel for both the tractor and the car.

Sitting on the tractor, he studied the top of the shifter knob and was relieved to see the gear-shift pattern. He had trouble shifting it into reverse until he depressed the shifter first and then slid it forward.

Manually going through the gears while it wasn't running showed him where each gear was. While he was on the tractor anyway, he thought it might be a good idea to get familiar with its operation. Finding a key, he turned it on and pressed the starter switch.

After a few turns, he pulled the choke lever and then the engine started. He tested the hand throttle and, with the clutch pushed down and reducing the engine speed, he then pushed in the choke and shifted it into reverse. Slowly letting out the clutch, he backed the tractor out of the shed and into the yard.

Smiling to himself he felt pleased with his accomplishment. While things were going good, he figured he might as well take advantage of the situation and go for a ride. There was a trail leading toward the park and so he drove along this at a leisurely pace. The land had a gentle roll to it, and it didn't look like it had been used for much in the last few years. The lawyer had informed him that that was the case when he had seen him the day before.

There was a stream that ran across the property near the park border. The runoff from the melting snows in the distant mountains had probably been used as a source of water for irrigation and livestock a number of years ago, but that was long before his uncle had taken ill.

Close to the border of the park, he found the remnants of an old well. Stopping the tractor, he walked over to it and lifted the protective boards on top. There were a multitude of spider webs to be cleared away before he risked looking down into the darkness. The walls of the well were made of stone, and about four feet across.

It was dark and he could only see part of the way to the bottom. Picking up a small stone, he dropped it and counted the seconds to when he heard a splash. If his estimation was correct, the well should be close to sixty feet deep.

It must have been quite an undertaking to have dug this well and lined it with the stone. This was an indication that at some point the stream must have dried up and the well used during the dry spells. Re-covering the well opening, Farley continued the tour. He was surprised at how large the property actually was. Being from the city, he wasn't used to the wide open spaces. It would take some time to grow accustomed to it. An hour later, he was back at the house, parking the tractor in the shed.

The mirror and the other things brought from Houston were in the shed with the car. He thought he would use the car to go into town the next day. Farley would have to change the title on the vehicle to his name as well as the rest of the things the law required. In the house, he'd take stock of items he needed in the food department too.

All in all, he was very happy way out there by himself. Before going inside he went to the shed to retrieve a box of books he'd accumulated as a priest. His bibles and books on church doctrine, along with many others, were a fount of information.

CHAPTER 85

A week went by with Farley rearranging things in the home. There were several possessions his uncle had had that were of no interest to him, so he took them to town and dropped them off at the local thrift store.

When the person running the store found out that Farley had been in charge of the Goodwill store in Houston, he tried immediately to get Farley involved with this one. For the time being Farley declined. "I am going to have to do a lot of work on the ranch, and it is quite some distance to and from here. I may pop in now and then, but that is all I can promise for the time being."

Having cleared out some of his uncle's possessions, there was a little more room in the home. Farley surveyed things and tried to determine where to place the things stored in the shed. Each time he had walked past the shed, there had been a feeling pulling him toward it. The feeling was similar to the one he had in the thrift store in Houston. He felt he should take the mirror into the house and hang it.

There were other things in the shed that required his attention too, so he might as well get to work on them.

Most of the secular books, except the old traditional masterpieces had already been donated. This left room in the bookcase for his books of substance.

Looking around he wondered where a good place was to hang the mirror. The bedroom he slept in was small and already full, so he looked around and came to the conclusion that the living room, over the fireplace mantel, would be the best spot for it. There was a set of deer antlers there, which he cared for not at all. Moving a chair close to the fireplace, he lifted the rack off its holder and took it outside. Bringing the mirror into the house alone proved to be no easy task. He finally did manage it, with a bit of imagination by using a wheelbarrow to carry it.

Struggling with it, he manhandled it as close as he could to the doorway. Weighing between forty and fifty pounds, it wasn't overly heavy, but the size made it awkward to handle. Farley was unable to lift the mirror high enough to get onto the mantel, so he sat and thought about it for a few minutes. With it leaning against the wall, he wracked his brain for a method of lifting it higher. Measuring the distance between the hooks on the back of the mirror, he found and installed heavy screws into the wall studs.

Walking back to the work shed, he looked for something that might assist him in his task. In the corner were a number of low, flat wooden crates. Leaning against the wall was a narrow door, which gave him an idea. He carried the crates into the house positioning them in two stacks three feet high.

The spare crates he put beside the pillars within easy reach.

The door was brought in and laid on top of the two stacks, close to the fireplace, and supported so the mirror could be placed on top, face down. Each stack had another crate placed under the door and the mirror was slowly elevated to the same height as the mantel.

Farley slid the mirror so the bottom edge was on the mantel and then tipped the top edge up until it was standing on top of the mantel and leaning against the wall. He found that he needed to rest for a moment before removing the door and crates.

Another half hour and he had the mirror hung up. He smiled with satisfaction at a job well done. This type of work wasn't his specialty and so he was rather pleased with himself. The crates and door were put back in the shed and, by the time that was done, it was time for supper.

The evening was spent reading the bible and getting his mind right. Now that he had a home of his own and money in the bank, he could relax, not having to concern himself with this aspect of life. What he would do with the ranch was still a question he would have to find an answer to. Looking at the fireplace, he wondered if he should look into whether or not he would require more firewood to keep him supplied for the winter. There was a small fuel oil furnace in the house, but a real fire might be nice to have burning on those cold winter nights.

Putting the bible down, Farley got ready for bed. When he lay down in bed with the window open slightly, he heard the sounds of the night. Having lived his entire life in the city, it took a bit of getting used to. The sound of coyotes howling in the distance seemed louder than the previous night and was a trifle unnerving for him, so he closed the window. Soon, because of all the exertions of the day, he was fast asleep, snoring softly.

CHAPTER 86

While still in Houston, in its excitement at having such a valuable asset within reach almost got the better of the entity, Drakmar. This was what he once, so long ago, had been called at a time when he had roamed the Earth, doing as he pleased.

The former priest would be an asset of great power, once he could be drawn into the mirror. It would, however, be difficult to draw this one in, but if great care was taken, Drakmar might be able to bring this about. There was a large store of energy within this newest target. Drakmar was certain this victim would give him the strength to finally break the bonds that had held him prisoner for what had seemed an eternity.

He felt an excitement building in him, as a long-sought-after goal was now within reach. The glass had been his home for so long, and before it was too late, he needed to free himself from it.

In his attempt to seize some control over the priest immediately, he almost gave himself away. The disillusioned man of the cloth immediately knew something was wrong, and Drakmar had been forced to restrain his

efforts and wait for the proper time to initiate the takeover.

The time was at hand and the work began, but great
care would have to be taken not to alarm this final victim.
A sense of peace came over the entity. The end to the
long struggle was in sight as it reached out gently to the
sleeping man in the next room.

CHAPTER 87

As Farley slept, there was a gentle soft voice faintly contacting his mind. Because his bedroom was next to the living room, and the mirror a trifle farther away from the target than it had been in the past, contact had been somewhat diminished. This, of course, was only a minor inconvenience for the entity, because the home was small and the distance actually negligible. It would just take a little longer, that was all.

In the morning, Farley awakened rested for the most part, but his muscles ached from the exertion of the day before. It took a while for him to loosen the muscles and, as the morning progressed, the achiness started to leave.

From the kitchen, Farley's gaze landed on the mirror across the room. "My, that is a handsome addition to the room. I am most fortunate to have had it come into the Goodwill store when it did."

Turning his attention back to the job of making lunch, he got ready to eat. The afternoon was spent on the tractor, as Farley continued to explore the ranch. He ended up at the border of the park, where an old rickety gate in an even more dilapidated fence was opened. He drove into the park to see what there was to be observed. When he ran across a trail, he parked the tractor and, taking out the key, walked among the trees.

It wasn't long before he came across the stream that went through the ranch. It was about six feet across and two maybe three feet deep, depending on where he stood. As he washed his hands, the water cooled him down. He was tempted to take a drink, but caution told him this might not be a good idea. Who knew if some dead animal had fallen into the water upstream or not? This had the potential to make him very sick, so no drink at this time. In the future, he would have to remember to bring water with him.

Another hour found him back at the house. As he walked to the front door, he decided to inspect the house for needed repairs. With winter coming in the next few months, the time for repairs was the present. The weather was good for anything that may require attention.

As he walked around, he saw that there were only a few small items that could use attention. Some nails and new paint would take care of these things. He had already seen the paint cans in the shed and would tackle the jobs in the morning. There were plenty of nails and a couple of hammers in the shed. He noticed the woodpile could use some building up, so he would look into it next time he was in town.

The evening was used to inspect the rifle that his Uncle Albert left in the closet. It looked like an army issue .303 caliber model. There was a box and a half of bullets on the shelf and, although he had never fired a weapon before, he would take a few shots in the morning. Since the rifle was there, he might as well know how to use it. One never knew when it might be needed to frighten off some animal.

That night was like many others for the entity. It continued to work on the subject. Farley knew nothing of the game being played for his life. If he was to have any chance of survival, he would have to become aware of the thing in the mirror. This had not happened often in the past but had, however, happened more often than Drakmar liked.

When Farley awoke the next day, there was a feeling of unease in him. Instinctively, he knew something wasn't quite right. He had, in his life as a priest, run across some peculiar things. Once many years ago, he was witness to an exorcism. This event had caused him much unrest for several years.

The episode shook him up and made him deeply aware of some of the dark evil running amok in the world. He never came across it again himself, but he had heard stories of these occurrences in other parts of the world.

Aware of this fact, the entity realized it would have to proceed more slowly. This was a victim of great value, and care must be taken not to lose him.

The day continued as Farley made the repairs and soon the disturbing thoughts left his mind. In the afternoon, he moved a rocking chair onto the porch where the warm sunlight shone.

Picking up a book left by his uncle, he was quickly lost to the world. The *Grapes of Wrath* told a story of hardship and the perseverance of man.

With the services all hooked up, he had a telephone, which chimed and brought him back to the present. Picking it up he asked, "Yes, who is this please?"

Mister Perkins, the lawyer in town, said, "I just wanted to make sure that everything has been completed to your satisfaction, and if there is anything else that you require."

"Thank you for calling, things are well here, and I am getting used to this new way of life. There is one thing maybe you can help me with. Do you know of anyone who can show me how to attach the front-end loader to the tractor here?"

"As a matter of fact, I do. Would you like me to give him your phone number and he can call you himself?"

"Yes, thank you. That will help considerably." With this, the conversation was concluded.

The next morning, Farley woke again with the feeling something was not right. He thought about it for a while and came up with no logical answers. Something he heard long ago nagged at his memory. He once heard a troubled person mention an occurrence that would shine a light on these circumstances, but what it was failed to materialize.

At ten-thirty, the phone rang and a man with an English accent spoke to him, "Mister Perkins asked me to give you a call. My name is Keith Essex. I'm a farmer five miles away from you. He said you needed to be shown how to hook up the front-end loader on your tractor."

"Yes, Keith, I could use your services. I'm from the city and don't have any experience with this type of equipment. I figured out the tractor, but the loader is a bit beyond me."

"I can be there in an hour if you like."

"That works just fine. Would you like to stay for lunch? It seems the least I can do?" Farley asked happily.

"Certainly, that would be nice. See you in an hour."

As it turned out, the job of hooking up the loader was fairly straightforward. While Keith was there, he showed Farley how to use the unit by having him scoop up large rocks near the shed. After fifteen minutes, Farley learned how to handle the tractor and loader well enough for any jobs he would have to do.

The two had lunch together and chatted for the next hour. When Keith found out that Farley was a retired priest, he asked a few questions concerning eternity and what he must do to get to heaven. By the time Keith was ready to leave, the two were on good terms and felt this could end up being a firm friendship.

As he walked with Keith back to his truck, Farley asked about where he could get some firewood.

"I have a friend that delivers my wood. I'll call him and have him drop off a couple of cords."

"Thank you so much, that would be a great help."

As Keith drove away, Farley thought that he liked this down-to-earth man. Keith had not been much of a churchgoer, but because he was getting older too, he was becoming concerned about an afterlife.

The loader had been removed and the tractor parked back in the shed. It was three o'clock and still some time before supper, so Farley put the chair on the porch and rocked back and forth. The occasional crow landed on the shed and cawed. A barn swallow flew back and forth, catching little insects out of the air and landed in the tree next to the house.

The elm tree was about thirty feet high and was full except for the side nearest the house. Uncle Albert must have had someone trim it periodically in order to keep it from damaging the home. The sparrow had its nest in the tractor shed which he saw earlier. In the tree, the bird stopped for a moment, looked and chirped at Farley, causing him to smile. He enjoyed the time outside as life went on around him.

After the evening meal, he sat for a time and, as it got dark outside, he prepared for bed. As he was about to drift off, during that few seconds between wakefulness and sleep, the voice softly started to enter his mind.

The feeling that something wasn't right hit him again. Startled, he sat up in bed, "What's going on in here?" he asked.

Getting up, he grabbed hold of a light and searched the house. Finding nothing, he looked outside for an intruder. Again, he found nothing that could have made the noise he thought was made by a person.

Sitting on the bed, he thought things over, trying to piece the scene together. He was tired, though, and soon turned the lights out and pulled the covers over him. As he lay there, he attempted to listen for any sounds that would give him a clue as to what may be transpiring. All was silent as he fell asleep. Soon after, however, the soft voice in his mind started again and the process of takeover slowly began.

With this mind more aware than those in the past, greater care had to be taken to advance slowly. Up to this point, a few mistakes had been made. With the end of the battle in sight, being too eager had been the biggest one.

Another week went by with the process taking a deeper and deeper hold on Farley, as the entity slowly attempted to take control of the sleeping man.

As the time passed, the feeling of tiredness became more pronounced than it had been previous mornings. Dark circles were forming under Farley's eyes, and he felt more drained with each passing day. With an uneasy sensation coursing through him, he got out of bed in the morning and headed to the kitchen. As he passed the mirror, there was a tiny movement seen out of the corner of his eye.

Turning quickly, he looked at the glass hanging on the wall above the fireplace. Studying it, he saw nothing. *Am I going crazy? Good Lord, what is happening here? Ah, it must have been a bird flying past the window and I caught the movement reflected in the glass,* he thought, feeling a bit silly.

As the morning progressed, the tiredness stayed with him. Taking a cup of black coffee, Farley sat on the porch and tried to figure out what was occurring in this house. One by one, he revisited the incidents that had given him cause for concern. He started with the most recent and worked his way backward.

Step by step, he cautiously attempted to ascertain the root cause of the strange phenomena. At first, he came to the conclusion that this all began when he moved into the home. This made him wonder if there was something in the home that may be out of the ordinary.

Continuing the process, he remembered when he was still in Houston, the strange episode when he first saw the mirror. The excitement he felt when he looked at it was not something he normally would feel toward any material possession. Farley had based his entire life on serving others and living a simple life.

Instinctively, he took his mind back to a time when he was much younger. Recalling the sensation he had during the time of the exorcism of the young man, he compared it to what was now occurring.

During the exorcism, there was an attempt to enter his mind by whatever evil was in the young man. Whatever was there, was looking for an escape, and chose Farley as the most likely candidate because he was the newest to the priesthood and the most vulnerable.

The feeling he had all those years ago resembled the one he woke up with now. A chill ran through him as he realized what he may well be up against. He felt totally unprepared to deal with a situation such as that. He was waking up each morning more and more drained of energy. He was beginning to doubt that he could fend off whatever was assaulting him in his sleep. He suspected that he had little time left to take action.

Picking up his jacket, he locked the house and used the car to go to town. After asking for directions, he parked in front of a small Catholic Church. Moving as fast as he could, he knocked on the door, where he saw a man through an open window. A priest turned and asked, "May I help you?"

"I want to speak with the senior priest please."

"The youngish man smiled. "I am the only priest here I'm afraid. Why do you ask? I am quite able to help you in any of your needs."

Farley explained who he was and told the young man of his background. Hesitantly he explained what he believed was happening in his home and what help he thought he required.

The look on Father Richard's face showed him to be highly skeptical.

"I'm sure this all is foreign to you, but I have been part of an exorcism before, and I can assure you that this is quite real," Farley stated emphatically.

"I am sure you believe it is. However, I have never come across anything like this and, even if I believed it myself, I haven't the faintest idea what to do about it. I can see by the dark circles under your eyes that you are suffering from something. Have you taken the time to consult with Doctor Beatty? He is quite good, and may find that you are only suffering from some deficiency, or have picked up a bug."

Looking at the floor during the last statement, Farley quickly looked up and saw the smirk on the young priest's face. This was obviously a waste of time. The young priest thought he was sick, and no more. Farley realized that he was on his own, and this young priest would be of no help whatsoever.

As Farley was about to leave, he stopped to ask, "Where is the nearest large church with a priest near my age?"

Thinking for a moment, the young man answered, "I believe that will be Father Gioni in Billings, Montana. It's about a four-hour drive from here. I think I have a number you can call in order to speak with him." He opened a drawer in the desk and, after a brief search, came up with a paper. Copying the name and number down on a scrap piece of paper, he handed it to Farley.

Driving home, Farley felt let down. Father Richard was of no help at all. In fact, the young priest didn't believe a word of what he had told him. Hopefully, Father Gioni would be more receptive.

Once he got the older priest on the line, Farley explained his dilemma. The older priest said, "My goodness, I have heard of these things, but I've never witnessed one. I wish I could be of help, but I am recovering from an accident where I fell down a flight of stairs."

"I'm sorry to hear this. Do you have any advice as to how I can handle this myself?"

"Do you have a copy of *Exorcism Rites* by Baskenelli?" Father Gioni asked, after thinking for a moment.

"Yes, as a matter of fact, I do. I'll familiarize myself with it before I tackle the problem. Thank you. I'll let you know what occurs when I'm finished if I can," Farley said softly, hoping he would still be able to.

"I'm sorry I can't be of more assistance. If I was able, I would come to you and help rid you of this thing. I will pray to the Lord Almighty. Only he can help you defeat this unholy adversary."

"Thank you, Father, I will do the same. I'll get to work on this as soon as I educate myself with the rites," Farley replied.

The two said goodbye and Farley picked up the book and started reading. The first big suggestion he found was that he must get some distance between himself, and the dwelling place of what he thought could be a spirit attempting to control him.

Moving his chair to the shed he continued to study. It was late afternoon by the time he came up with the idea of how to remove the mirror from the house.

CHAPTER 88

If I spend another night in the house with that thing, the attack will come at me full strength and I don't know that I can withstand it anymore while I'm asleep. The time to act is now, while I'm aware of the power I'm up against. God, I feel so tired."

Resting for a time, trying to regain some of the spent energy, Farley formulated a plan of action. Gathering two planks about seven feet long, he brought them into the house and placed one end of each on the mantle under the mirror. There was a familiar tugging at his mind as soon as he entered the living room. Running out of the house, he picked up two concrete blocks, one at a time, and placed them against the end of the planks on the floor. That, he thought, should prevent the planks from shifting when he did what he planned to do. All the while he was in the house, he felt something trying to get into his head. The only thing that saved him was the fact that he knew what he was fighting.

Back in the shed, he looked for something that was less than four feet high, for him to stand on while he took the mirror off the wall. In the corner, he spotted a short ladder that would work just fine. Bringing it into the house, he stood it as close to the fireplace as he could between the planks.

As he climbed the ladder, the attack intensified. Tendrils wormed their way into the portions of his mind that controlled his will. He could feel the desire to remove the mirror lessoning. He fought this control as hard as he could, but unless he hurried, he knew he would fail.

Down the ladder, he went and ran out of the house until he no longer felt the invader. Resting, he sat on the wheelbarrow in the shed. "My goodness, this is as close as I've ever been to falling victim to an evil presence. I need to pray for the strength to overcome this. I have dedicated most of my life to the church. Now I need help all the help I can get to defeat this thing in the mirror. How many people in the past have fallen victim to that cursed thing? What can I do to help them? Is there *anything* I can do to help them?"

Looking at the tractor, he got on it and hooked up the loader. With it attached he drove the unit to the front of the house and lowered the bucket to the ground with the front of it angled upward. He could feel the tugging even at this distance, so he ran back to the shed to pray and reinforce himself against this enemy. Fear threatened to overrun his faith, and this he knew he had to overcome in order to fight the battle of his life.

When he felt ready, he made his move. Grabbing the tarp as he headed toward the house, he brought it in with him. Steeling himself for the confrontation, he climbed the ladder, throwing the tarp over the top of the mirror, and hooked it behind so it wouldn't fall off. He braced himself in position, got his hands under the mirror, and heaved upward.

He felt the invasive attack on his mind building rapidly\, but managed to hold out as the mirror unhooked from the supports. He lowered it as fast as he could, resting it on the mantel. Freeing his hands, he felt himself starting to lose the battle, bit by bit.

Unwilling legs were forced to move and step down the ladder, missing the last step. This caused him to stumble backward, putting a little distance between him and the mirror. The control was lessened just enough to allow him to stagger out of the house.

Farley was in the fight of his life and knew he had just come close to losing it. Sitting in the shed, he tried to come up with a way that would allow him to do what he must while still maintaining at least some distance between him and his adversary. Having the mirror in his hands was allowing the demon or whatever was in the glass to enter his mind too easily.

The closer to the mirror he was, the more strength it had over him. Searching the shed and the workshop, he took inventory of the items available to him. He noticed a good length of rope that might come in handy. Off to the side in the work shed was a ten-foot long wood pole, two inches in diameter. A couple of metal hooks with a small loop at one end hung from a beam.

An idea came to him as he collected the pole, rope, and hooks, bringing them outside the shed. Searching the tool boxes, he found a number of clamps. He used two clamps to fasten a hook to the end of the pole. Unraveling the rope he tied a hook to the end of it.

While he felt somewhat recuperated, he took hold of an old two by four. Running into the house, he placed it on the floor against the two concrete blocks holding the planks in place. Out he ran again before he was subjected to the probing tendrils for too long.

When he felt ready, he grabbed the rope in one hand and the pole with the hook tied to it in the other. Winding a few loops in the hand holding the hook, he quickly re-entered the house and placed the rope with the hook, on the floor near the ladder, unwinding the rope as he exited the house again.

Even these short exposures to the influence of the thing in the mirror took its toll. He found that he needed to pray and regain his internal strength. Fifteen minutes later, he approached the house with the ten-foot pole that had the hook tied to the end, in his hands.

Steeling himself once more, he quickly entered the house and placed his foot on the two by four he had set against the concrete blocks. Raising the pole, he hooked the top of the mirror and pulled. The mirror fell toward him. He kept the pressure on the back of the frame and pushed it against the planks so it didn't bounce and fall off and onto the floor.

Smoothly, it slid on its tarp down the planks, coming to rest when it made contact with the blocks. Out of the house, Farley ran again as he felt the assault on his mind. His hands were shaking with a fear he had never before experienced. It was now close to five-thirty. He would have to get this all done before it got dark in about three hours.

Slowly his reserve built up again. When he felt strong enough, he used the pole with the hook to grab the hook on the rope. Lifting and pulling, he drew the rope over the mirror frame. The hook on the rope was hooked over the rope as it came out from under the mirror and was tightened around it. Backing out the front door, he pulled the rope tight and started dragging the tarp-covered mirror across the floor toward the door. It got caught up on a chair and then a table leg, but a hard tug freed it until it got to the door.

There it jammed itself in the opening. Resting yet again from the onslaught of the groping fingers trying to get a foothold in his mind, Farley sat by the shed. At that point, he wondered if he had the resolve to finish this last phase of the job without succumbing to the forces within the mirror.

Using the hook on the pole once more, he hooked the far side of the mirror, lifting the piece up on its edge, and pulled on the rope. A quick jerk and it was freed, and then he managed to pull it through the door and off the porch. Using a combination of rope and pole, he maneuvered it close to the bucket of the loader.

In order to get it into the bucket, he was forced to start the tractor and lower the bucket flat on the ground. Again the attack was made and the strain of the fight weakened him further. If this continued for too long, Farley knew he wouldn't have the strength to resist, and he would lose this battle of wills.

He found he needed to recuperate once more as mental fatigue was wearing him down. Back in the shed, he surveyed the scene and attempted to come up with a viable plan that would enable him to get the cursed thing away from the house. His resistance was weakening, and he didn't know how long he could hold out.

The rope was laying on one side of the tractor and the pole on the other. All he had to do was to pull the mirror into the bucket and the worst part of the job should be finished. As fast as he could, he threw the rope over the back part of the tractor. Quickly he went to where the pole was on the ground and picked it up, hooking the frame closest to him. He pulled the rope and the pole at the same time, and the mirror was yanked into the bucket.

Two more quick dashes to and fro with the bucket tipped back, and the mirror was fastened to the bucket in a way that would allow for easy untying.

The tractor was still running while he rested one more time. His hands had been trembling for some time as the close encounter with the spirit, or whatever it was, had waged a battle for its latest victim. This victim, however, was determined to keep his freedom.

Looking in the direction where the state park was located, Farley saw a relatively flat land with no obstructions. A plan formed and so, getting hold of a short piece of thin rope, he jumped on the tractor, depressed the clutch, and ground the gears as he attempted to slam it into reverse too fast.

Finally, he got it in gear and backed up enough to head it toward the border. Putting the transmission into first gear, he got the tractor rolling and, using the rope, tied the steering wheel so the tractor could drive itself toward the park.

Farley felt his control slipping through his fingers. The tendrils gripped his mind tighter as he stood on the tractor swinging his right leg past the gear shift. With a last ditch effort, he threw himself sideways off the tractor, narrowly missing the large back wheel. The hard rubber brushed against his pant leg as he fell to the ground.

He landed on his side in the dirt with the wind knocked out of him. Slowly the tractor continued its journey away from him. After a time lying in the dirt, he got his breath back. The groping at his mind dissipated as tractor drove away.

Dizzily, he got to his feet and, at a distance, followed the tractor. He had come so close to being taken over that he almost started to cry. The tractor continued for half an hour before Farley ran beside it and shut the key off, removing it, and then ran away again. He didn't have the strength to fight this thing anymore that day, so he went home, leaving the tractor and its cargo in the field near the border.

CHAPTER 89

By the time Farley got home, darkness had started to fall. He was as exhausted as he had ever been. That night, he felt safe for the first time since moving to the ranch. The mirror was over a mile away and, at this distance, could do him no harm.

The following day, he would have to decide what his next move should be. While he was being attacked the last time before jumping/falling off the tractor, he felt the presence of other people/souls within the mirror. The ones trapped in the mirror had been there for various lengths of time.

The thing in the mirror, he realized at that last instant, was counting on his capture to break loose from a prison too long endured.

The trapped entity, revealed itself to him to be more vile and evil than anything Farley had ever encountered. The fear at that moment almost overrode everything and any emotion in him. What a horror the people/souls in the mirror must have endured.

It was time to put this all aside, because he needed sustenance and rest so badly. As he walked in the door, he turned on the lights. A plain simple meal would have to suffice for the time being. His body drained of all its energy needed to sleep.

For the first time since having the mirror in the house, Farley slept well and woke far more rested. He did, however, have a dream that upset him when he remembered it. Of course, it related back to his harrowing experience the day before.

After breakfast, he called Father Gioni saying, "I wanted to let you in on the events that have transpired. I believe that there are souls trapped inside the mirror by something evil." He told the priest about the battle he had yesterday and how it had almost turned out against him. Farley continued by saying, "I have called you because I need advice on how to free these souls I believe are trapped in the mirror."

"I have been looking into this since you called me the other day. In the book I mentioned, *Exorcism Rites* by Baskenelli, chapter twenty-seven, on page two hundred and seventeen, and also chapter thirty-one, deals with your situation. Study these and I think you may have your answer."

"I'll do that before I attempt to free the souls in the mirror. Thank you for your help."

"Please be careful, Farley, and let me know how it goes. I'll pray for you."

The conversation finished, Farley picked up the large heavy book and turned to the pages Father Gioni had indicated. He studied the various rites in detail and found a few exorcism rites he could use as backups. By mid-afternoon, he felt armed well enough to tackle the job. At least he hoped he was.

He took a supply of holy water, which he had obtained from Father Richard in Cody. Farley had considered asking the priest to accompany him, but in the end, felt the man would be more of a liability than a help. He brought other items such as rosary beads and a large cross. At two o'clock he started the walk back to the tractor. Apprehension filled him.

CHAPTER 90

As the tractor came into sight, Farley stopped. For fifteen minutes, he prayed to God for help in dealing with the task at hand. He knew that he wasn't strong enough by himself to defeat this foe. He studied the rites preparing for the upcoming confrontation. Pulling the key out of his pocket, he moved as fast as he could, jumped up into the seat, and started the tractor.

Immediately he felt the tugging at his mind, but he was now able to resist better because of the preparations he had made and the night's rest he'd had. Shifting into third gear, he drove as fast as he could to the well. Raising the bucket, he stopped when the front edge was just over the top of the well.

By this time, he could feel the invasion digging deeper into his mind as it attempted to regain control. He knew he had lots of gas, so he left the tractor running, set the brake, and then retreated, almost stumbling because of the severity of the attack. He desperately needed to put distance between him and the mirror, in order to regain his strength.

When he felt ready, he steeled himself, ran to the well

cover, and, quickly as he could, pulled the boards off. The attack began right away, and he felt the invasion going deeper into his mind this time. Knowing his time was limited, he ran away far enough to get the book and pray for a few minutes in order to build his resolve.

The tractor ran quietly as he approached chanting loudly the passages of the rites. The tone of the encounter changed as the entity realized what was happening. Farley kept going, shouting louder and louder as he felt the desperate attempt within the mirror that tried to stop him.

The battle for supremacy continued for an hour. Farley was attempting to free the souls within, and that was the last thing the entity could have happen. It would mean being trapped forever within the glass.

The mirror took on a quality that made it glow whenever a dark cloud covered the sun. The glass had a flowing appearance as Farley's red perspiring face concentrated on the book and his voice cracked from the strain.

Feeling the time was right, he switched to a rite he had found farther in the passages. He began using the holy water, sprinkling it on the glass. This rite was one that he hoped would complete the release of the trapped souls.

Loudly he called out, "In the name of the Lord Jesus, I command you to release the captured souls held in the mirror by you, this evil being." Over and over he repeated the rite. His strength, at that point, was starting to fade, and he felt that if he couldn't finish this soon, he would have to retreat and start again later.

The battle had been extremely difficult, and he had no desire to go through it again the next day. With one last valiant attempt, he gave it everything he had. Shouting and concentrating, he focused his entire being on the rite and the mirror.

A ghostly figure exited the upturned glass then another and another. They went straight up into the air and disappeared. Finally, at the height of his efforts, a flash of transparent figures exited and disappeared into the air. He kept chanting as he grabbed a lever controlling the bucket and tipped it downward. The mirror slid off and dropped into the well. The grip on his mind faded as it fell deeper and deeper into the hole.

After what seemed an eternity, there was a splash as it hit bottom, and he could finally relax as he felt what had been trying to control him fade to almost nothingness—almost. There was still a faint feeling as he leaned over the edge of the opening. He pulled back, not wanting to experience that sensation ever again.

Seeing what he believed was the freeing of the captives helped to make this endeavor more worthwhile. The horror that the prisoners must have felt couldn't be imagined by the living.

Farley felt good that day.

CHAPTER 91

It took over an hour to compose himself and revive his body to the point he could do what he felt was required to finalize his task. Using the tractor, Farley dug up several buckets of sandy soil and dumped it into the well.

When he dropped a stone, he no longer heard a splash, so he dumped in three more buckets of soil. By the time he had done this, it had been close to supper time. He was starving and jittery by that time, so he drove the tractor back to the shed, parking it for the night.

The next morning, he called Father Gioni and told him what had gone on, saying, "This is the most difficult thing I've ever done. The freed souls are now gone, and the Lord will deal with them as he sees fit. I pray for them. Thank you for your help in this. Maybe we will meet one day, and we can discuss this at length."

"You're welcome. I'm happy it turned out well, and I look forward to the time we can visit."

Farley had breakfast and, when he felt ready, walked to the shed. Filling the gas tank on the tractor, he drove to where the rocks were piled. He filled the bucket as much as he could. Driving to the well, he dumped them in. He did this several times and then dumped some more fine soil in the well, in order to fill the gaps between the rocks in the deep hole.

The well was almost half full as he broke apart the portion of the rocks and mortar that was above ground. It then broke off several feet below ground level. He then filled the well with soil to the top, and driving the tractor back and forth over the dirt, he packed it down.

By the time he was finished, he stopped and said a prayer over the site. On his way back to the house, he vowed to keep an eye on this place, just to make certain the well remained hidden. He was sure that some settling of the soil, would occur over time, but he would deal with this as it was required.

As he drove away, a feeling of peace came over Farley. "A job well done and now a life to live," he said.

CHAPTER 92

In the Mid-West, the main gate of a prison opened, and a man was released. He had been incarcerated for many years. It had been a difficult time, and he felt angry as he left. He never committed the crime for which he was sentenced, but because of his attitude all those years ago, a jury had found him guilty. This attitude had softened over time, but he still resented the fact that he had served time for something he hadn't done.

Getting a job had been very difficult. As soon as employers found out he had spent time behind bars, they no longer wanted him working for them. The only real work he managed to hang on to was seasonal work picking fruit, or working on farms around the country.

Three years of roaming the country, working at various short-term jobs had finally landed him work on a farm in Wyoming. The cattle ranch provided him with some sense of stability. He liked working there and got along well with the owner. Now and then he had a few days off, and he used them to go camping in the great outdoors.

Here, he felt at peace, and the trials he had had to go through seemed to fade away. There was a time long ago when he had been married. His wife, because of his harsh attitude had been a very unhappy woman. She died of consumption and left him with his children. It was difficult trying to raise them himself. Having had time to mature, he saw that he was the problem, not her. His children were taken by children's services and adopted many years ago. He had tried to locate them, but this proved to be an impossible task.

He was resigned to the fact that this phase of life was not meant for him, at least not, unless he met a woman with children of her own. He had no idea where he would meet someone like that out there in the middle of nowhere. The owner of the farm had recommended he go to church, as a way to meet someone, but he wasn't sure about trying that.

The upcoming weekend he planned to go camping in the state park not too far away. Ben, his boss, had agreed to let him use the truck to drive there, so all was good.

The day had come and he was in the park, hiking to a spot where there was a stream for washing and cooking. The map showed a farm bordering the park and the land leveling off at this point. After a day of hiking, he was ready to camp for the night. Setting up his tent in a nice level place just outside the park on the unused land of what must be an abandoned farm, he got ready for the night. The stream was not far away and this spot seemed to call to him.

A campfire completed this scene as he ate in the open air. He relaxed for the evening and when it started to get dark, he turned in. As he lay down, he let his mind drift off as he enjoyed the freedom of being in the wilderness. Looking up into the sky, he saw the stars twinkle. The moon overhead cast a glow across the land and life seemed better. There was a cool gentle breeze taking away the heat of the day.

As he was about to fall asleep, a faint voice entered his mind. There was a familiarity to this voice. He had heard or, more accurately, felt this thing in his head once before, many, many years ago.

Jumping up, with a fear he hadn't felt in years, he realized where and when he had the similar experience before. As quickly as he could, he dismantled the tent and camping gear. He stuffed the things in a large canvas bag and hightailed it out of there.

He hadn't stopped running until he came to the main road leading into the park. Not knowing which direction to head, he sat by the roadside till daybreak not daring to sleep. Studying the map in the daylight he located where he needed to go and walked back to the truck in the parking area.

During his wait by the side of the road that night, he figured out exactly where and when he had had the experience before. The crime he had been sent to prison for involved the disappearance of a girl he had bothered too much. When he was outside her bedroom window, there had been a horrible pain and a feeling that something had entered his head. It scared the hell out of him at the time.

He was absolutely certain that what tried to enter his head in the campsite was the same thing. How on earth it found him after all those years was beyond him. There was no way he would ever go back to that place again. Because it had never bothered him in all the years since that first time, till now, made him realize that the thing now resided in that open field.

His hands trembled at the thought of encountering the thing again. He drove back to the farm and went back to work. He didn't leave the farm for six months. This caused the farmer to ask why, but he received no real answer.

James, after that time, decided to take the farmer's offer of going to the local church. He needed to find the peace again that had been momentarily interrupted by his camping experience. A month later, he met a nice woman with a boy and a girl. They had hit it off and soon were serious about forming a permanent union. Life had finally turned around for James.

EPILOGUE

Deep in the ground, Drakmar resided in the mirror. Buried beyond the reach of most minds, he waited. One day, the familiar musings of a mind encountered so long ago gave him a momentary hope. In his eagerness, he tried to contact this mind. This had turned out to be a big mistake. He should have waited till the target was totally asleep before attempting contact. Spooked, the occupant of the portable dwelling far above him ran in fear, never to return.

Since that time, he had not felt the presence of any other minds. The wait grew longer and longer as the years slipped by. He had started to believe that it would be his permanent home, unless of course, the one who placed him in the mirror came back to collect him. With the escape of his captives, he no longer had a bargaining tool to use. If his captor returned for him, he himself would be taken to a new and even more unpleasant place to spend eternity. He was not sure which was worse, the waiting, or the return of one more evil than himself.

The terror others had felt, and he had lived on, was now his own as Drakmar sensed that the day he had feared was coming. He was headed for a far worse home than this and knew it would be soon—very soon.

The End

About the Author

Leonardus G. Rougoor was born in the Netherlands. His parents and most of his family moved to Canada to start a better life years ago. He was raised on a dairy farm, which made for an abundance of work. Educated in southern Ontario, he tried a number of different jobs before he ended up in a major tool and die shop, starting a lifelong career.

Having a heart for the underdog, although causing many sleepless nights, has been the driving force in a writing career. He now writes in three genres: crime, young adult mystery adventure and the supernatural.

"If you like rejection, become a writer."

www.ingramcontent.com/pod-product-compliance
Lightning Source LLC
Chambersburg PA
CBHW060935120726
47910CB00002B/334